OCTAVIO SOLIS:

RIVER PLAYS

(El Otro, Dreamlandia, Bethlehem)

NoPassport Press

Dreaming the Americas Series

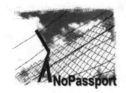

Octavio Solis: River Plays

(El Otro, Dreanlandia, Bethlehem)

Copyright © 2010 by Octavio Solis.

"Borderline Drama" copyright © 2010 by Douglas Langworthy

Cover photo: *Dreamlandia* at Dallas Theater Center, courtesy of lighting designer Steve Woods.

NoPassport Press Dreaming the Americas Series

First edition 2010 by NoPassport Press, PO Box 1786, South Gate, CA 90280 USA; NoPassportPress@aol.com

ISBN: 978-0-578-04881-9

No Passport is a Pan-American theatre alliance & press devoted to live, virtual and print action, advocacy, and change toward the fostering of cross-cultural diversity in the arts with an emphasis on the embrace of the hemispheric spirit in US Latina/o and Latin-American theatremaking.

NoPassport Press' Theatre & Performance PlayTexts Series and its Dreaming the Americas Series promotes new writing for the stage, texts on theory and practice, and theatrical translations.

Series Editors:

Jorge Huerta, Randy Gener, Otis Ramsey-Zoe,

Stephen Squibb, Caridad Svich

Advisory Board:

Daniel Banks, Amparo Garcia-Crow, Maria M. Delgado, Elana Greenfield, Christina Marin, Antonio Ocampo-Guzman, Sarah Cameron Sunde, Saviana Stanescu, Tamara Underiner, Patricia Ybarra

Contents

The author dedicates this volume to the
memory of Luis Saguar

Borderline drama

El Paso, Texas, with its shadow twin Ciudad Juarez, has had a lifelong hold on playwright Octavio Solis. Although he has long since left his arid hometown for the cooler climes of San Francisco, he has set nearly all of his plays in this Texas border town, continuing to explore borders both literal and metaphoric. His emotion-packed, often violent dramas are filled with transgressions: whether breaking the law, cheating on a spouse, or illegally crossing the border.

For the Latino characters in Solis's plays, the international border becomes a line of demarcation between the two halves of the Mexican-American psyche. Identity is tautly stretched in a contentious tug of war between both shores of the Rio Grande. The Spanglish Solis's Chicano characters use gives voice to their bifurcated souls, mixing and matching Spanish and English like so much oil and water. The melting pot, for Solis, is a hollow myth.

The price one pays in a Solis play for transgressing is steep, often erupting into raw violence and death. Passion propels the characters. A strong sense of fate hangs over his plays, whose plots unfold with the inevitability of Greek tragedy. Even though many of his plays revolve around parents and children, these families have more in common with Clytemnestra and her clan than, say, the Cleevers. Multiple interwoven storylines give his plays an epic, even Shakespearean, scope. Time is fluid in Solis's work, with flashback, fantasy and internal monologue frequently interrupting a play's rising action.

His use of language is layered and heightened, making liberal use of the collision of Spanish and English: "*Sombras*. Shadows. Gassy dreamfuckers. As if *que si*. As if *que no*." (*Dreamlandia*). Solis plays with language, often punning or coining new phrases by turning a familiar idiom on its head: "The world is topsy turdy" (*El Otro*); "misery loves Mexicans", "one awesome apoca-lipstick day" (*Dreamlandia*). And it's important to note here that Solis's plays, even the ones with tragic outcomes, are leavened with wry humor.

The three plays in this volume, *El Otro*, *Dreamlandia*, and *Bethlehem* share these qualities to varying degrees. They are all set in or around El Paso, all are violent, involve border-crossings and investigate issues of identity and parentage. The plays are also strikingly different from one another: *El Otro* is a cross-border road trip centered around a young girl's search for her father; *Dreamlandia* is an adaptation of Pedro Calderon de la Barca's Spanish Golden Age drama *Life is a Dream*, with its attendant focus on dreams and reality; and *Bethlehem* is a journalist's exposé of a murderer that morphs into something far more personal and frightening.

El Otro, subtitled "a river play," takes place on both sides of the Rio Grande. The action consumes one fateful day—the birthday of Romy, a thirteen year-old girl with a troubled relationship with her parents. Her first stepfather, Lupe, is a drug dealer while her second stepfather, Ben, is a soldier at nearby Fort Bliss. Lupe undertakes a journey with both men to discover who her real father is. With her mother in pursuit, they all end up swimming to the *otro* (other) side of the river. There they meet *El Charro* (the cowboy), a cryptic character who can see into past and future, who can arrest time to describe the whizzing arrival of a bullet fired at Lupe that took "the long way around" to reach its target:

> EL CHARRO: And out of the vanishing point where border meet border in the wish and never was of sun and dark and real and bones one eye of Romy see

a teeny ball of lead heading straight this
way and with her other eye see the best
part of her dad and the one quarter inch
of pure that never know sin open up its
mouth to receive to admit to recognize
and a wiz go past her face and the teeny
ball is received and recognized and
understood and then you know what.

El Charro has many answers to Romy's most
burning questions, including those concerning
death:

EL CHARRO: Dead's a relative term in
El Otro. When people die, they become
story, and when stories die, they
become myths, and dead myths become
tattoos. I'm a purgastory thirteen years
and half a crime old. Suffice to say I'm
what's left of an old myth.

And as a tattoo artist himself, El Charro stands
ready to serve those transitioning beyond their
mythic state—he completes Lupe's unfinished
tattoo as he lies dying. The play is broken up
by Romy's out-of-time poetic riffs that give free
reign to her inner life. In this example, Romy
tries to calm her mother's fears as she attempts
to cross the dangerous river:

ROMY: Mama don't cry the reeds sway
and rattle in the green-black current that

carries me along the bank of wildflowers and alfafa that witness my sinkin' don't cry I see my dyin' is a pretty one among the yellow fleshy bubbles of gathering foam with the soft muddy floor sucking my toes under and the sky all asunder and you know what Mama the water tastes like skin like a man invading my mouth his whole self slipping in my shell like the tiny crayfish in the rushes no Mama don't cry just hear and don't cry.

The story is told in two time frames—the sequential, forward-moving trip, and a series of flashbacks that fills in the story of Romy's mother Nina and the men in her life. All the characters meet up at a *rancho* (a crossroads of sorts) where Anastasio, Romy's real father who was bludgeoned to death by Lupe before her birth, is magically channeled through Ben. Romy is critical of Ben, a first generation Mexican-American, because he doesn't speak Spanish, while Anastasio is fluent. Even though Lupe is killed, the ending is relatively uplifting with mother and daughter reconciled, and Romy having gained new respect for her new stepfather Ben.

A contemporary retelling of a Spanish classic, *Dreamlandia* follows the plot of *Life is a Dream* fairly closely, the story of a father who, receiving a prophecy to beware of his son, has him locked away until he is fully grown, and then decides to release him, with disastrous consequences. In both stories, the father's fear of his son becomes a self-fulfilling prophecy; he turns the boy into a savage who inevitably brings on the ruin that he so fears. Celestino, the father in *Dreamlandia*, has Lazaro, the son, locked in chains on an island in the middle of the Rio Grande. To occupy his time, he is given piles of women's fashion magazines and TV guides. His captors keep him pacified by occasionally filling his veins with heroin or "T-Rex." When the woman who has cursed Celestino dies, he has Lazaro drugged and brought to the family estate, where he is awakened and told that everything he remembers was a dream. But still very wild, the first thing Lazaro does is tear the ear off of Frank, his jailor. Frank, it is revealed later, is the father of Blanca, the beautiful young Mexican woman who has crossed over looking for her real father. Blanca, dressed as a man, gets a job tutoring Lazaro, who falls in love with her even though he thinks she's a man.

Set in the business world and drug underworld of El Paso/Juarez, Celestino runs a television manufacturing company as a front for his illegal drug dealing empire. Celestino is ruthless; when he catches his wife, Sonia, in bed with Lazaro, he dumps her in the middle of the Juarez desert where so many young women have gone missing. At the end of the story, Celestino is left stranded on Lazaro's island, while Lazaro and Blanca walk slowly into the river.

Among its many themes, *Dreamlandia* explores what it means to be a hyphenated American. Pepin, Blanca's brother, at one point says: "Lookit where you're standing, *Jefita*! Right on the *linea* between U.S. and U Lose." Blanca, having discovered that Frank, a white man, is her father, considers her own complicated racial identity:

> Races, *Ama*, these races, they grow
> fathers, mothers, daughters, sons and
> gods, these *raices* brown as a book,
> white as a bond, black as tar, they tell us
> who we are and punish what we're not.
> I'm brown, I'm *India*, then Spanish, then
> white, or half white which is worse than
> being all, I am all, Ama, all that I denied
> me! What am I? What race dries up and
> another grows? I saw him, saw the
> blood with blood matched up and it was
> mine. I'm a white lie, lie of this Sincero,
> his half-truth, half-breed, half Blanca, all
> *desmadre*! My father with his *raza*

stripped mine off and slipped me half of
his and left me with no race at all.

In *Bethlehem*, Solis explores the darkest corners
of the human psyche. Lee Rosenblum, a
journalist, wants to get an exclusive interview
with Mateo Bonaventura, accused of the
savage murder of a teenager named Shannon
Trimble. In order to get the interview, Lee
agrees to let Mateo help guide the
conversation. As Mateo begins to ask Lee a
number of personal questions, Lee becomes
more sympathetic toward him, and even
begins stepping in for Mateo as certain
memories are played out. Central to the story
is the bizarre fact that Mateo received a heart
transplant from a young girl just before
committing the murder, and in fact blames the
murder on the transplanted heart. When
Shannon's body was found, her heart was
missing.

Lee's own identity is confused—born Leandro
Guerra, his parents separated when he was
young, and his mother married a Jewish man
and moved with Lee to New York City, while
his Mexican father returned with his sister
south of the border. Lee is very conflicted
about his Mexican heritage, not only because of

his separation from his father, but also because his father beat (and possibly sexually abused) him when he was a child. Mateo senses Lee's vulnerability and sticks his finger in the wound:

> MATEO: I look in your eye. That red tomato edge in your eye and it look Mexican to me. It got that shredded Mexican pride in it still. Overripe. Sore to the touch. Sleepless. The pride that never sleeps, but waits. Waits for something just outa reach of this world. Your clothes are a mask. Your name is a mask. That makes you white. But what makes you Mexican like me is your soul itself is a mask.

Stylistically, this play, like the others, works on multiple planes. There is the present tense story of getting the interview, there are flashbacks in which Mateo and Lee sometime exchange roles, and there are moments of time-stoping direct address. The farther Lee proceeds with the interview, the more his objectivity is drained by his increasing identification with Mateo: "I want to loathe you, Mateo Buenaventura, I want to be morally repulsed by you. But all I feel is pity. I pity your sorry ass. I wish I knew why."

The play's title comes from Belen, a town in Mexico where Mateo says his sister Sonia lives, a town that translates in English as Bethlehem. Since Lee's sister is also somewhere in Mexico, this parallel draws the men even closer. When Lee discovers late in the story that Mateo has made up his sister, Lee feels he has finally gotten inside his subject:

> LEE: I am sitting in your skin feeling this crazy numbness strangle me. Then I know. I understand. Right there. In the interstice, right on the fucking F-stop. What you need is Sonia. But there is no Sonia. There never was any Sonia in your life to show you love, no matter how depraved. You don't know how to love, Mateo. You don't know how to feel. This numbness you only know as Belen, that's what you are. Not even this new transplanted heart can make you feel love.

The line between Mateo and Lee, the border between love and death, dissolves completely when Lee commits a horrible act. Lee confesses with new-found fervor: "I've gone down to that darkness and sought the wicked out.... I have stood where killers stood and put my hand on death."

As these plays suggest, Octavio Solis is a gifted, imaginative storyteller. The plots he invents grab you by the throat, take you on a wild ride and ultimately release you satisfied as after a five-course dinner. As Lee says at the end of *Bethlehem*, "As in the beginning, so in the end. Standing on the cusp, past and past, the same bag, the ending of the story inside." There is a fulfilling circularity to these plays. After taking you somewhere extreme, they leave you shocked and awed in a place that is both beginning and ending, with the sense that life will never be the same, and yet at the same time, life will go on.

Douglas Langworthy

EL OTRO

a river play by Octavio Solis

Cast of characters:

Romy, the kid, about 13

Guadalupe (Lupe), her dad

Ben, her other dad

Nina, her mom

El Charro Negro, a tattoo

Alma, the maid

Polo (Apolonio), the gardener

Ross (Cowboy), the cowboy

The Border Patrol Officer, the guardian

Anastacio (played by BEN), Romy's Stranger

Time: Sometime in the 1980's, on a Monday.

Place: El Paso, the border, El Otro

EL OTRO

2009 Production Credits

@ Thick Description, San Francisco, CA

<u>Cast:</u>

Romy, the kid, about 13: Maria Candelaria
Guadalupe (Lupe), her dad: Sean San José*
Ben, her other dad: Johnny Moreno*
Nina, her mom: Presciliana Esparolini*
Ross, the cowboy: Lawrence Radecker
Alma, the maid: Wilma Bonet*
the Border Patrol Officer: Michael Bellino
Polo, the gardener: Richard Talavera
El Charro Negro, a tattoo: Rhonnie
Washington*
Anastacio, Romy's stranger: Johnny Moreno*

direction by Tony Kelly; music by Vincent
Montoya, with Seventy and the Tattooed Love
Dogs; lighting design by Rick Martin**;
costume design by Todd Roehrman**; stage
management by Danielle Thomsen*

* Members of Actors' Equity Association, the union of Professional
Actors and Stage Managers.
** Members of United Scenic Artists, Local USA-829 of the IATSE,
representing designers for the American Theater.

EL OTRO was originally commissioned and developed by Thick Description.

Thick Description owes special thanks to these people and organizations for their help in the 2009 production:

Kip Gould and Broadway Play Publishing, Inc.; Pinata Art Studio Gallery; Bindlestiff Studio; Asian American Theater Company; Golden Thread Productions; Intersection for the Arts; The Potrero Hill Neighborhood House; Union Bank; Tom McCarthy, John Garibaldi, and Northern California Carpenters Local Union #22, and the residents of the Goodman 2 building.

Thick Description and the EL OTRO company dedicate the 2009 production to the memory, spirit and family of Luis Saguar.

Act One

(ROMY emerges from the darkness. The shadows of two men loom large behind her.)

ROMY: La Romy knows the way she knows the way it goes sun yanked out by the roots at dawn *y en la noche* buried in the ground like an old bone that's how long we got that's all it takes to live

(A MAN's voice, singing softly.)

MAN: *Eres mía para siempre*

Aunque vengas de la vientre

De tu madre

ROMY: Barely time enough to love *casi nada la Romy* knows the way it goes *mas que nada* you come you kiss and die that's the *cuento* only story we got time to tell 'cause there it goes there goes my sun

MAN: *Ése vicio, ésa hambre*

Éstos huesos, ésta sangre

Son del padre

ROMY: He's leaving his Romy and she's ready to die she's taken all day to die and there it goes up toward the blue above us, the sun over Romy and these two *babosos* in the parking lot of the Hidden Valley Shopping Center who don't feel the fire that Romy feels

MAN: *Cuando mi peor enemigo*

      Es el más conocido

      No vale la pena amar

      Hay que morir o matar.

ROMY: But Romy knows before she knows *simón* she knows the way and she's about ready to take it.

> *(LUPE stands beside her. BEN in army uniform appears opposite them.)*

LUPE: Are you him?

BEN: Yeah.

LUPE: Where's she?

BEN: Watching Good Morning America. She gave me the keys and said pick her up.

LUPE: Is that uniform supposed to impress me?

BEN: No.

LUPE: 'cause it don't.

BEN: Good.

ROMY: It don't impress me neither.

BEN: Nobody asked you, kid.

LUPE: *Trucha.* That's my kid you talking to, freak.

ROMY: I can take him.

BEN: Give her a birthday kiss and let's go. C'mon, Romy, your mother's waiting for you at the house.

ROMY: Uh-uh. Ain't goin' back.

BEN: Romy...

> *(LUPE strides up and plants his face almost against his. He smells him.)*

LUPE: Two eggs, over easy. *Chorizo* with onions. Wheat toast, margarine, coffee, lowfat milk.

BEN: You got a good nose--

LUPE: Cheap cherry lipstick. Tall glass of pussy juice.

BEN: That's enough, Lupe.

LUPE: You going down on my wife, Sarge? She what you have for a fortified breakfast every morning?

BEN: She's not your wife anymore. And I'm not a sergeant.

LUPE: What's his name, sweetheart? What do dogturds like this go by nowadays?

ROMY: Ben.

LUPE: Benjamin. I got a question for you. When does a wife quit being a wife? When she says? When he says? When the court says? I always thought it was when a life quit being a life, *ese*.

BEN: It was over long before I showed up. You were outa their lives months before.

LUPE: I don't question that. It's love that mystifies me. It must got the properties of water. Sometimes ice, sometimes it's a gas, sometimes it's all wet. Is that clever? Fuck me, I don't mean to be clever. It don't become a man like me to use wit on a fool like you.

BEN: Are you gonna wish her a happy birthday or what?

LUPE: You're no fool now, though. *Vato's* husband number two.

BEN: This is it. After today, you don't see her no more.

ROMY: Don't make me go with him, Apa. He's a loser.

LUPE: He's your new father, baby.

ROMY: I don't care. I hate him.

LUPE: She hates you, friend.

BEN: She'll get used to me.

ROMY: Make me go with him and I'll kill myself.

LUPE: Shit, she's starting to sound like me. You better take her off my hands, Ben, before she really makes some trouble.

ROMY: NO! FUCK HIM! I'M STAYING WITH YOU!

BEN: Cmon, we gotta get you ready for school.

ROMY: DON'T TOUCH ME, CHUMP.

LUPE: *Romelia Maria. Portate bien, mijita, o te doy tus chingazos.*

ROMY: *Si, Papi.*

LUPE: She's yours. Watch your fingers.

BEN: What you tell her?

LUPE: Be cool or be kicked in the teeth.

(LUPE kneels and faces ROMY to make his goodbyes.)

LUPE: *Oye.* Lemme see your eyes. *(He peers into them.) Ay te watcho, mijita.* Take care of your mother and don't be such a fuckin' pain to her. Remember these things: the razor in your sock in case you ever need to hitch a ride somewhere. Don't ever drink outa someone else's beer unless you helped pay for it. Always, always, speak Spanish to spite your teachers. And if this doofus walks by in his underwear in front of you, report his ass. Is that the lip? Don't give me the lip. Quit it, c'mon, I got you a present.

(He searches his pockets for it.)

LUPE: Shit. Hold on. It's gotta be in my car.

(He goes, leaving ROMY crying with BEN.)

ROMY: *Since when* Romy says since when he ever look her in the eye when except to say goodbye gotta figure out a way to die gottagottagotta be gone gottagottagotta be gone

(LUPE returns.)

LUPE: Damn, Romy, I had a present for you, but I musta left it at the *chante. Orale*, Ben, think we could take ten minutes to go by the house--?

BEN: We'll wait for you.

LUPE: No way, man. Come along. We'll go in my car. Ride with me, *ese*. I'm not so bad a guy as Nina makes me out.

BEN: Once you're done, I'm supposed to go straight home.

LUPE: Ten minutes. Just a couple blocks. I'll drive us there and back. It's her present, man.

BEN: Ten minutes?

ROMY: I'm not sitting next to that chump.

LUPE: Shut your ass. *(to BEN)* Ten minutes.

ROMY: Then la Romy *y los dos babosos* in the car and then her in the back seat and them in the front and then seeing El Paso streak by like bad laundry and then she hears the doofus saying...

(All three in the car.)

BEN: So I told Nina maybe it was harsh for the court to strip your visitation rights. You're entitled to see her at least once a year.

LUPE: Nina told you about me?

BEN: Not really.

LUPE: Then how do you know what I'm entitled to?

BEN: Well, you're her father, aren't you? *(No reply)* Anyway, I hope the last visitation you got to spend together was worthwhile.

LUPE: *Simón, cabron.* Tell him what all we did on your last visit, honey.

ROMY: We went to Dairy Queen.

LUPE: Awesome shit those parfaits.

ROMY: And then we went to the movies.

LUPE: Some kickboxing thing.

ROMY: And then we saw those people.

LUPE: She kept me company while I drove around and scored a couple deals.

BEN: A couple deals?

LUPE: A little this, a little that. I got some exceptional medication people are talking about.

BEN: What kinda medication?

LUPE: NASA of the mind. Show him, Rome.

(ROMY shows him the bag.)

BEN: Now I get how come the courts stripped your visitation rights.

LUPE: Don't worry about her, Benny. I brung her up right. What's our motto, honey?

ROMY: Just say no.

LUPE: What else did we do? Oh yeah! We keyed this guy's car and shot his dogs for cheating a friend out of some bricks for his patio. Dogs, man, they don't know when to give up the ghost. It was kinda funny.

BEN: Ha ha.

ROMY: And you know what? this Romy knows the way she's got it right in her lap the way out of the story *hijola* these little buds of peyote these dream givers she could eat em and quietly join all those other suns that ever set so she puts a few buds *en su* pocket and eats one and begins to feel it break slow like a secret like a little black secret inside

LUPE: Did you hear something?

BEN: No.

LUPE: Something whizzed. I felt it whizz right by us, shooom, right through these open windows, this wee chunk a righteousness.

Shoom, right under our noses, didn't you feel it?

BEN: Maybe it was a bug.

LUPE: I need to see this guy.

ROMY: And then we stop in front of this house.

> (ROSS the cowboy comes out, his
> ear bleeding profusely.)

ROSS:Hey, Lupe! *¿Como te va, guey?*

LUPE: Damn, Ross, what the fuck happened to you?

ROSS: Nothin'. It's nothin'. Who's the soldier boy?

LUPE: My competition. Ben from Ft. Bliss. Are you okay?

ROSS: Yeah, yeah. I'm fine.

LUPE: Your ear looks pretty bad, white boy.

ROSS: It's fine. I feel like a million.

BEN: What are you talking about? You're bleeding all over yourself.

ROSS: Loop, is this guy, like, trying to make a point or something? 'Cause if he's trying to make a point, he should come right out and make it and not sit on his fucking hands all day.

LUPE: No, shit no, nothing of the kind.

ROSS: I don't appreciate smart ass sergeants.

LUPE: He's cracking a joke. *Un chiste.*

BEN: And for your information, I'm a private first class.

ROSS: You must be frying in that uniform. Listen, I'd ask you all in but things are a bit of a mess.

LUPE: *¡No mames!* Let's break open some sixes.

ROSS: Things are a real mess. I couldn't let you in, Loop. Way too messy for the eyes of innocents.

LUPE: Whatever you say, Ross.

ROSS: So what you got, buddy?

LUPE: Premium boogie, no fat, all natural ingredients.

ROSS: Vacu-packed for freshness?

LUPE: For your chewing satisfaction.

ROSS: Awright. Come around side of the house.

(They go.)

BEN: You really shoot those dogs?

ROMY: He did, I just saw.

BEN: No wonder your mama's concerned about you.

ROMY: Crock.

BEN: She cares about your feelings, Romy.

ROMY: More crock.

BEN: She wants to help you adjust to the new situation.

ROMY: *Ese, no seas tan mamón.*

BEN: What?

ROMY: What kinda Mexican are you? You don't even know Spanish. Man, you're embarrassing.

BEN: Look, kid, I want to work this out. It doesn't have to be this ugly. We're trying to do right by you.

ROMY: Then how come nobody checked with me? How come nobody asked if I wanted a doofus in the house?

BEN: Okay, your mom shoulda told you. But it doesn't matter anyhow. We're married and that's that.

ROMY: Then my feelings don't count for shit, do they, Ben?

BEN:*(touching her shoulder)* Romy, I-

> *(ROMY violently recoils from his touch.)*

ROMY: Don't you fucking touch me! Pervert!

BEN: I was... I...

> *(The lights change, casting an eerie glow on BEN.)*

ROMY: And then everything's water and she looks at Ben and Ben stares at the sun and then looks back at La Romy with a fierce whiskey in his eyes and whispers in another voice

BEN: *Eres... mía*

ROMY: the voice of the stranger who been messing with my sleep showing up in my dreams in tatters of blood and muck

> *(The lights resume. LUPE and ROSS return.)*

LUPE: Thanks a lot for waiting up, Ben. Ross ain't no loose honky, he's a stand-up guy. He's the Boss Ross. Right, *ese*?

ROSS: You don't got a tarp in the trunk, do you, Loop?

LUPE: Sorry, man. What for?

ROSS: My house is in a grievous state. Damn place turned to hell on me. Gotta clean up. Do a midnight dump-run.

BEN: And take care of your ear.

LUPE: More army humor.

ROSS: I will take care of my ear, sir. Your benediction gonna make me right. Cuz a you I have the balm to make my pains holy. Cuz a you I'ma have me a spectacular day!

> *(He takes out a prescription vial and crams his mouth with pills.)*

BEN: What do you mean cuz of me? What is that shit he's taking?

ROSS: Sir, my poor decrepit ass is shittin' gratitude for you. I just hope the *Charro* knows how fuckin' good his angel is.

ROMY: The *Charro*.

BEN: Who's that? What *charro*?

(LUPE raises his shirt, revealing an array of tattoos. Prominent on his back is a large tattoo of a <u>Charro</u>.)

LUPE: *El Charro Negro*, Ben. Got to be.

ROSS: Pray for me, sir. Pray that I get a tarp before nightfall.

LUPE: Check with my ex-, Ross. She'll fix you up.

BEN: Can we go now?

(ROSS goes.)

ROMY: And you know what? I'm feeling a tingle like when you get up too fast and the blood rushes to catch up with you and you see little holes in the air. And with this tingle comes a music and I see the back of Lupe's head as he drives on and on and on and on

BEN: What happened back there? Why was he bleeding? And what was he thanking me for?

LUPE: You asking too many of the wrong questions, bud. Just know that Ross respects you now.

BEN: What did you tell him?

LUPE: I told him you were taking over. I told him you were sleeping in my place. Was I outa line? Tell me if I was, Ben.

BEN: That looked like a gunshot.

LUPE: Probably was.

BEN: I got that address memorized.

LUPE: Bitchin.

BEN: This kid doesn't need to be seeing stuff like that.

LUPE: I'm with you there.

ROMY: And you know what: I'm there too.

> *(Lights change. LUPE's apartment.*
> *LUPE points and goes.)*

LUPE: Make yourselves at home. I gotta take a leak.

BEN: Where's all the furniture?

ROMY: He don't got none.

BEN: Where are we supposed to sit, on the floor?

> *(She does. He sits beside her.)*

BEN: Hey, back there. I didn't mean anything by that.

ROMY: Why don't you go fight some war and die so we can scratch your name on that dumb wall?

BEN: You know what? I get it. Who wants to break up a family? Even one like yours. But she's the only woman ever made me feel like somebody, and I'm the man she needs right now. And with or without you, we're gonna have us a baby--

ROMY: That's gross!

BEN: I want my own kid. Someone to start us off clean, bless the house, someone to--

ROMY: Replace me.

BEN: That's not what I was gonna say.

ROMY: You go try and make a baby with her. I'll take this razor and slit that baby in its sleep, I swear to God I will.

BEN: I wonder how much of your daddy are you.

> (*Lupe enters with a beer in each hand.*)

LUPE: Fully 50 percent. Least that's what I been told.

BEN: A little early in the day for me.

LUPE: If you're serious about taking on this spitfire, be serious about this.

(Ben takes the beer.)

LUPE: Sorry about the digs. Sold everything last week and chucked the rest in the dumpster out back. Kept nothing but my old Zippo lighter. I used it to keep time to all her pretty songs.

BEN: Nina sings?

LUPE: Pipes like Vikki Carr. She serenaded me all the time.

ROMY: Did you find it?

LUPE: What?

ROMY: My present.

LUPE: No. It's around here. Go look in the kitchen.

(ROMY goes, grumbling to herself.)

BEN: Can I borrow your phone to call Nina?

LUPE: Just cut off the service. Relax. I'll get you back to your car. Where do you hail from, soldier?

BEN: Chicago.

LUPE: Cool.

BEN: Second generation. Working-class Mexicans from Pilsen.

LUPE: We must look like hicks to you. Why'd you join the service?

BEN: I needed some discipline in my life. Army's a good place to start. The chain of command is clear, PFC to God. Why are we talking about this? We should be going back.

LUPE: I'm not done with my beer, pal. Tell me how you met my wife at the cafeteria.

BEN: I dunno. I like chili-cheeseburgers and she happened to cook them to my specifications. What can I say? I was lonely and she was there. In a town where I don't know a soul and people don't talk much, it was nice that she was nice.

LUPE: Yeah.

BEN: Nina in that funky white uniform and her little name tag. She gave me a new lease.

LUPE: So wassup with you and my daughter?

BEN: What do you mean?

LUPE: How come she call you a pervert?

BEN: What are you insinuating?

LUPE: I ain't insinuatin' shit. I'm saying I heard both of you back at Cowboy's. Wassup with you? She what you come to my house for, Ben? Is this what you mean by needing some discipline?

BEN: Lemme tell you one thing, before you jump to any more conclusions. I didn't know about this kid. I never heard two words about her until after I proposed to Nina.

LUPE: You expect me to believe that?

(ROMY re-enters.)

BEN: I don't care what you believe. The fact is in all the times I went out with her, not once did the name Romelia pass her lips.

ROMY: You're a liar.

BEN: It's the truth. She was a free and single woman so far as I was concerned and your little ass never came up. Not till after we got the rings. I'm willing to raise you as my own *(turning to LUPE)* but not how you're suggesting. So don't even go there, okay? Let's get back to my car.

LUPE: Lemme find that present first.

(LUPE goes.)

BEN: Fuckhead.

ROMY: La Romy sitting there staring at the wall feeling her momma's denial start to seep through the cracks and then she see that old lady coming already feel her pressure she's coming she's about to

> (*An old woman, ALMA, enters, furtively. She becomes very distressed when she sees BEN.*)

BEN: Yes? You know this lady, Romy?

> (*ROMY shakes her head. ALMA is visibly rattled.*)

BEN: Are you looking for someone, ma'am?

ALMA: (*in a hushed voice*) Dios mio. Dios mio. *Dueño de mis dolores.*

BEN: Ma'am?

ALMA: Face so pale, eyes so pure, still the boy we knew. Do you know who I am? *Los pesares del mundo, los renuncio todos.* There are lies which come true and nights with opened veins. (*taking out a small alarm clock*) Numbers on the palm of the hand and little bones in the clock. Ants in my water and regrets I daily light candles for. *Ticka ticka tick.*

BEN: Are you with some church or something?

ALMA: It is the time, *mijo*, which picks us. The sins ripen. Fall at our feet. Open up like ulcers. Proclaim our souls to hell. For our crimes, *Anastacio*, forgive us.

ROMY: Who?

ALMA: *(turning to ROMY)* And you! You who deliver us. *Santísima flor.* For you, *virgencita*, on my knees, I receive your host.

> *(ALMA thrusts ROMY's hand into her mouth.)*

ALMA: Hmm. You are my sacrament.

> *(LUPE enters, sees her, and seizes her by the collar.)*

LUPE: FUCK! What are you doing here! Get your ass away from my daughter, bitch!

ALMA: ¡*Perdón, perdón!*

LUPE: Shut up! Ben, I'm disappointed in you.

BEN: What, she came in, I didn't know what--

LUPE: Are you all right, baby? She hurt you?

ROMY: No.

BEN: Who is she?

LUPE: This hag? This filthy crone? She's my maid. Alma the fucking maid. She comes here every Monday to clean the house for me.

BEN: What's there to clean?

LUPE: Tell him.

ALMA: The floor, the walls, the sink in the kitchen, the vegetable bin in the refrigerator, the toilet bowl, the windows-

LUPE: What did you tell him? Tell me what you told him.

ALMA: *Nada, señor.* Not a thing. I just... wanted to see.

LUPE: Alma, you sick cow, tell me who the fuck you think this is.

ALMA: *No sé.*

LUPE: This is Ben from Ft. Bliss. Ben from Chicago. What the fuck is your last name?

BEN: Cortez.

LUPE: Benjamín Cortez.

ALMA: *Señor Cortez.*

LUPE: Now what did I tell you? Didn't I make it clear that you were to wait at the ranch? Don't you know you almost messed everything up? What kinda fuckin' maid are you anyway!

> (He produces a handgun, which he levels at her head.)

BEN: Whoa! Lupe! What are you doing?

LUPE: This domestic is an incompetent, Ben. A pervert who don't know the first thing about raising children in a positive environment!

ALMA: *¡No, señor, por favor!*

LUPE: I pay her well, Ben, don't I pay you well, and all these years I kept her because I thought I should depend on something, I thought she might give the world some credibility, Monday comes, maid comes, Monday comes, maid comes. Only now I ain't so sure the routine makes any sense. Mondays are starting to feel like a bitch to me. Maybe if I do away with the maid, Mondays won't come. That would suit me fine. What do you think, Alma?

> (ALMA urinates on herself, creating a small puddle.)

LUPE: Get a mop.

> (Ben starts to go.)

LUPE: Not you. You.

(ALMA goes.)

LUPE: She's the maid.

BEN: You gonna put that away?

LUPE: Thought you were accustomed to seeing firearms in the Army, Ben.

BEN: Put the gun away or there's going to be a situation.

LUPE: Whoa. Hubby number two grows some balls.

ROMY: Is that my present?

> *(ALMA returns with a mop and mops up the floor.)*

LUPE: What? No, honey. This ain't even loaded. Check this out.

> *(He aims at the floor and slowly pulls the trigger. A nasty click sends a shudder through ALMA.)*

LUPE: See?

ROMY: Where's my present?

LUPE: I dunno, babe. Alma, have you seen...?

ALMA: *No señor.* But it can only be at one place.

LUPE: Where?

ALMA: *Al otro lado.*

BEN: Where?

ROMY: The other side.

ALMA: *Allí en el rancho estará.*

BEN: What *rancho* is she talking about?

ALMA: You know what *rancho, mijo.* It's where you rode, Anast-

LUPE: Shut your hole!

(keeping his gaze on ALMA)

LUPE: What have you heard about me, Ben?

BEN: What do you mean?

LUPE: What have you heard on the street? Have you heard like, that Lupe, *ese,* he's bad news, he's into some shit, like, he's killed some kid or somethin', *ese.* Have you heard that?

BEN: No.

LUPE: Have you heard anything about me killing a maid?

BEN: No.

LUPE: Me neither.

ROMY: *Apa,* I want my present.

LUPE: What you thinkin', Ben?

BEN: Let's get her present.

LUPE: Alma, go back to where you were. And stay put.

ROMY: *Pero La Romy* can't stay put in her own head cuz the little buds are breaking up inside her slowly bringing up her Mom one secret at a time so I can tell her: how could you pull this shit how could you deny me to that chump *Ama*

> (*As she speaks, the others recede into the darkness and NINA emerges, coming toward her in a slow glide.*)

NINA: Romy...

ROMY: Mom...

NINA: *Mi gatita...*

ROMY: *Ay, Ama...*

> (*NINA bursts forward. A large bruise under her right eye.*)

NINA: Don't you come near me! Don't come dragging those shoes into my house! Lookit you, *loca*! What is that!

ROMY: Horseshit.

NINA: *Pos* take your shoes off! Take them off! *Valgame*, where in this crummy neighborhood did you get horseshit from?

    (ROMY sits to take off her shoes.)

ROMY: A horse. Damn, quit being such a mom.

NINA: You quit being a smart mouth. Don't wipe your hands on me, girl. Damn, I come home from work and not a minute's rest!

ROMY: -- Hey! What happened to you?

NINA: *Nada.* Other shoe.

ROMY: Your eye's all swoll up!

NINA: I don't want to discuss it.

ROMY: D'you two fight again?

NINA: I said, I don't wanna discuss it.

ROMY: I can't believe it. What did you tell him that he did this to you?

NINA: I told him don't hit me. Now, what horse you talking about?

ROMY: The one in Mr. Tovar's backyard.

NINA: The Tovares? The Tovares have a horse? Are you sure?

ROMY: I heard it whinny this morning. So when I got home from school, I changed pants and went to see.

NINA: You went to their house? The socks.

ROMY: *(as she takes them off)* To the alley *atras*. I climbed up the metal fence he keeps there, but I couldn't see it. So I jumped over and landed in this big ol pile of *caca*. But there it was.

NINA: You saw it?

ROMY: *Ama*, it was a colt. This skinny thing with legs like willow branches and a white hanky stain on its nose. He made this little snort and shook its head to one side like it was calling me.

NINA: Did you get close?

ROMY: I couldn't move 'cause he was staring right at my kneecaps, but he came to me, *Ama*. He came slow and he let me touch him.

NINA: *Mija*, that's a trait you get from me. I have this way with horses. They come to me like I'm one of them. Their hides ripple when I run my hand across their backs. I learned to love when I learned to ride.

ROMY: You rode horses? When did you do that?

NINA: Way before you were born, kid. Did Mr Tovar catch you?

ROMY: No. I felt someone watching me the whole time, though. So I split.

NINA: Don't be jumpin' into people's yards. It's trespassing. The Tovares, especially.

ROMY: How come we never see them? How come they never come out or nothing?

NINA: They're sad people, *mija*. They gave up all their horses years ago when they lost their only boy.

ROMY: How come they got that colt now?

NINA: That's what I'd like to know. Hose off. You stink.

ROMY: I can't. You got the sprinkler on.

NINA: Then do what I woulda done, stupid.

ROMY: What.

NINA: Run through it!

> (She dashes into the shower of the 'sprinkler' screaming and laughing as ROMY follows suit.)

ROMY: IT'S COLD!

NINA: IT FEELS GOOD!

ROMY: YOUR UNIFORM!

NINA: HELL WITH THAT!

ROMY: LET ME GO! I'M GETTING WET!

NINA: GOOD! GET YOURSELF CLEAN!
CLEAN ALL OVER! CLEAN TO THE BONE!

ROMY: *¡ANDALE! ¡AMA!* QUIT!

NINA: ALL RIGHT! ALL RIGHT!

> *(They run out and stand by their
> shoes, panting with delight. ROMY
> finds a small note NINA dropped by
> the sprinkler.)*

ROMY: And you know what from Ama's soul
a petal fall inside the ring of water a note of
secrecies and La Romy see it pick it and save it
for no reason why...

> *(She puts it away, unseen by
> NINA.)*

NINA: I'm not letting him in the house again. I
told him. This is the last time.

ROMY: He's my dad.

NINA: I can't be married to that man no more. *No mas.* C'mon.

ROMY: What.

NINA: I'm not drinking by myself. One beer. A toast to the new colt on the block. But first... *(turning to the 'sprinkler')* One more walk through the water.

> *(NINA slowly courses through the invisible rain, feeling the cleansing drops on her face. ROMY watches her go.)*

ROMY: La Romy sees you Mom and sees something scared hurt something hidden from even you *Ama* wishin' you could hose yourself off hose off years of shit but you know what it won't wash off ever ever ever and ever

> *(BEN and LUPE enter, LUPE holding his shoes and socks in his hands.)*

LUPE: You ready, babe?

ROMY: Uh-huh.

BEN: Hold on a minute. What's going on? What are we doing?

LUPE: We're crossing the river, Ben.

BEN: What for?

ROMY: To get to the other side, stupid.

BEN: Hey, they got bridges for this last I heard.

LUPE: They're not available routes for me anymore, see what I'm saying? You want her to get her present. Take your shoes off and roll up your pants.

BEN: I don't think this is legal, Lupe.

ROMY: We should leave him here.

LUPE: Ben, the Law is an outmoded thang. It's just an excuse to make people do what they don't want to do. Shit, the Law's even moved into my bedroom. Laid down these fuckin' rulings that don't make no sense. Custody, property, restraining orders, it's all bullshit.

BEN: I'm not letting you take her across.

ROMY: Why not?

BEN: Because you could drown, you idiot.

ROMY: Pffft.

BEN: Yeah, you say that now.

LUPE: It's not deep in this part. Trust me.

BEN: No way.

LUPE: *Oyeme*, Benjamin, what's the deal here? Are you establishing the chain of command? You pulling rank on me, babe?

BEN: There is no present for her, is there? Is there?

ROMY: I don't know how you even think you can be my Dad. You don't got the guts to cross the damn river cuz you ain't no real Mexican.

BEN: I'm Mexican. I got Mexican blood in me.

ROMY: Don't go foolin' yourself, Ben.

BEN: I'M A MEXICAN, GODDAMMIT!

> *(A BORDER PATROL OFFICER leaps out, aiming his flashlight at them.)*

OFFICER: Did I hear someone say Messican?

ROMY: Oh-oh.

BEN: Hey, how's it goin. We were just leav--

OFFICER: Stay right where you are, brother. Don't make me chase you down.

BEN: Whoa, take it easy. I'm trying to tell you, they wanted me to go with them across the river--

OFFICER: Really. To that side.

BEN: That's crazy, right? They wanted to cross right here.

OFFICER: You sure it wasn't the other way around? You didn't just swim from that side to this?

BEN: C'mon. Do we look like illegals? (to LUPE) Clear things up with this character and let's get the hell out.

LUPE: *¿Como?*

BEN: Tell him, Lupe.

LUPE: *¿Que dijo este buey?*

ROMY: *No se. Creo que ya nos chingamos, Apa.*

BEN: Aw, cut it out! Talk English, both a you!

LUPE: *No hables así, mijita o te doy por la madre.*

ROMY: *¡Si me pegas, te doy una patada en los meros huevos!*

BEN: We're American.

OFFICER: I heard Messican.

BEN: C'mon, the uniform, I'm an enlisted man. Wanna see ID?

OFFICER: That would be helpful. *(ROMY starts to run. The OFFICER aims his gun at her.)*

¡ALTO! ¡NO SE MUEVA 0 LE DOY UN BALAZO POR LA CABEZA!

BEN: SHIT! ROMY! WHAT THE FUCK ARE YOU DOING! DON'T RUN!

> *(ROMY freezes.)*

LUPE: *Por favor, señor,* no keel my leetle chile. *¡Es mi hija!*

OFFICER: EVERYONE! On the ground! Now! You too, *jovencita*!

BEN: Do as he says.

> *(Everyone lies flat on their stomachs. The OFFICER frisks the men for weapons.)*

OFFICER: So what's the motivation, sergeant? Don't like the pay in the Army? Feel you gotta diversify by takin' on wetbacks?

BEN: I'm not a coyote. And they're not illegals.

OFFICER: Uh-huh.

BEN: The girl is my step-daughter, the man is her father. He was trying to get me to wade across the border to Mexico. And I'm not a sergeant.

OFFICER: *(finding the bag full of peyote)* Well, hi-de-hi-hi-ho.

BEN: oh fuck.

OFFICER: What are these for, sergeant, your allergies?

BEN: I have nothing to do with that.

OFFICER: *(finding the gun)* How about this?

> *(No reply.)*

OFFICER: All right. *Quítese la ropa, por favor.*

BEN: Say what?

OFFICER: Start stripping.

BEN: What for?

OFFICER: Just do it.

BEN: Lupe. Say something. Tell him you're American.

LUPE: *Soy Americáno.*

OFFICER: Peel. *(They strip to their shorts.)* In all my ten years on the Border Patrol, never ever have I come across anyone trying to sneak from the US side to the Messican. That's a good one. Why would anyone give up living in the richest country on earth and go live in that shitpot? What could possibly be there that can't be had here?

LUPE: Maybee chee ees ded.

OFFICER: Whut?

LUPE: Ded. Joo cahn dress her op in jools an fine closs an put mucho make-op on her fase. Joo can get een bed weeth her an mahke sex weeth her an mahke beleef dat chee ees good an muy linda, but joo canna fool joorsef. Chee ees a rotteen corpse an chee duzznt eefen know joo are der. Cos la *verdad, señor,* ees dat chee ees ded to joo an maybee alwaz has bin.

OFFICER: Are you talking about America?

BEN: He's talking about his ex-wife.

LUPE: We haf too go bahck, *señor.* We canna leef in dee same box weef da ded. *Tenemos que devolvérnos.*

OFFICER: I can't let you go.

LUPE: *¿Porque no?* It ees our right.

OFFICER: But it's our job, too, to protect the border from--

LUPE: To keep us out, dat ees joor yob. To send us bahck ees de same ting.

OFFICER: *(seeing them in their nakedness)* Well, one sure for sure: I don't much see the difference between Messican and Merican now. Alla you look like wetbacks to me.

LUPE: Dat ees what we are. *Mojados*. Eliens. Whatefer border wi cross.

OFFICER: I hate this job. I really hate it. I tell Lucille, Lucille, this job is the sickest job there is. To have to pick up them poor people and haul them to the station like strays to the pound, it's terrible. And to see that... that dread in their eyes. To deal with that on a daily basis, cutting people's hopes off right at the knee, right as they set foot in the USA, to bag 'em right there and knock 'em back across, it's a crime worse than the crime they commit. I go, Lucille, I'm a barb wire fence with Ray-bans. She just stares back at me like I'm not even there. I hate this damn job.

(tossing their clothes back to them)

OFFICER: You wanna go back, I can't stop you.

LUPE: *Vamonos.*

BEN: You're letting us cross? Are you crazy?

OFFICER: Get.

ROMY: Thanks, mister.

OFFICER: *Señores*, if I see you on this side again, I'll perform my duties to the letter and you'll be sorry for it.

LUPE: Joo weel be doeen us a faybor. *Gracias.*

> *(LUPE and ROMY go as BEN yells at the OFFICER.)*

BEN: You can't let us go! You can't! That girl could drown in that water!

OFFICER: She seems to be fordin' it all right to me.

BEN: Oh shit! ROMY!

> *(BEN runs off after them, past ROMY who stands downstage. The OFFICER takes ROMY'S shoes and goes.)*

ROMY: And then we're toe-deep then ankle-deep then knee-deep in water that is more syrup than water and it feels good to La Romy and then you know what swooosh we're deep like that I see two heads in front of me bobbin' and chokin' an' swooosh La Romy starts to go under swimmin' with old tires and bottles and tennies and La Romy feels a long hand crammin' in her mouth goin' down her lungs clawin' at the breath she got left and swooosh she can't see a thing she think she drownin' but she think a Mom my Mom my Mom my Mother MAMA!

> *(Lights change. NINA appears.)*

NINA: I hear you, baby. *(She turns and calls loudly.)* COWBOY! COWBOY, I KNOW YOU'RE IN THERE! GET YOUR ASS OUT HERE RIGHT NOW! I'M GONNA CALL THE COPS, ROSS! I MEAN IT! GET OUT HERE!

> *(ROSS enters, really stoned, his wound cursorily dressed with a bandanna.)*

ROSS: Hi, Nina. I didn't hear ya. The waffle iron was on.

NINA: Jesus Christ. What the hell happened to you?

ROSS: Me and Marie. You know how we mess around. It was a accident.

NINA: Oh shit. Marie! Ross, what have you done? Is Romy in there? You got my little girl in your house?

ROSS: No, no, Nina, listen, you can't go in, you can't, they're not here!

NINA: They were here, though, right? That's what you're saying, am I right?

ROSS: You wouldn't have a tarp, would you?

NINA: Listen to me, Ross. My man was supposed to be home with Romy hours ago. I been looking everywhere for them. Nobody's seen them and nobody's seen Lupe. But I know he's got *mija* and my new guy and you're the only one I know who can figure things out for me. Now where the fuck did they go?

ROSS: Dunno. You know Loop, movin' target. Boy, these pants are finished.

NINA: Ross, goddammit, I'm talking to you!

ROSS: Hey, take it easy!

NINA: How long we known each other, Cowboy? How many times you come to my house and cry on my shoulder about your girl? How many bottles been passed between us? We're losers, *ese*, rank amateurs when it comes to doin' what's right. We deserve what's coming to us. But not *mija*. She's got nothing to do with this. If he hurts her, if he so much as touches her, we're all fucked for life.

ROSS: If I only had a tarp, I might--

NINA: I don't have a goddamn tarp, Ross!

ROSS: You checked the trunk?

> (*She looks at him askance, then goes. Pause. She returns dragging a large tarpaulin.*)

ROSS: Lord in fuckin' heaven.

NINA: How did this end up in my car, Ross?

ROSS: It's perfectamundo.

NINA: When did you and him dig this up?

ROSS: A few days ago. Can I have it?

NINA: Where are they?

ROSS: I used to bust horses, you know. A ranch out by Abilene. I would get up at five, eat cold beans out of a can, and take the meanest horses and ride 'em till they broke. Took pride in my bloody boots. It was a damn good livin'. But you just can't treat a woman like that, can you?

NINA: No, you can't, Cowboy.

ROSS: They got spirit won't quit till they do. *Chíngao.*

NINA: I told that girl to leave you. Poor thing loved you too damned much.

ROSS: I'm sorry.

NINA: Where are they?

ROSS: I used to bust horses, Nina. Did I ever tell you that?

NINA: Take this thing in there and clean up your mess and do what you have to do. And this time don't miss.

> (ROSS drags the tarp off. NINA holds back tears.)

ROMY: Mama don't cry the reeds sway and rattle in the green-black current that carries me along the bank of wildflowers and alfalfa that witness my sinkin' don't cry I see my dyin' is a pretty one among the yellow fleshy bubbles of gathering foam with the soft muddy floor sucking my toes under and the sky all asunder and you know what Mama the water tastes like skin like a man invading my mouth his whole self slipping in my shell like the tiny crayfish in the rushes no Mama don't cry just hear and don't cry

NINA: I hear you, baby.

> (She goes. Lights change. ROMY falls to her knees, out of breath. LUPE and BEN stagger on, wet, cold, panting, their drenched clothes in their arms.)

BEN: Oh my god! Oh my god! Jesus Christ!

LUPE: That was some ride! Yeah! That's the way to live! Goddamn!

BEN: I thought you said it wasn't gonna be deep!

LUPE: That's the river, *ese*, she one treacherous bitch! Ha!

BEN: That water was twenty feet at least! It was spinning us around like twigs! We coulda drowned!

LUPE: Like I said, Ben, that was some ride! You gotta be ready, you gotta keep the blood red, the fists clenched, the teeth grit down, 'cause now we're on the other side, *cabron*! WOOO!

BEN: Uugh. What am I gonna tell my C.O. about my uniform?

LUPE: Fuck your uniform! When are you gonna learn, brother? The army don't mean shit here. God ain't no American and he don't wear no uniform and he don't give a shit about PFCs. We're on the Other, Ben! The Other!

BEN: This is crazy.

LUPE: You're catchin' on. How are you, sweetheart?

ROMY: Okay.

BEN: What do you mean okay? You nearly went under, you brat.

LUPE: He's right, Romy. We almost lost you. *De chiripada este cabron te salvó.*

ROMY: What?

LUPE: He dragged you ashore by the scruff, didn't ya, ace?

BEN: You quit stroking and let yourself go. What was I gonna do, let you sink?

LUPE: The fact is, he saved your ass.

BEN: You scared me, kid.

LUPE: It was a sight, babe. He had you one arm around your neck, and he was holding your head up, and his face was real near to yours and his hand, you know, kinda rode down over your breast, and *mano*, it was a sight.

ROMY: Is that true?

BEN: Dammit, Lupe, what are you doing?

LUPE: *Nada*, Ben. Just trying to find us a place where we can watch the moon pus up in the sky without the chiggers crawling up our ass.

ROMY: Were you really trying to feel me up?

BEN: I was keeping your stupid head above water. You're gonna catch hypothermia if we don't get you some place warm.

LUPE: Sit down, relax, commingle.

BEN: Fuck you.

(BEN goes.)

LUPE: I feel sorry for you, Rome. Your father's a nerd.

ROMY: He's not my father.

LUPE: Hey, listen. You wanna be rid of him? I can do that, you know. Right here, right now. You want me to do that?

ROMY: (pausing for a moment) No.

LUPE: I'm just clownin' you! What up? Are you pissed at me? Huh?

ROMY: No.

LUPE: ¿Como está tu mama?

ROMY: I spend the whole weekend with you and this is the first you ask of her.

LUPE: How is she, I said.

ROMY: Better. She ain't sittin' up in the kitchen all night smoking cigarettes or talkin' to herself in the mornings and wipin' those red puffy eyes. She's not alone in the evenings. She's actually starting to look younger.

LUPE: So this soldier makes her happy?

ROMY: I guess.

LUPE: That's too bad. Your mama and me were made for each other, you know.

ROMY: Oh sure. You hardly showed your face and when you did you were drunk and you trashed the house and took Mom's money and made fun of her food like she couldn't do nothin' right and you never took us out to dinner even, *Apa*! Mom couldn't keep any friends 'cause they were afraid of you. And junkies were always callin' for you or if it wasn't them it was the police, and then she said you hit her. Yeah you were made for each other, all right.

LUPE: You **are** pissed at me.

ROMY: You don't have to go, *Apa*. You can change.

LUPE: I have. I've gotten worse.

ROMY: You can't let this guy be my father.

LUPE: I dunno, babe.

ROMY: You're my dad. Just tell him that. Tell him you're my real dad!

LUPE: Lissen to me, you little cunt. You keep the fuck away from me! You should've stayed with your mother while you had the chance!

You got me all wrong! I ain't your father! I never been your father!

> *(He turns away from her as BEN enters, carrying a rolled up old quilt.)*

BEN: I found this. It's filthy but it's dry.

> *(He places it on ROMY's shoulders. She violently shrugs it off.)*

BEN: What's wrong? What happened?

LUPE: She's touched by your goodness, Ben. Such a heart a gold, I just wanna cut it out and put it by the dice on my dashboard.

> *(BEN places the quilt over her shoulders and turns to LUPE.)*

BEN: What you tell her?

LUPE: Nothing she don't already know-- *(suddenly ducking, forcing BEN down with him)* Heads!

BEN: What is it?

LUPE: Din't you see it?

BEN: What, another bug?

LUPE: Ain't no bugs, Ben. This is a bullet.

BEN: A bullet? I didn't hear no gunshot.

LUPE: Why would you? It's not meant for you. *(to ROMY)* Did you hear it?

ROMY: Nope.

(NINA enters in her bathrobe.)

ROMY: And then La Romy feel another chemical vision riding on the back of bad memory she don't say nothin' as Momma come from that day past when I was sleepin' in my bed

NINA: Hey, deadweight.

LUPE: Yeah?

BEN: I wonder what Nina's thinking of us right now.

NINA: You gonna watch TV all night *o vas a venir a la cama*?

LUPE: Where's Romy?

BEN: Over there.

NINA: Sleeping in her room. Or trying to. She keeps having these nightmares about some man trying to grab her. Comes out of the earth and grabs her.

LUPE: It's all them zombie movies.

BEN: Nina says there wasn't any heat between you.

LUPE: There wasn't.

NINA: Well, coming to bed or not?

LUPE: Nina, why is it that when I look at you and see the flesh of your lovely tits peekin' through your blouse by the little cup at the base of your neck and then I catch a whiff of the sweet oil of your sex, why is it that when I start to get it up for you, I get overwhelmed with this numbing guilt?

NINA: 'cause you're a Catholic.

BEN: She said you hate her more than anything in the world.

NINA: Don't you love me anymore, Lupe?

LUPE: I do.

NINA: Maybe that's what you feel guilty about.

LUPE: The lengths I went to. Things I did.

BEN: What did you do?

LUPE: Unspeakable things.

NINA: Then don't speak them. (They kiss.) How's your guilt now?

LUPE: Harder.

(They kiss again.)

ROMY: And then in bed La Romy hear them thumping away thumping away thumping away heaving gasping scratching making that messy sex that always scare her cuz how could La Romy have come from that noise that rage that desperation and how come she didn't just dissolve in the shower that they take after and how can all of that mean love how can it possibly mean love.

BEN: Was there ever a time that you opened up to each other?

LUPE: No.

NINA: Can I be real honest with you, Lupe?

LUPE: Sure.

NINA: Back then, when you did what you did, and washed that bat in the river, I was crazed with fear.

LUPE: So was I.

NINA: But I was turned on, too. It got me so hot. To see what you would do for me. Kill a man for me. Fuck. Is that sick or what?

LUPE: Pretty damn sick.

NINA: Nobody loved me like that. Nobody went that far. I just didn't know I was worth that.

LUPE: You still are, babe.

NINA: Uh-uh. These days, I don't feel like much of anything. Even sex with my old man feels like adultery.

LUPE: What's your point?

NINA: You're fucking someone else, aren't you?

LUPE: If I was, you think I'd tell you?

NINA: I would.

LUPE: Okay. (Pause.) Are you?

NINA: You're gone for days sometimes weeks at a time without a word and just like anyone else I'm a woman who wants. I ain't gonna stand around and wait for you to show. It's lonely in this damn house and I get tired of hearing myself pine.

LUPE: Who is he?

NINA: Nobody.

LUPE: You bring him in this house?

NINA: I still got scruples.

LUPE: Here, lemme wipe them off. *(He slaps her.)* Shit. What the fuck am I doing? Nina...

NINA: *(taking out the same gun seen before)* Uh-uh. Kiss your ass goodbye, Loop.

LUPE: Nina...

NINA: You won't stay and you won't stay away. I won't have strangers hitting me. Romy, the older she gets, the more she adores you. The bigger shit you become the more she likes it. It's gotta stop, Lupe. Right Fucken Now.

LUPE: Gimme that--. *(She fires it. Huge bang. LUPE flinches.)* Pendeja. You missed.

NINA: Uh-uh. My bullet's just taking the long way around.

(He turns away. She goes.)

BEN: She told me she once fired a gun at you. Was that true?

LUPE: *(staring off after NINA)* Na. Nina likes to dramatize things.

ROMY: And then you know what La Romy shivers at the nearness of lead and pees where she sits out of fear and coldness

BEN: Assholes never told me the desert could get this cold.

LUPE : Who?

BEN: Officers at Ft. Bliss. Yeah, right, Bliss.

LUPE: *(singing softly to ROMY)*

Perla de mi vida

No me dejes solo aqui

Prefiero el infierno

A el mundo frio sin ti.

> *(A moment passes, then ROMY crumbles into LUPE's arms. They hold each other tightly. A shaft of light pierces the dark.)*

BEN: What's that?

ROMY: *¿Apa?*

> *(LUPE stands, faces the source of the beam. An OLD MAN with a flashlight comes up to him.)*

OLD MAN: *(planting his circle of light on one of his tattoos.)¿Qué significa eso?*

LUPE: Serpent. For the sin of Envy.

OLD MAN: And this bleeding rose?

79

LUPE: Is for the sin of Lust.

OLD MAN: And this knife?

LUPE: The sin of aggravated assault.

OLD MAN: *Eres maldito, Lupe.*

BEN: Does he know you?

LUPE: This is Polo. My gardener.

BEN: How did he know we were coming?

LUPE: Crink in the shorts of Time, Ben. His incident got together with our incident and made coincident. Kinda like with you and Nina.

POLO: This is him?

LUPE: Ben from Ft. Bliss.

> *(POLO stares intensely at BEN then turns to ROMY.)*

POLO: She don't look so good.

LUPE: That's cause she's coming under his custody.

BEN: Romy, you got a fever?

ROMY: Keep your hands to yourself. I'm fine.

LUPE: Let's get the fuck outa here.

ROMY: And then La Romy the two babosos and the old man Polo like the game like the Italian guy who went to China we're all crammed in his old pick-up and La Romy is sitting on my *Papi's* lap and for no reason at all but maybe night she start to cry

LUPE: I see the lip. No lip, Rome.

BEN: Where exactly are we going?

POLO: *El rancho.*

BEN: What *rancho*? Where is it?

POLO: *Allá.*

LUPE: We're on the Other, man. Didn't I tell you?

POLO:*El Otro.*

ROMY: What's your problem?

BEN: I'm itchy.

LUPE: Don't scratch. You'll rip the bodies off but leave the heads inside and get infected.

BEN: What are you talking about?

LUPE: Ticks. They were all over the blanket. I got them too.

BEN: Aw... SHIT.

LUPE: It's okay, *ese*. We're almost there.

ROMY: And then La Romy see the old white stucco walls gleaming even on this moonless night and she see the heehaw of the donkey come flying through the air covered in cornspit and she know we're there

POLO: *¿Quieren frijoles?*

LUPE: *(as POLO goes)¡Orale!* Pot a beans and tortillas for the starchy farts, Ben! Eat while I look for my Romy's present.

BEN: Fuck her present! I want to go home! I'm covered with ticks! *(LUPE embraces him, lifting his feet off the ground.)* What are you doing!

LUPE: Mingling bloods, *ese*! Trading these little eight-legged whores and filling their fat little stomachs full of the wine of you and me and making you and me *CARNALES* inside them! BRODAHS!

BEN: We're infested, you crazy fuck!

LUPE: Chill. I know how to get them off. Follow me.

> *(They go. POLO enters with a bowl. He sits and watches ROMY as she staggers to the ground.)*

ROMY: I don't want it.

POLO: You have to eat. You the only good thing that's ever come out of that man.

ROMY: He said he wasn't my father.

POLO: Consider yourself lucky.

ROMY: I wish he was different. If *Papi* was more like Ben, I could like take him home and make us a family again. Leave that doofus here.

POLO *(as ALMA enters and stands quietly in the background)* Tell me about the doofus.

ROMY: He came outa nowhere. All of a sudden he walks in wearing this uniform like it entitles him to me.

POLO: Ben is his real name?

ROMY: Yeah. I guess.

POLO: Has he ever said the name *Anastacio*?

ROMY: *(spotting her)* No. But she has. How come?

POLO: *Come tus frijoles.*

> *(POLO joins ALMA and they go.*
> *LUPE and BEN enter a corral.*
> *LUPE carries a bottle in each hand.)*

LUPE: Time for our ablutions, sergeant.

BEN: Our what?

LUPE: *(proffering one of them)* Mescal. It'll kill the ticks. Take your shirt off.

> *(Lupe takes his shirt off.)*

BEN: What for?

LUPE: They're going start laying eggs on you.

> *(BEN takes his shirt off. They rub themselves down with the liquor, occasionally swilling from their bottles.)*

LUPE: I can see what she likes about you.

BEN: What are you gonna do, now that you're cut loose?

LUPE: Cut loose, I guess. What about you?

BEN: I dunno. I got some ideas.

LUPE: How do ya like the brew? Fermented in oblong casks of dried oak and hammered tin, then buried in the earth like a dead man. What are you thinking?

> *(LUPE offers his back. BEN rubs mescal into it.)*

BEN: What if I was you.

LUPE: What if you was?

BEN: I don't know how I'd live with myself. I don't know if I could give up on my woman, but I know for damn sure I'd never give up on my child.

> (BEN offers his back. LUPE rubs the stuff on.)

BEN: What if you were me?

LUPE: Bitch, I'd probably kill myself.

BEN: Ha ha.

LUPE: So I'm curious. What is this lack of discipline? What did you done that was so bad you had to get your ass straightened out with Uncle Sam?

BEN: It wasn't nothing.

LUPE: Nothin' ain't nothin', Ben.

BEN: I was young. I fucked up a lot. I was high on all my fuck-ups.

LUPE: What kinda fuck-ups.

BEN: The kind that make you feel alive. The kind that make you wonder whose heart is pounding in your chest. Anyway, I was out of control. My old man suggested the armed forces and that's where I atoned.

LUPE: *Carnal*, you ain't even started.

(LUPE takes out a baseball bat.)

BEN: What are you doing with that?

LUPE: Say hi to Louisville.

> *(LUPE viciously smashes the bat on the ground by him.)*

BEN: HEY! What's going on, man?

LUPE: You tell me. Smartass fucking sergeant.

BEN: I'm not a sergeant--

LUPE: Don't you think I know that! Don't you think I noticed your bones?

BEN: What?

LUPE: The same fine bones in the face. Same high-tone look in the eyes. The same heart pounding in your chest.

BEN: Where's Romy? Romy, get your butt over here now!

LUPE: You're not taking her. She ain't yours to take.

> *(BEN starts to run but LUPE smashes his leg with the bat and grips his head in a vise. ROMY's body jolts with a vision.)*

ROMY: And all a sudden La Romy feel her *corazon* swell up like a gourd to receive the *cuento* that bedevil my Dad and make hell inside him

LUPE: You never know when to quit! The past too horny to stay past! Well, I seen you! I seen the two of you!

ROMY: two shapes standing in the dark

LUPE: Making out like dogs right in this corral!

BEN: NO!

LUPE: And I seen what you look like!

ROMY: a thin boy pale so pale you see the green stems of his veins spread along his arms fragile but unafraid of life

BEN: Stoppit! Lupe!

LUPE: In the arms of my goddamn bride!

ROMY: a young girl a living heart smooth skin big dark eyes the boy kissing love-notes on her shoulder blade

BEN: NINA!

LUPE: BUT I TOOK CARE OF YOU THEN, DIDN'T I! DIDN'T I!

ROMY: a devil aiming death at the boy the boy's veins bulging his face red his eyes clenched with tears and blood gathered in his mouth

BEN: FUUUUUCK!

LUPE: I caught you full in the temple, motherfukkah, POW went the crack of bone and Nina gasping and me cussing and *pinche* Louisville finding fractures. Boom. Boom. Boom.

ROMY: nothing but a black and shiny mess where his pretty face was, all open blood and muscle and the nightsky smeared with clouds

LUPE: I did it once, I can do it again!

BEN: WHO THE FUCK AM I SUPPOSED TO BE? WHO!

ROMY: And the last thing La Romy see is horses and a name come to her in a mouthful of blood

LUPE: ¡ANASTACIO! *(LUPE stands over BEN, the bat raised for murder.)* You and me, we got business, we got hell, we got shit there ain't no word in English for, we got the *rio*, the Migra, the liquor, the *sangre*, El Paso and the Other Side, parasites and *penitencia*, mescal and parfaits, death and daddyhood, we got it all

between us, *carnal,* and its fuckin' time we
settled that sin.

> (*ROMY raises the bowl to drink*
> *when a brilliant light introduces EL*
> *CHARRO, epic, ominous, dressed in*
> *the glittering finery of the Mexican*
> *cowboy. His spurs clink as he steps*
> *forward and raises the broad brim of*
> *his spangled sombrero.*)

EL CHARRO

Donde está el baño.

BLACKOUT

End of Act One

Act Two

(ROMY and EL CHARRO. As
before. Utterly still. Braced for the
changes to come. Then grotesque
images flash in nightmare color
around them:

LUPE viciously smashing the bat
down on the tarp

Torrents of blood, bloodletting, and
gore

Equine shadows soaring overhead

POLO carrying a simple casket on
his back

NINA with her gun aimed at Lupe,
who laughs at her

ALMA holding up the alarm clock

The gun firing with a tremendous
roar.

All the images disappear.

Eerie Mexican accordion plays,
punctuated by ghostly neighing

And shrill cries.)

ROMY: And then everything's water and she looks at Ben and Ben looks back with a fierce whiskey spilling out his eyes and whispers

BEN: *(in a ghostly voice-over) Eres mía*

> *(In the far distance, the neighing of a single horse.*
>
> *EL CHARRO finally takes a step to clink his spurs and utters-)*

EL CHARRO: *La cuenta, por favor.*

ROMY: Hey. You.

EL CHARRO: *La cuenta.*

ROMY: Are you Death?

EL CHARRO: *Dónde está la playa.*

ROMY: I just wanna know: Are you Death?

EL CHARRO: *Soy Charro.* I'm *El Charro Negro.* Exile. Mister *Penitente.* The guilty conscience of my poor misbegotten land. I'm Death, all right.

ROMY: Then make yourself useful. Help me to die.

EL CHARRO: What you want to die for?

ROMY: Livin' ain't worth the trouble. Too much pain. I seen terrible things in my head that can't be true, and if they are, all the more reason to die.

EL CHARRO: What you got there?

ROMY: Peyote in my bean soup.

EL CHARRO: Spicy.

ROMY: I wanna eat it but I can't.

EL CHARRO: You ain't done your penance is why. You gotta purge your sins.

ROMY: How do I do that?

EL CHARRO: You turn to me. Get on your knees. Roll up your sleeves. Hold this spoon. *(She does all this. EL CHARRO sits before her.)* Keep it very still.

> *(He pours a small black goop on the spoon then turns a Zippo lighter on under it.)*

EL CHARRO: Now freely confess.

ROMY: I hate my mom. I hate her for bustin' us up. I hate her for not makin' the effort. But mostly right now I hate her for makin' like I never existed.

EL CHARRO: She denied you?

ROMY: Uh-huh.

EL CHARRO: Like Peter at the cock's crow. Go on.

ROMY: I hate my *Apa*. He's acting real strange to me. Him, too, he said he wasn't my dad, wasn't ever my dad, then he takes it back. Fuck his ass, I say. Seems like nobody wants me, except...

EL CHARRO: Yeah?

ROMY: Ben. But he's a nerd. Don't even know jalapeño from serrano, he's so white.

EL CHARRO: So?

ROMY: So I can't be with him. How come you're dressed like that?

EL CHARRO: And this terrible thing you've seen?

ROMY: I dunno. A man getting killed. My Dad doing it. *Ama* there with them. That's a dream though. Peyote yankin' my chain. What's with the get-up?

EL CHARRO: It's my vestment, it's how I been stamped. This is how you die.

> (*In one motion, he undoes his belt
> and straps it around her forearm. He*

*produces a thin blade, dips it into the
serum in the spoon and applies a
tattoo to her arm.)*

ROMY: Ow. What are you doin'?

EL CHARRO: This is how your daddy and me
met. I remember the day. Juarez in the spring.
Birds singing. Flowers blooming. Dogs lapping
up blood of a knife fight. He walked into my
dementia. Wanted someone to confess to. So he
had me branded on his back for company.
Poured his damned soul out to me. Keeps me
au courant on all his mortal sins. There.

ROMY: What is it?

EL CHARRO: A wee horsey. If you wanna die,
ride that pony down.

> *(He takes ROMY's hand and they
> move across the dark.)*

ROMY: And then La Romy feel him tugging
her chemical heart down down follow that sun
down to where it goes when it goes down at
night and she know this man will lead her
there

> *(NINA enters with a covered tray
> containing several items.)*

NINA: Into Dark. Night.

ROMY: ¡*Ama!*

EL CHARRO: Whoa, girl. She in her own space now.

(BEN enters from the opposite side.)

BEN: Can I turn the light on?

NINA: No. Sit on the floor.

ROMY/BEN: Why are you whispering?

NINA: Just be quiet. Here.

BEN: What's this?

NINA: Salsa piquante. And a bag of chips. And these. *(Rubbers)*

BEN/ROMY: What's going on?

NINA: You start.

BEN: I'm not into chile, Nina.

NINA: You have to. If you're here to say what I think you're going to say, you have to.

BEN: Is it hot?

NINA: Four alarm.

ROMY: Whoa.

BEN: Did you bring water?

NINA: Straight up. *Dále.*

> (He dips a chip and bites it. During the following sequence they eat chips in hot sauce, getting progressively burned.)

NINA: Do you think you know me, Ben?

BEN: I think I do.

NINA: Have you been looking for me all your life?

BEN: Yes.

NINA: 'Cause I sure been waiting for you all of mine.

BEN: I'm not complicated, I don't ask much of life, except a good job, good weather, a good woman.

NINA: You're a good man.

BEN: Do you know how long I waited for you? I would've stayed a virgin if I knew you were coming this soon. But it was that or a bullet through my head. Between dying and loneliness, there's no contest. Dying's quicker.

NINA: *Es la pinchi verdad.*

BEN: Ohhh. This is hot.

NINA: And yet you haven't touched me once. You haven't once asked me to bed.

BEN: I don't wanna fuck you. I've done fuck. Fuck is what bodies do. I want to love. To make love. Don't you see?

NINA: What would you do for me, Ben, what would you do?

BEN: Anything, anything. Ow god.

NINA: Would you die for me (yes) would you surrender your life for me (yes) would you give up your soul (yes) would you be poor (yes) would you still want me the way I am?

BEN: No matter what.

NINA: You are a dream, *cabrón*. Something out of my past. I don't deserve you.

BEN: Kiss me, Nina.

(They kiss.)

NINA: *Ay*, Benjamin, if you knew my trials, my years of silence, my sentence of guilt and hunger, all the times I wished myself dead, all the times I died in that man's arms in our bed, all those times I prayed for evil shit...

BEN: What evil shit.

NINA: I prayed never to get pregnant and the only time I did, I prayed to God he'd flush it out of my body. I prayed it would die before it gave light, my god, oh my god...

BEN: Shh. Nina. Don't cry.

NINA: No, I'm telling you, I wished her dead but it--

> (BEN *drinks the contents of the jar.*
> *He burns.*)

BEN: Marry me, Nina! I wanna take care of you, give you the love you need, work with you for life and give you children. Look, rings, honey. I got the rings.

NINA: Oh Ben!

BEN: I'm serious as all shit. I sold my car, my bomber jacket, and my mother's Saint Christopher medal for this. I'm bound to my choice with gold, Nina. 14 fucking carats.

NINA: First there's something you have to know.

ROMY: Mom.

BEN: Who's that?

NINA: Oh. That's another thing we gotta talk about.

BEN: Is that…?

NINA: My Romy.

BEN: *Your* Romy?

ROMY: Mom.

NINA: If you've always been waiting for me, you've been waiting for her, too.

BEN: I need a glass a water.

> *(BEN goes with the tray. NINA looks at the rings.)*

ROMY: Ama, you wished me dead.

NINA: I did, honey. But that was when I thought death was better than being around me.

ROMY: And now?

NINA: I wish you home.

EL CHARRO: He may not know Jalapeño from Serrano, but he takes 'em both in the mouth like a man.

ROMY: He was telling the truth. He didn't know about me. So how can I blame him for not taking so good to me?

EL CHARRO: He's a father before he's a father. The world is topsy-turdy, home fries. Even for this chump.

> (The BORDER PATROL
> OFFICER appears on the river shore
> with the gun and Romy's shoes
> cradled in his arms.)

ROMY: I know that buttface.

EL CHARRO: I figured. He's got that pinched anality round the mouth.

ROMY: What's he doing here?

EL CHARRO: Doubt if even he knows.

> (NINA regards him.)

NINA: That's my gun.

OFFICER: Whut?

NINA: That's my gun you got.

OFFICER: I disarmed... some desperados.

NINA: And that's my girl's shoes. What are you doing with her shoes?

OFFICER: They went in.

NINA: You mean to the other side? Did you see her make it across?

OFFICER: I saw them go in. I saw the current carry them around the bend. After that, it was just water.

NINA: And you let them take her.

OFFICER: She wanted to go.

NINA: And you let her go? What's the matter with you?

OFFICER: I'm lost. My compass is all thrown. What's north, what's south. I'm all froze up in this damn hole and everythin's spinnin' around. I can't move!

(NINA feels the earth at his feet.)

NINA: Oh no. Oh no.

OFFICER: What is it, lady? Where am I?

(NINA addresses ROMY, whose presence she senses.)

NINA: This is where he lay, baby. This is where for thirteen years he hid from the world and kept it guessing.

ROMY: Who?

OFFICER: I can't lift my damn feet. It's like I'm dying inside.

NINA: A night of eruptions, *mija*. All I see is a bat blowing a million specks of blood all over, my face and dress catching all the spatters. I feel sick and I throw up on the gravel and just then I feel another eruption inside me like a light coming on! I feel it! A pressure. A promise. Sweeping from the pit of my gut to all my bones and vessels. Eyes turn to grey and I hear horses.

ROMY: *Ama,* what happened? What did you do?

NINA: I only wanted to see his horses. Just like you.

OFFICER: I never caught anyone sneaking southaward. Yearning for the other side. It threw my compass. The whole world's turned on us. Black is white, white, black, death life, life death, Donny Marie, Marie Donny. What the hell am I guarding! A line! A dadburn line in the water! *¡Alto alto! ¡Un balazo por la cabeza! Me need ver tu passaport! ¡Muy impassaportante!* Your no *hombre, por favor!¡Aqui se habla ingles! Pais de los muertos,* land of deceased, *mi casa es su* fricken *casa! ¡Bienvenidos!*

NINA: Always dead men giving us pause. Grabbing us by the ankles every time. At least I have a chance to keep my girl clear. Wherever she is.

ROMY: Right here.

NINA: I can't lose her. *(turning out toward the water)* ROMELIA! DON'T YOU BE DEAD, GIRL! DON'T YOU DARE HAVE SUNK TO THIS FUCKIN' RIVERBOTTOM! I still need you around, baby, it's not finished, please, honey, be alive, it's not finished.

(To the OFFICER) Dump that gun in the *rio* and go home, border fool.

> *(She takes up the shoes. She starts slowly stepping toward ROMY.)*

ROMY: What is she doing?

OFFICER: Are you going in?

NINA: If I make it across, that's where I'll find her. If I go down, that's where she'll be.

ROMY: No, Mama! Go back! Go back!

NINA: Romy, little shit, I'm coming.

ROMY/OFFICER: It's deep! You're gonna drown!

NINA: *Sigo en tus pasos*, baby. *Voy donde tu vas.* Right behind you.

ROMY: No! Go back!

NINA: Life or death, *Ama* is on the way.

103

(NINA continues wading in a circle around ROMY with her shoes held high over her head.)

EL CHARRO: Your mama's fearless, girl. Taking danger in the mouth.

ROMY: 'cause she loves me.

OFFICER: *(calling after NINA)* If you drown, miss! Miss, if you drown, could you wash ashore on the Messican side? Then I'll know which side is which!

(He goes. ROMY and EL CHARRO watch as she makes her slow march across the river till she vanishes.)

ROMY: Where she going?

EL CHARRO: Somewhere kneedeep, waistdeep, neckdeep, souldeep.

ROMY: Is she dead, Charro?

EL CHARRO: Dead's a relative term in *El Otro*. When people die, they become story, and when stories die, they become myths, and dead myths become tattoos. I'm a purgastory thirteen years and half a crime old. Suffice to say I'm what's left of an old myth. And that's what *he's* gonna be.

(LUPE steps out, carrying a roller attached to a long pole, a paint pan and a tarp. He paints an invisible wall between him and ROMY.)

EL CHARRO: A man with more faith in his heart than his heart had in him and thereby a rift between them. Exile been his home address. You, child, slipped in the mail slot.

ROMY: Is that my dad? What are you doing, *Apa*?

LUPE: Pressing white paint into the walls of white people, *mija*, it gets me to thinking. And my mind comes to you, before you even show your little brown ass, I see you not a boy 'cause what do I want with a boy, a boy would most likely turn out like his father, but a girl, *dios mio*, a girl might just turn out like her mom.

(POLO and ALMA enter behind him. ALMA with her alarm clock.)

LUPE: That would suit me fine. *¿Y sabes que?* Your name comes to me. Romelia. Thinking up your name is the last good thought I'll ever have.

POLO: Guadalupe.

LUPE: *¿Si?*

POLO: *¿Es usted Guadalupe Madero?*

LUPE: That's me... How did you get in?

POLO: *Señor*, I am Don Apolonio Tovar and this is *mi señora*, Doña Alma.

LUPE: *Para servirle.*

POLO: *Señor* Lupe, we have a ranch not far from here full of quality stock, and with the help of our son we plan to—

ALMA: Our plans are *mierda*! Our boy is with her, *pendejo*, open your eyes! Open your eyes, you idiot, they are doing each other like dogs!

LUPE: Wait. What?

ALMA: Your wife and our son are lovers!

LUPE: *¡Mentiras!*

ROMY: Lies!

POLO: Believe it! Our son and your wife.

ALMA: *¡Como perros!* Go see. See if she's home. See if she's waiting for you in your bed. See if she's there! *¡Baboso! ¡Idiota! ¡Te pone los cuernos y ni te das cuenta!*

LUPE: How do you know this?

ALMA: WE SEEN THEM, YOU STUPID!

POLO: It's not the first time. We tried to stop them once before. We tried to reason with him.

106

She's not for you, *hijo*. She's a married woman now. She could bring disgrace on us all. *Piensalo bien, Anastacio.*

ROMY/LUPE: *Anastacio.*

POLO: But he won't listen. He wants to be with her. This cannot happen. We have plans for him at the ranch. Everything comes to breeding.

LUPE: I can't believe I'm hearing this.

ROMY: Then don't, Apa!

ALMA: As God is my witness, that little bastard walked out on me! Left me talking to myself! My own little *puto* and he treats me this way! God is my witness, he is not having her another night!

LUPE: What do you want me to do?

ALMA: What do you think?

POLO: This very night, they plan to run away. She is leaving you, *Señor* Lupe. Stop them. Talk to her. Remind her of her vows.

ALMA: Keep your bitch in her own house and tell her to stay away from our son.

LUPE: But what if—

ALMA: There is no if, *baboso!* (*flashing the clock at him*) There is no time! Are you a man? *¿Eres Mexicano?* Do what you have to do.

POLO: We thought you should know.

(*They leave.*)

ALMA: *Centro de mis amores por toda la eternidad no quiero Señor resistir mas--* ... Do what you have to do!

(*LUPE somberly takes the roller off the pole and rests it in the paint pan.*)

ROMY: *Apa...*

LUPE: No, baby.

ROMY: *Apa,* you don't have to listen to their shit. You know *Ama's* good.

LUPE: Yeah, real good.

ROMY: Don't do it.

LUPE: Don't do what.

ROMY: Don't go over there.

LUPE: Where am I going, Romy?

ROMY: Ranch.

LUPE: What am I doing once I get there? *(ROMY hesitates.)* Tell me, honey. What is it they expect me to do and do you think I already done? 'Cause I'm confused, I'm so fucked up, I don't know which end is up. What do I do, Romy?

ROMY: Go home.

LUPE: I can't do that.

ROMY: Please, Dad.

LUPE: Someone has to stop them.

ROMY: Then talk to her. Tell her you love her. She'll stay if you tell her that.

LUPE: She's a whore, baby.

ROMY: She's good. Forgive her.

LUPE: I would. But it just ain't my style.

(He starts to head out.)

ROMY: PLEASE, *APA*! DON'T KILL HIM!

LUPE: Is that what I do? What do I use? A gun? Knife? The bat in the bed of my truck? *(ROMY reacts to the last suggestion.)* Thass it. *Pinchi* Louisville. Be a Mexican they said. Well baby, I'll show that brother some Mexico. You watch me.

(He twists and wrenches the tarp in his hands.)

LUPE: I'll roll him up in this. He'll lie rolled up in tarp three feet under river silt. Won't he.

(He gathers his things into the tarp and rolls it up.)

ROMY: *Apa*, I love you.

LUPE: What was that name I gave you?

ROMY: Romelia.

LUPE: Oh yeah.

EL CHARRO: Romelia Maria.

LUPE: Hell of a name for retribution.

(He goes.)

EL CHARRO: There he goes.

ROMY: What's goin' on, Charro? I feel like I'm making this shit happen! But how? How? I never knew this, did I? How could I know it?

EL CHARRO: There are things our bodies know before we do. Little secrets rolled up and slipped in the flutes of our bones. Mystery loves, mystery griefs, longings so private that we act on them before we even feel them.

ROMY: I feel them.

EL CHARRO: *El Otro.*

ROMY: All asudden everything's all bony the trees the walls the moon all got bones showing through their skin and even time is all bony and then La Romy see the dogs

> (*Eerie barking and howling of dogs. ROSS enters, his whole left side drenched in blood, dragging the rolled-up tarp.*)

ROMY: the big ol' dogs *Apa* shot dead circling around eyes bald fangs bared sense of smell all gone their bodies thin as shadows on the wall and then she see the dead walking

ROSS: Kid.

ROMY: The Cowboy

ROSS: You don't wanna look in there

ROMY: All pasty faced

ROSS: Not for the eyes of innnocents

ROMY: Bleeding out his head

ROSS: That's a burden for grownup fools like me to tug and drag on.

ROMY: Ross what are you doin'? Get your ass to a hospital, man.

ROSS: Too late for that, kid. My medulla oblongata took a shotta penitent lead.

ROMY: Huh?

EL CHARRO: Blew his brains out.

ROMY: What you pull shit like that for?

ROSS: 'Cause a love. Love that don't know when to quit. Love that goes too far. You can't treat someone you love like a horse, you know.

ROMY: What are you talking about, Ross?

ROSS: I'd rather accuse than excuse her. I'd rather kill than lose her. I lose her anyways. What remains is the remains.

ROMY: What's that smell?

ROSS: My baby ain't what she used to be. Nothing ain't.

ROMY: Wait, Ross. Hold on. *¡Esperate!*

ROSS: You can't treat someone you love like a horse. You can't. Too messy for the eyes of innocents but you're innocent no more. No more.

> (*ROSS staggers out. EL CHARRO and ROMY silently regard the rolled-up tarp for a moment.*)

EL CHARRO: That tug you feel in your heart is hunger. Hunger's what passes for gravity in *El Otro*.

(*NINA enters and regards the tarp.*)

NINA: *Muchacho bravo*. How am I going to live without you—

> (*She takes a razor from her sock which she places against her throat.*)

ROMY: No. *Ama*. Rolled up inside of you, a seed of me there. Feel me?

Feel me?

NINA: I do.

ROMY: Open that vein and I die. And you never see me. And I never grow. And I never get to feel your love, or hear your lullabys, or keep you up nights with my crying—

NINA: I could do without that.

ROMY: And I never get to know what school is, and never get that ten-dollar bill from your purse, and never feel what walking through a sprinkler with you is like—

NINA: What ten-dollar bill?

ROMY: Mom, forget it, you never missed it, anyway.

NINA: You've been through my purse?

ROMY: *Ama*—

NINA: You've been through my purse, *caraja!?*

ROMY: Get off my case, *esa!* How else am I supposed to know you, what kinda person you are, what secrets you keep? You won't tell me squat! I figure you out by the kleenex you keep, the lipsticks you wear, by the little things you collect, the coupons, matchbooks, sticks of gum, and those little notes to yourself.

NINA: Notes?

ROMY: You write little poems and prayers to me, Mom.

NINA: I do?

ROMY: Little songs wrote out of need and fear. Valentines scribbled in these tiny letters, *Ama,* like they were wrote down with that razor. Here.

> *(She takes out a slip and passes it to Nina.)*

NINA: *Tus susurros y tus besos*

Del sabor de aceituna

Como golondrinas vuelan

Al cuerno de la luna.

> *(She cries softly, putting the razor away.)*

EL CHARRO: All I gotta say is… you owe that lady ten bucks.

ROMY: I saved her, Charro, didn't I? Didn't I save her?

EL CHARRO: Yeah, but not from the hurt that never goes away. What you care about living, anyway? Ain't you decided on dyin'?

ROMY: Well, yeah, but…

EL CHARRO: You're not having a change a heart, are you?

> *(LUPE enters.)*

LUPE: Nina –

NINA: No.

LUPE: Nina, *ven.*

NINA: Get away from me.

LUPE: It's all over. It's done.

> *(He approaches her. She points the razor at him.)*

NINA: I don't know you, *animal*! I'll kill you if you come near me. I swear I will.

LUPE: Then go ahead. Put an end to it. Do it!

> *(LUPE steps closer. NINA, aiming the razor, sings.)*

NINA: *La voz de mi Amante*

> *Resuena en mi pensamiento*
>
> *Es la musica de mi soledad*
>
> *Es todo mi alimento.*

LUPE: Cut me up. I'm dead anyway.

NINA: We're doomed, Lupe. *Bien chingados.*

EL CHARRO: And then he touch her. And then she feel it. And then he kiss her neck. And the sickness, the hate and the fear in her flood to her lips and an amazing thing happen...

NINA: I kiss him.

EL CHARRO: And the hate, fear and sickness in his heart rush to his hands and an amazing thing happen...

LUPE: I hold her.

EL CHARRO: Not forgiveness but desire overwhelm their bodies now bound forever by this death, desire like a crime, and then an amazing thing happen...

NINA: I'm going to have a baby.

LUPE: His or mine. His or mine.

NINA: Mine.

> *(LUPE carries her up and starts slowly out. NINA sings softly as they drift off.)*

NINA: *Tus susurros y tus besos*

> *Del sabor de aceituna*

> *Como golondrinas vuelan*

> *Al cuerno de la luna.*

EL CHARRO: Don't you think she sounds like Vikki Carr?

ROMY: Is this what death is, Charro? Hearing things I can't bear to hear. Seeing people cut each other up? Seems to me living's just another way of dyin'. You just... feel it more.

EL CHARRO: Maybe you should verify that with the one man who's nigh on to his myth-hood by now. All rolled up in his meat burrito death.

(ROMY eyes the tarp and with a single heave unscrolls it. BEN rolls out, his body completely caked with blood and offal.)

ROMY: Ben?!

(He opens his eyes and rises to his knees. He speaks as ANASTACIO, the voice which sang at the beginning.)

ANASTACIO: *Muchos días.*

ROMY: Say what?

ANASTACIO: *He estado muchas días… abajo.*

ROMY: Wait, you're talkin' Spanish.

EL CHARRO: He has so many days… been down. Primroses and rye have sunk their roots in him.

ROMY: Anastacio?

EL CHARRO: In pieces. Fragments you can fill a gourd with.

ANASTACIO: Where is she?

ROMY: Who?

ANASTACIO: I had her in my arms a moment ago. Have you seen her?

ROMY: No.

ANASTACIO: ¡NINA! ¡NO ME DEJES SOLO!
¡TENGO FRÍO!

ROMY: She's not here.

ANASTACIO: Can you tell me where she is?
A girl with brown eyes. We played checkers
with the stars, counted headlights by the levee,
rode horses by moonlight. Do you know her?

ROMY: I think I do.

ANASTACIO: She's waiting for me. She
knows I'm going with her. ¡NIIIIINA!

ROMY: It's too late. She's gone.

ANASTACIO: But I have my bags. We're
running away. I told my father so. Didn't I?

EL CHARRO: You did, son.

ANASTACIO: We are in the *corral* at night.
Seeing my horses for the last time. *Mis caballos
sementales*. Twitching hides. Then a breach in
my temple, blood in my mouth. And then...

ROMY: Yeah?

ANASTACIO: Nothing. This room where I
wait and wait and wait. I miss something and I
don't know what. I feel my eyes water and I
don't know why. I can't move. A million

mouths inside me, none of them crying for Jesus. Still the dust proclaims me Anastacio.

ROMY: That's cuz you're dead.

ANASTACIO: Then it's up to you.

ROMY: Me?

ANASTACIO: Your eyes, the way the tears give them color, heat. The way the lips make that little rose. *Eres de Nina.*

ROMY: She's my mother. My name's Romy.

ANASTACIO: Then I'm not dead.

> *(He reaches his hand out. She recoils.)*

EL CHARRO: Love what you can, Romy. The days decompose.

> *(He lightly caresses her cheek.)*

ANASTACIO: When you see her, tell her my wounds still call her name. Tell her they blame her for none of it.

ROMY: But my dad. It was him that smushed your head in. He busted you up.

ANASTACIO: Your father is blameless. His only crime was love.

ROMY: Huh?

ANASTACIO: When it's time, you'll know him. Bones in the clock. Ticka ticka tick. I'm cold.

ROMY: Anastacio...

> *(The light darkens. LUPE enters, bat in hand.)*

LUPE: Having a bad night, honey?

ANASTACIO: Light slips away. Sockets darken.

LUPE: Having bad dreams again?

ROMY: He said you didn't do it. How can that be?

ANASTACIO: *Eres mía.*

> *(He rolls himself up in the tarp and is still.)*

ROMY: Didn't you beat him dead? Didn't you? How can he say my father is blameless?

LUPE: No-one ever is.

> *(LUPE swats the rolled tarp with the bat.)*

EL CHARRO: Now we're dyin'.

ROMY: What you doin', *ese*! CUT THIS *PEDO* OUT!

EL CHARRO: Can you feel your own Romy soul turning to ash and mold?

LUPE: Don't look at me like that, kid. I'm just trying to be your dad.

> *(He bludgeons the tarp viciously. ROMY feels a dizzying nausea.)*

EL CHARRO: Feel yourself steeped deeper than any sun ever gone feel the little crumbs of life drifting and the light going all tarblack and cold?

LUPE: *(baying like a madman)* GET YO' INK READY, CHARRO! WE GOTTA *PACHANGA* TONIGHT!

> *(The place explodes with dangling strings of colored Christmas bulbs, bathing the place with eerie garish light. Present, somber and still, are ALMA and POLO. EL CHARRO has vanished.)*

LUPE: Check it out!

> *(Suspended high over their heads, a multi-colored piñata of a horse, which POLO controls by rope, ceremoniously descends.)*

LUPE: There, *mija*, over the *corral de los Tovares*, your motherfuckin' present! See the sign, the flying horse clopping at the air like a crime come home! A *caballito, pochita*! Aaaay-aayy!

> (*LUPE shouts and laughs and dances under the piñata.*)

LUPE: Wooo! This night you gonna do it! This night this bat will join you with your daddy! Bust open the *pinche* shell of our lie and shower us with penance! Manna, baby! Wooo!

POLO/ALMA: HAPPY BIRTHDAY, ROMELIA! *¡FELIZ CUMPLEAÑOS!*

LUPE: *¡VIVA ROMELIA, PATRONESA DE LOS MALDITOS!*

POLO AND ALMA: *¡VIVA!*

> (*LUPE guzzles from a bottle of mescal.*)

LUPE: *¡Orale!* Check out the *jefita*! It's grabass time for our little Romy and the old sow's lighting candles like it's Lent! Who you praying to, *esa*?

ALMA: *La Virgen de Guadalupe.*

LUPE: My namesake! Ask her who she favors in the Cowboys game! I got some *feria* running on that show.

POLO: Let's do this, Lupe. Esta *piñata* weighs a ton!

LUPE: Apolonio! What's your problem? Weren't you some bigass horse breeder? Don't you know how to rope them in?

> (*ALMA ties the bandanna over ROMY's eyes.*)

LUPE: ¡*Hechale las mañanitas!*

> (*POLO and ALMA grimly sing as LUPE places the bat firmly in ROMY'S hands and slowly twirls her about.*)

POLO/ALMA: *Estas son la mañanitas*

> *Que cantába el Rey Davíd*
>
> *Hoy por ser día de tu santo*
>
> *Te las cantamos a tí.*

> *Despierta mi bien despierta*
>
> *Mira que ya amaneció*
>
> *Ya los ya pajarillos cantan*
>
> *La luna se metio.*

LUPE: This game is all about the woes of the world. The way we purge ourselves with *sangre*. Played right on the border between the riches of bliss-- *(kisses her)* --and desertion. Strung on a wire, the shape of all our *desmadres*, a child's game, Rome, but like all childrens' games, it cuts deeper than we see.

> *(He places the tip of the bat on the head of the horse and steps back.)*

LUPE: One good whack, *mijita*. All the woes turn to candy.

> *(ROMY searches blindly for the piñata. POLO makes it weave and dance around her. Everyone is breathless with anticipation.)*

LUPE: *Orale. Dale madre, mija.*

POLO: *¡Andale, Romelia!* You can do it.

ALMA: *¡Pegale!*

POLO: *¡Fuerte!*

LUPE: C'mon, Romy, show 'em what you got!

> *(ROMY winds up.)*

ALMA:*¡Por Dios Santo, Romelia!* Break it open and he's ours!

POLO: Lupe said! He said you would break the *piñata* and reveal the miracle of our son!

ALMA: Anastacio!

POLO: He said be his maid and gardener for one day and play his game and before the night is done, he will return our son intact!

ALMA: All the years we've waited! All the hours prayed and counted, over and over like a rosary! Ticka ticka tick!

POLO: We been nothing but dust since he left us! All we do is grieve and go mad and wait!

ALMA: For you, *mijita*! You are the one who absolves us! Bring our son back!

ROMY: How!

ALMA: One swing of the bat! One good smash on the belly of that horse! And our hell is over!

POLO: Anastasio! I know you're there, *mijo*! I know you're hiding out there! Forgive us, son! Forgive us!

ALMA: We've seen you already! Please don't punish us so!

LUPE: Don't keep them waiting, Rome. Hit it.

(She keeps still. LUPE places the tip of the bat right on the piñata. Still, she does not swing.)

ALMA: ¡Pegale, maldita!

LUPE: GODDAMMIT! WHAT ARE YOU WAITING FOR! HIT IT!

(ROMY walks deliberately to the tarp and strikes it. It violently unscrolls and BEN, gashed and bruised, erupts like a madman.)

BEN: YAAAAAHHHH!

(ROMY takes off her blind as BEN pulls on the halter around his neck and turns his bloodied face around.)

BEN: you….fucks…

ALMA: Is this him?

POLO: What have you done to him, Madero?

LUPE: Just cured him a little bit, *sabes*, like you cure jerky.

ROMY: Ben?

LUPE: No, baby. This is Tovar.

BEN: …no…

POLO: Anastacio Mario Enrique Tovar.

ALMA: So many days, so many years, waiting. Nights with open veins, ants in my water. God and this devil bring you back.

BEN: I'm… not…

POLO: *Hijo mio.* Don't you know who we are?

ALMA: We're sorry for the way things turned out. Forgive us for telling him. We didn't know what you'd do.

POLO: We just wanted the best for you. That girl was trouble. But never did we think you would go away for so long. *Perdónanos.*

BEN: *(pushing them away)* I… I don't know you.

LUPE: You brought it on yourself, broda. Banged my old lady. Ruined my life. Gave us the *mal de ojo.* You give it every goddamn night, every time I look in my girl's face, and I see your *pinchi* eyes looking back. You know what that does to a man?

(*He takes the bat from ROMY.*)

LUPE: This time, Tovar, Romy stays with me.

BEN: No.

(*LUPE strikes him with the bat.*)

ALMA: ¡Lupe! ¡No!

ROMY: DAD! Stop it!

LUPE: You don't want her. Say it.

BEN: No way.

> *(LUPE strikes him again.)*

POLO: *¡No lo golpees más, Madero!*

LUPE: She's not yours! SAY IT!

> *(BEN shakes his head. LUPE hits him.)*

ROMY: TELL HIM, BEN! TELL HIM YOU DON'T WANT SHIT TO DO WITH ME!

BEN: I can't. The choice isn't mine. It's yours. Lying rolled up in that tarp I learned something. I'm not afraid to die. We've been there, you and me. You know me. And I know you.

ROMY: What do you mean.

> *(BEN extends his bloody hand to her.)*

BEN: *Eres mía.*

> *(NINA enters the corral, soaking wet, her uniform muddied and torn, with ROMY's shoes in her hands.)*

NINA: The last thing he said. You. Are. Mine.

ROMY: *Ama…*

NINA: Hi, baby. Ben, you alright?

BEN: I think so.

ROMY: I saw you in the water. I'd knew you'd make it. I knew it.

NINA: Put the bat down, Lupe.

LUPE: Remember this corral, Nina?

NINA: This ain't Tovar, Lupe.

LUPE: Got Tovar in him, though. Check out the bones.

NINA: Tovar's dead, Lupe.

ALMA: *¿Como?*

POLO: *¿Que dice?*

NINA: *Sr. y Sra.* Tovar, I'm sorry. My ex- has lied to you. We both have. This is my husband, Ben from Ft. Bliss.

BEN: I don't even know who Tovar is.

ALMA: You are him. I know you are.

BEN: I'm sorry. No.

ALMA: *(studying his face closely)* Oh god. You are not him. Not him!

POLO: Where is our son, Lupe!

NINA: Where is he, Lupe? He's not where you buried him.

ALMA: Buried him? Oh no. No. WHERE IS OUR SON?

> (LUPE turns and smashes the piñata
> with all his might. It breaks apart
> and a steady stream of old dusty
> bones, ash, and rotting frays of cloth
> come tumbling out in a small pile.)

ROMY: This was my father.

> (NINA goes to the bones.)

NINA: *Muchacho bravo, mi Tovar, mi prieto,* we knew each other before we even met. Barely a man, Romelia, but I was barely me. They tried to tear us apart by sending him south, and I married Lupe. The price I paid for losing hope. Because Anastacio came back with the light hotter in his eyes for me. And here he is, *mija,* sitting in our mess.

BEN: Why didn't you tell me?

NINA: I was afraid to lose you.

ROMY: Is that why you didn't tell me?

LUPE: You already knew. Deep in your own body, you knew the *cuento*. You knew it had to end this way.

ROMY: How?

LUPE: This way.

(He levels the bat at BEN's head.)

ROMY: Apa. Don't. He went the distance. Not 'cause you led him like a dog. Not for Mom. For me. Me.

LUPE: So?

BEN: So hubby number two grows some balls, hubby number two in el otro! I am private first class benjamin cortez, washed by river, kissed by ticks, thickened with mescal, browned by fucken bat! That man you think I am, their son, he's gone, died in the stink of your sin, and he's taken that other Ben with him, the one who can't go back to Chicago, they're both dead, but no siree uh-uh I do not die like that. I have me a mission that mission is Father and I promised I would see my daughter home and by God Almighty I Will See You Home.

LUPE: Have it your way, sergeant.

(He arches back to swing the bat.)

ROMY: He's not a sergeant, Apa. *(Pause.)* He's a private. First class.

LUPE: Oh shit.

ROMY: It can't be the same. I can't live with you now.

LUPE: *Simón.*

NINA: Put the slugger down, Lupe.

LUPE: What do I have to do to be your father?

ROMY: Let me go.

> *(He nods, then winds up to strike ROMY. The bat freezes in midair. EL CHARRO enters, his silver-tipped finger tracing the trajectory of the bullet. He is seen only LUPE and ROMY.)*

EL CHARRO: And out of the vanishing point where border meet border in the wish and never was of sun and dark and real and bones one eye of Romy see a teeny ball of lead heading straight this way and with her other eye see the best part of her dad the one quarter inch of pure that never know sin open up its mouth to receive to admit to recognize and a wizz go past her face and the teeny ball is received and recognized and understood and then you know what:

133

*(EL CHARRO's finger finds
LUPE's exposed back.)*

LUPE: *¡PUTA VIDA!*

*(LUPE drops the bat, groans
hoarsely, and falls to his knees.)*

ROMY: Apa.

BEN: What's happened?

NINA: I told you, *ese*.

LUPE: Fuck.

NINA: I told you it'd catch up with you. It was just taking the long way around.

LUPE: I didn't even hear it.

BEN: I don't believe it.

*(EL CHARRO takes out his tattoo
kit. He tears LUPE's shirt off and
straddles his back like a horse.)*

EL CHARRO: Now you ripe for some new ink, brother.

LUPE: *Me rompió el corazón, Charro.*

ROMY: Nothing's wrong. Get up, *Apa*. C'mon.

LUPE: Too late, Romy. I got my *Charro* on.

ROMY: Charro! What are you doin', *ese*?

EL CHARRO: Finishing what I started. Here on the ass-side of *corazón*.

ROMY: No way. You can't take him.

LUPE: *¡Romelia Maria, apórtate bien o te doy tus chingazos!*

NINA: He means it, baby.

BEN: We better get her out of here.

> (*They pull her away from LUPE,*
> *who sinks into EL CHARRO's*
> *arms. ALMA goes to LUPE as*
> *POLO proceeds to gather the bones*
> *in the tarp.*)

ALMA: *La vida no vale señora sagrada sus hijos son todos condenados*, all the sons of adam all damned forever. (*She viciously kicks LUPE.*) *Demonio.*

POLO: Romelia, we saw you in our yard with the colt. If you want, come by again. Whenever you want. The little horse is yours.

> (*ALMA and POLO place the bones*
> *into the coffin crate.*)

NINA: She needs a real father, *viejo*.

LUPE: Enjoy yoor affair weet thee beauteeful cadaver, *señor*. Lyeen weet her may kill joo, but also joo may breen life bakk to her. Now fuck off.

ROMY: Shitty the way I wailed on you, Ben.

BEN: It's okay. Just get me the hell outa Mexico. It's sick and strange and as close to hell as I ever want to come.

NINA: I'm sorry you feel that way, honey, 'cause this ain't Mexico.

BEN: What?

NINA: We're still in Texas. You swam across the river at the point it heads north and the border goes west by fence.

BEN: But I thought this was *El Otro*.

NINA: That's just my ex- talkin'.

EL CHARRO: We know where it is, don't we, Lupe?

LUPE: *Ya pelense.* You're gonna miss Good Morning America.

NINA: *Ay te watcho, loco.*

EL CHARRO: Next time you're in El Otro, Romy, look me up. I may be lucid.

*(ROMY starts toward LUPE, but
his singing halts her.)*

LUPE: *Ay mamacita no te vayas*

¿Que no ves que te quiero más que nada?

Si te vas, te hecharé de menos

Y luego te hecharé a la chingada.

*(ROMY turns to go with NINA and
BEN. POLO and ALMA slowly
carry the bones off.)*

EL CHARRO: Pony up your penance, brother.
*(muttering in his ear) La cuenta, por favor. La
cuenta.*

*(He continues tattooing on LUPE.
ROMY returns and faces LUPE.)*

LUPE: Is that the lip? Don't be giving me no lip
now.

ROMY: Not the real Romy but la Romy of his
mind come back and look with love on her *Apa*
and feel the hole in his back and the fissures in
his heart long enough to believe he can take it
back to say the words he's never said say them
now *Apa* there's time there's air there's a ghost
of me here to hear you

LUPE: It ain't my style, sweetheart.

137

(ROMY *kisses his forehead. LUPE*
groans.)

ROMY: Your present.

And then *la Romy* she leave to catch up with
herself sitting in Polo's truck with *ama* on one
side and *apa* ben on the other tearing down the
dirt road that lead to the paved street that lead
to the interstate that take them like the wind
take the desert pollen to their rightful place the
house already booming with good morning
america.

(ROMY *sits by EL CHARRO as he*
works on LUPE's back. LUPE
quietly dying. TABLEAU. Slow fade
to black.)

End of Play

DREAMLANDIA

A river play by Octavio Solis

(based on "La Vida Es Sueño"
by Calderón de la Barca)

Revised October 29, 2009

World Premiere by the Dallas Theater Center
May 2000

Richard Hamburger, Artistic Director

DREAMLANDIA

The cast:

BLANCA (ALFONSO), Young woman

LAZARO, Young man

PEPÍN, Blanca's brother

CELESTINO, The Father

SONIA, His mistress

FRANK, Border Patrol Sector Chief

DOLORES, Dead, a ghost, Blanca's mother

SETH, Border Patrolman

CARL, Border Patrolman

BUSTAMANTE, played by Dolores

VIVIAN, CELESTINO's wife, played by Sonia

The snatches of lyrics sung in Spanish are from "Amor Eterno" by Rocio Durcal.

Dreamlandia

Commissioned by and performed at the Dallas Theater Center on May 16, 2000

Directed by Richard Hamburger, Artistic Director

BLANCA (ALFONSO): Zabryna Guevara

LAZARO: Carlo Alban

PEPÍN: Felix Solis

CELESTINO : Gino Silva

SONIA: Maggie Palomo

FRANK: Bernie Sheredy

DOLORES: Dolores Godinez

SETH: Scott Phillips

CARL: T.A.Taylor

BUSTAMANTE: Dolores Godinez

VIVIAN: Maggie Palomo

Set Design by Russell Parkman, Lighting design by Steve Woods, Costume Design by Claudia Stevens. Sound Design by Marty Desjardins, Stage Manager Christy Weikel, Assistant Director Marisela Barrera, Lisa Holland Artistic Office

Casting by Elissa Myers

Act One

PEPÍN: A night big as the state of Tejas with Pepín inside.

> *(Pounding rain, punctured by lightning. Howitzer thunder. VIVIAN on a bed, screeching in pain. PEPÍN on floor by the bed, an open suitcase at his feet.)*

VIVIAN: *OH GOD* this *thing* eating me eating me eating me whole CELESTINO!

> *(CELESTINO rips through the storm dragging DOLORES after him. PEPÍN rushes to her side. FRANK enters behind them and remains at a distance.)*

CELESTINO: There! Hurry! She needs you! *¡Ayudala!*

DOLORES: *Señor*, what can I do? *No se--*

CELESTINO: *Partera*, they call you! *¿Eres Partera?*

DOLORES: *Si pero--*

CELESTINO: Deliver this baby! Save my wife! Do it!

VIVIAN: Burning! My insides all black!

FRANK: Do it!

DOLORES: She belongs in a hospital! *¡Mira, sangre!*

PEPÍN: Mami, I wanna go home!

CELESTINO: I can't take her to a hospital! No-one can know! No-one can know anything!

DOLORES: I can't help her, *señor! ¡Tiene el Mal de Ojo!*

CELESTINO: *¡Mira!* I'll get you papers, a passport, I'll make you legal!!

DOLORES: *¿Papeles?*

CELESTINO: Everything! Just deliver my baby!

FRANK: He means it!

DOLORES: My cords, in the case! *¡Pepín, espera afuera!*

VIVIAN: Pain filling me with flies, millions of flies.

PEPÍN: Mami pries the legs apart like a curtain.

VIVIAN: My breath become smoke.

PEPÍN: Mami thrusting hands inside the mulch of blood and birth.

VIVIAN: AYY!

DOLORES: *¡No quiere salir!* The wretch is afraid of the light!

CELESTINO: Soon, *mi amor! ¡Ya mero!*

VIVIAN: OH GOD!

FRANK: Don't speak! Don't try to move!...

PEPÍN: Rope in her fists, rope around his little crown, pull against the neverlife, pull against blood, Mami pulls, her veins thicker than lightning, thunder in her throat, pulling--

DOLORES: Come!--

VIVIAN: *Bastards!---*

CELESTINO: Wait! You're hurting her! STOP!

PEPÍN: A whole mess of *tripas*, intestines roping the bed, dragging him back and then Mami says

DOLORES: *¡TENGO QUE ABRIRLA!*

> (FRANKS slaps DOLORES his knife. The VIVIAN screams as an

infant wails. DOLORES hoists the
wet child.)

FRANK: OH SWEET JESUS!

PEPÍN: Hanging like meat, a bald pale pigbody limp and dripping with *mamasangre*.

> *(Lightning, then black, then a*
> *riverside. Rain swells the raging*
> *current. DOLORES, PEPÍN and*
> *CELESTINO with a gun.)*

CELESTINO: My beloved. My Vivian.

PEPÍN: Right on the lip of *Señor Grande*, his black tongue licking our shoes.

DOLORES: She was too sick. The cocaine made her slack.

CELESTINO: So much blood in a woman, who knew?

PEPÍN: River and night become one.

DOLORES: I did all I could, *señor*.

CELESTINO: Swim.

DOLORES: *¿Como?*

CELESTINO: Both of you, in the water.

DOLORES: I don't understand. You told me I would get papers.

CELESTINO: You killed my wife. For that, you want citizenship? Swim back to Mexico, *bruja*!

PEPÍN: ¡Mami!

DOLORES: Please! Not my boy! He'll drown!

CELESTINO: Go!

DOLORES: I delivered your son! I saved him!

CELESTINO: Keep walking!

> (*DOLORES and PEPÍN step into
> the rivertide.*)

DOLORES: *¡Celestino Robles, hombre desgraciado!
¡Ingrato!* I curse you, I throw my scorpion signs
at you, liar, *mojado*, yes, I know, *mojado* like all
of us, I spit ash and gravel on your name, I
swear the boy by the stars will be raped, by the
stars will he beget his rage, to shit blood on
your affairs, poison the kiss of your woman,
betray your own word, and love another man
better than he ever loves you! *¡Te lo juro,
demonio! Te lo juro!*

CELESTINO: SWIM, BITCH!

DOLORES: *¡SINCERO! ¡SINCERO! ¡DONDE
ESTAS! ¡SINCERO!*

> (*Blackout. CELESTINO and PEPÍN
> wake from the same dream twenty*

146

years later, on separate shores of the river.)

CELESTINO: Is that all it was? A dream?

PEPÍN: *Sueños sueños son.*

(FRANK walks on.)

FRANK: You know, cowboy, if I had a fifth of pity, I sure wouldn't waste it on you.

CELESTINO: I don't want your pity. I want your allegiance.

FRANK: Well, I am your dog, sir.

CELESTINO: I would've cut you loose years ago, Frank. I would've spared us both the obligation that keeps us eating off each other's plate.

FRANK: And I woulda thanked you. But I reckon misery loves Mexicans.

CELESTINO: Maybe so. But I'm not a Mexican.

FRANK: Right. So what was it this time? What sick little peach pip a conscience set you on this midnight dosey-doh?

CELESTINO: Vivian.

FRANK: I ain't hearing this.

CELESTINO: I saw her, Frank.

FRANK: I don't care.

CELESTINO: She was my wife!

FRANK: And my sister! Don't you forget that!

CELESTINO: Then why don't you dream her! Why doesn't the grief play over and over in your sleep? Why don't you hear the screams like I do?

FRANK: Maybe I got less to feel guilty about.

CELESTINO: It doesn't change the facts between us, brother.

FRANK: Only fact I live by is on that island out there.

> (*Across the riverbank in Mexico, BLANCA drags with great heaving effort the drenched body of DOLORES.*)

CELESTINO: Listen!...

PEPÍN: *¿Mami?*

FRANK: I don't hear anything.

CELESTINO: It's not about hearing.

PEPÍN: Is Mamasangre drunk again?

BLANCA: I found her tangled in the rushes. Wrapped around an old tire.

CELESTINO: I think it's over, Frank.

BLANCA: *¿Como pasó, Pepín?* This morning when I went to work, she seemed fine. How did she end up in the river?

PEPÍN: She packed this case, and held me close to her liver which is brown like *cucarachas*, she said adios, said she was going back, said go to sleep, so I slept. Is she sleeping too?

CELESTINO: I think she's finally dead.

BLANCA: ¡AMA!

> *(She collapses in tears over her dead mother.)*

CELESTINO: The bones are all played out. I waited my time and my time is done, *bruja*. I win!

FRANK: What are you on about?

CELESTINO: What the dream meant, Frank. It's over. The woman that cursed my life is dead. Do you know what that means?

FRANK: I'm a Baptist, Tino.

CELESTINO: Bring him, Frank. Bring my son.

FRANK: No and hell no.—

CELESTINO: It's time.

FRANK: Them's not the terms we struck.

CELESTINO: I decreed him to that hyphen between his mother's name and mine, right in the middle of the *Rio*. Now I decree my son home.

FRANK: He's not the son you think.

CELESTINO: He's a Robles and he belongs by his father.

FRANK: You don't know what being a father means.

(FRANK goes.)

BLANCA: Why did you do it, *Ama*? What in that damn country did you drown yourself for?

PEPÍN: She said she was going for *Sincero*.

BLANCA: My father?

PEPÍN: En *mis* dreams, I heard her calling for him while this big *chingon*, Mr. *Migra*, stood by the *Rio* like the sheriff of *pinchi* Walmart.

BLANCA: Sincero. That name *es mi destino*. Without *Ama*, what home, what country, do I live in? All the country I got left is Sincero.

(pumping her mother's chest for air.)

Let there be one *suspiro*, one breath in my mother's lung, one little pocket of *Bilis. Coraje. Susto!* Breathe into me your torment, Ama!

> *(DOLORES emits a single gasp of air. BLANCA inhales it.)*

Asi. Asi. In your trances, you always walked the water. Now it's our turn.

PEPÍN: Blanca…?

BLANCA: *Vamonos, Pepín.* Let's bury Ama and get going.

PEPÍN: *¿A donde?*

BLANCA: *Yankeelandia.*

> *(BLANCA takes the suitcase and goes with PEPÍN. CELESTINO stands as lights change. The island…)*

CELESTINO: I feel you, boy, on the fringes of my sleep, hair parted, skin smooth and brown, little manicured fingers reaching for me, drawing me near, making me say… Lazaro.

> *(LAZARO charges out from his lair screaming like an enraged animal until the heavy chain on his neck jerks him back.)*

If I could, I would've sucked you in and held
you till the right day the right moon the right
sign and then released you to your mother and
let you be the son you were supposed to be.
But I couldn't and she's gone and you're what
family's left.

LAZARO: *¡Escuchame!*

    (CELESTINO goes.)

Sombras. Shadows. Gassy dreamfuckers. As if
que si. As if *que no.* You know what rise they
come from? Your cuts and punctures. Ghosts
slip out the seams and walk. Cry for the
homeblood. The wound is mouth. The mouth
has voice. Voice has blood. Blood is home.
Home bleeds Lazaro. And all the time the
voices are saying only no. *Cada vez que no.*
Every ever no. Never to be home. Never to see.
Never to feel. It makes *el pinchi* heart a gash.
Ay!

    (He violently yanks at his chain.)

Cadena. You one big motherfucking piece of
jewelry. Hang on me, sister. Hang your
shimmer on, your metal *luz*, your clink and
your clank and the weight of that sound, hang
your *pinchi* links on me and let me show the
world I may be screwed *pero*, honey, I know
how to accessorize!

O God, come to where the flavor is!

Gimme one day's good glossy full page dream *de* liberty!

Let me stand in the ad *de mi* own manhood long enough to feel *suave, y si no suave,* then *con puro* attitude! How can you leave me like this, in my own rags, with my body reeking me up *y mis* glossy girls smiling in my face! How can you let them treat me *como un animal*? I have seen Italian leather!

Es el mero skin of God.

Black me out, *ese*! Just black me out! I got no place but this, I got no recall, no friend, *nomas el* Sugar Man *con los* cc's of T-rex *y mi* Happy Meal! I got no hope to hang on. Just fucking black me out, just---

> (*BLANCA rises out of the water like a vision. He hides.*)

Whoa. *Ruquita.* Wass your game? What you play *en mi* sandbar? The dreamfuck sends me a cover girl. As if *que si.* Oh, *mira.* Her skin, not white but tinted-glass, full-page lips, the scent of Obsession in the Vanity Fair, issue 46, *pagina* 29, I be so good at these delusions.

> (*LAZARO steps out. They gape at each other in awe.*)

Hey.

BLANCA: Hey. Listen. Have you seen this boy? I lost him in the current.

LAZARO: *Senorita* Godsend.

BLANCA: Did you see my brother come ashore here?

LAZARO: *Aqui.*

> (*LAZARO produces a small portable radio. He turns it on.*)

BLANCA: What's your deal?

LAZARO: My deal? I live and he feeds me. I stay and he enlightens me.

BLANCA: What is this place? You live here? Smells like *mierda.*

LAZARO: My fully furnished hole. A water bowl and a dog dish. Every TV Guide *desde* 1976 *pero no* TV. I do the crosswords. What was Suzanne Somers' name on Three's Company?

BLANCA: Chrissie.

LAZARO: You <u>are</u> a godsend. (*The radio*) He needs batteries to live.

BLANCA: Duh..

LAZARO: I need pain.

*(He shows her his arms, speckled
with needle marks.)*

BLANCA: Why are you *encadenado*?

LAZARO: For my own good. That's what *Tio*
Sugar tells me. *Dice que* I'm a dangerous man.
My knowledge of things can shatter the world
to pieces. Do I look dangerous to you?

BLANCA: You look pathetic. My kid brother,
he's dangerous. He once whacked off a cat's
head with a hub cap. *Como el* Oddjob.
SSSHHOOOO!

LAZARO: Laughing hurts my throat.

BLANCA: You gotta lose that chain, *ese*. This
Uncle Sugar, he the one who put you here? Is
he your *jefe*?

LAZARO: This chain is my *jefe*. My *mami* is the
water all around. Can I touch you?

BLANCA: Uh-uh.

LAZARO: I won't hurt you.

> *(He slowly approaches her. Feels her
> skin.)*

Que piel, que piel, smooth receptive skin with a
healthy glow. Enriched with moisturizing

plant extracts. Velvety finish, rich and creamy for day-long comfort.

(Her lips.)

Safe and effective lip balm, imbued with rare florals for that treasured moment.

(Her hair.)

Ay, que maximum body and fullness. *Cada* follicle carefully revitalized for that healthy lustre and shine that nature gave you.

> *(He takes the ribbon from her hair and then smells her.)*

A captivating signature fragrance, allergy-tested for all skin-types. I smelt you before.

BLANCA: You have?

> *(He retrieves from his hovel a stack of fashion magazines Elle, Vogue, Modern Woman, etc. Sniffs earmarked pages.)*

LAZARO: Here. *(Sniff)* Here. *(Sniff)* You.*(sniff)* All of them you. But never dreamed you out. That took more T-rex than I could take. Who are you?

> *(Noises off.)*

BLANCA: Not now. Wait, okay?

LAZARO: Where you going?

BLANCA: I have to go!

LAZARO: You can't leave like that! *Tienes que* set free me!

BLANCA: Look, I'll be right back.

LAZARO: FUCK NO! BITCH! You have to let me go! GET YOUR ASS BACK!

BLANCA: Brother, I'm gonna tell you once! You're gonna have to wait. I'll be back for you. I promise. *Te voy hacer* free.

> *(She goes.)*

LAZARO: DREAMFUCKER!!!!

> *(He collapses in a heap, and rocks himself as he cries.)*

Wish her back. Wish her back. Wish her back. See her. Wish her back. Squeeze her out again!

> *(He squeezes his needle marks. FRANK and his two men enter.)*

FRANK: Hey, pilgrim.

LAZARO: *¿Eres tu?* Are you really there, Frank?

FRANK: Sure am. Look what I brung you. Claudia Schiffer in color. Beauty tips on Page 80. The new Fall Line.

LAZARO: mmgh.

FRANK: You don't sound too excited, son.

LAZARO: I don't need her no more, Frank. I seen the cover girl move.

FRANK: What cover girl?

LAZARO: I seen her shake her ass. She let me *tocarla*. Felt the ph balance of her skin. So rockin.

FRANK: Who are you talkin about? I didn't see no-one.

LAZARO: She's my ghost, Frank. She arose *de mis* sores.

FRANK: That can only mean one thing, son. It's time for you to check out.

LAZARO: *¿De veras?*

FRANK: Cmere, son.

> (*LAZARO goes to him. FRANK gently holds him.*)

I know, boy. I know. Been a hell of a time for both of us. But I'm gonna free you. I'm gonna quit that pain and deliver you from the bonds of this world. Bring me that thermos.

> *(They bring him the thermos. He opens it. Steam rises.)*

Fetch one of your cover girls, pilgrim.

> *(LAZARO tears a page from a magazine and hands it to FRANK.)*

She's pretty.

> *(FRANK tears the picture to little pieces and drops them in the thermos. Then he hands it to LAZARO.)*

Drink it all up.

> *(LAZARO drinks.)*

LAZARO: It's strong.

FRANK: Brewed the way a special lady taught me. Now on your back. That's it, boy. Close your eyes.

> *(FRANK unlocks the shackle from his neck.)*

LAZARO: I feel....like...kinda....free.

FRANK: That's darkness spreading you out.

LAZARO: Will I see cover girl there?

FRANK: Front row at the Latin Grammys. In a mink and black number slit up to here.

> *(FRANK's men slip a large sack over his head.)*

LAZARO: *Se siente* prickly. Does darkness feel so prickly?

FRANK: Darkness does, son.

LAZARO: I'm gonna find her, Frank. I'm gonna...hhh...

SETH: You don't have to do this, you know.

FRANK: Shut up, Seth.

SETH: Mr. Robles ain't the INS. You don't have to take orders from him.

FRANK: I said shut up. What the hell you know about this, dumbass?

SETH: Well, I know you like this kid more'n he does.--

FRANK: Dammit, Seth, this boy is an abomination to me: if it was up to me, he'd a been drowned long ago. It ain't up to me.

> *(CARL finds the ribbon.)*

CARL: Lookit this, Frank. Where'd he get this?

FRANK: Maybe cover girl paid a visit after all. Put him on the boat. And you, mister, remember yourself. You gotta badge to uphold here.

> *(They take up the sack and go.
> FRANK studies the ribbon.)*

Cover Girl? You mess with my pilgrim?

> *(FRANK goes as PEPÍN enters,
> crying out after BLANCA.)*

PEPÍN: Blanca! *¡Blanca Dolorida! ¡Blanca de mi vida!* Where are you?

> *(He sees the audience.)*

Oofas! Who the refried beans are you! Are you...waspichis? Ancient tribe of white people? Waspichis from the land of Wasp? *¡Chevre!* I thought *Americanos* were taller, like that *presidente, como se llama,* Rano... Rano...Rano Macdano! The big red hair! Mami admire him so much, she dressed me like him sometimes, put me on the street to do presidential tricks. I juggle, I breathe kerosina and vomit fire, make all the waspichi kiddies laugh.

Oofas, are you the *presidente? Orale,* presidunce, I got one thing to say to you: these *problemas* with the border that we got? I know how you can erase them all, *mano!* Switch

161

countries. That's right. Move the US to the south and Mexico up north, and watch how things change. Wait a minuto puto, ain't that whass happening already? *¡Chale!* You're a *chingon presidente!*

> (*BLANCA appears behind him dressed in a man's suit.*)

BLANCA: Pepín.

> (*Startled, PEPÍN stands at attention and checks his pockets.*)

PEPÍN: *Si señor.* I have *mis papeles.*

BLANCA: No, Pepín. It's me. Me.

PEPÍN: *¿Blanca? ¿Que te pasó, carnala?*

BLANCA: I'm a man now, okay? You gotta call me by my man's name, okay?

PEPÍN: But where are your *chi-chis*?

BLANCA: As soon as I set foot in *Tejas*, my hair fell off and I grew some things that I had to cover with man clothes. Follow me so far?

PEPÍN: So we're in the Land of Billy Bob! Yeehaw! *Andale*, Blanca's a cowboy! Yeeeehaw! Ride em, pardner!

BLANCA: *Escucha*, Pepín. My name is Alfonso now. *No me llames* by that other name. Noone'll bother us if we're boys.

PEPÍN: Is the same thing gonna happen to me? Can I have your *chi-chis*, please?

BLANCA: No, just me. I can't be a girl now. Not if I'm going to find him.

PEPÍN: Our father who art in Tejas?

BLANCA: Pepín, I want you to think. Does this look like the riverside in your dream? Are we close to that place?

PEPÍN: *¿Sabes que?* It's *un poquito* like it, but I think in my *sueño* it was this a-ways, gotta dream this a-ways, ooo-ooo-oooo!

> (He wanders off in a daze. BLANCA watches him.)

BLANCA: *Pobre loquito.*

> (DOLORES appears as PEPÍN exits.)

DOLORES: He was never meant to live.

BLANCA: *Ama.*

DOLORES: But he lives to spite us all.

BLANCA: *Ay, Ama. ¿Porque?* Why did you go in the river?

DOLORES: I had to, *mija.* Why did you bring Pepín? He's going to need a lot of care.

BLANCA: He's the only one who's ever seen him. He'll recognize him for me.

DOLORES: Your father.

BLANCA: You never showed us any pictures, you never told us anything but his name. A name you couldn't say without crying. In a house where from the ceiling hung all these herbs to dry and all these wooden *santos* stared out at me and the smells of healing filled my senses, there was no healing. This man caused you pain, Ama.

DOLORES: I had to die to stop it.

BLANCA: Now I got your pain. I have to stop it. Even if means coming to these *pinchis gringos*, I'll find him and I'll stop it.

DOLORES: Better make sure you got a green card, honey.

BLANCA: Is that all you have to say? Is that what you came for?

DOLORES: I came because I thought you were him. Those are his clothes you're wearing.

BLANCA: This... is his?

DOLORES: You stand like *Sincero* in those pants.

BLANCA: Oh god. They were in that old suitcase.

DOLORES: With those old records. Lucha Villa. Javier Solis. He loved those old Mexican boleros. *(Sings)* *"Tu eres la tristeza de mis ojos que lloran en silencio por tu adiós..."*

BLANCA: I can't wear it... I can't...

DOLORES: Wait, *mija*. Don't take it off. It does my swollen heart good to see his old coat filled with life again. You bring him back to me.

BLANCA: Who is he, *Ama*?

DOLORES: I'll tell you, honey, if you'll dance with me.

> *(BLANCA slow dances with DOLORES.)*

Your father is a good dancer. He holds my hand like it's this little bird and makes me feel special. Every night he comes to my house and sometimes drives me to the barrios where I bring in the songs of little babies. On Sunday afternoons, he helps me collect herbs for my healing and plays with Pepín in the garden.

BLANCA: He plays with Pepín?

DOLORES: Oh he loves him so, and he loves the taste of fresh corn tortillas, and has a smile the wingspan of a sparrow, and he touches the place where you are being formed...

>   *(BLANCA places her hand on
>   DOLORES' stomach.)*

BLANCA: Ohhh…

DOLORES: Shh, he says. No-one can know about us. We are a secret. Our love is a crime. Shh. Shh.

BLANCA: And then there is so much blood and lightning and then we are at the river

DOLORES: Deported in the worst of ways

BLANCA: On the worst of nights

DOLORES: Forced to swim across the *rio* like a wetback but backwards!

>   *(BLANCA roars back, ripping a
>   knife out from the pocket of her coat.)*

BLANCA: WHERE ARE YOU, *COBARDE!*
HOW CAN YOU LIVE WITH YOURSELF!
I'LL RIP YOU TO PIECES!

DOLORES: If the blade fits, *mija.*

> *(VOICES OFF calling: ALTO!*
> *ALTO! BLANCA hides the knife*
> *and runs. DOLORES turns to see*
> *CELESTINO enter.)*

I dream a man dreaming of me and this creature with no arms no legs and no face, this creature called night is dreaming us.

"Prefiero estar dormida que despierta..."

> *(DOLORES dances away. Lights up*
> *on NEXMEX.)*

CELESTINO: --*"De tanto que me duele que no estés..."*

> *(Sonia appears at her desk.)*

SONIA: I love how you sing to me, baby! *Dame un besito.*

> *(He kisses her.)*

CELESTINO: How's my darling?

SONIA: Busy like hell. I got these *pinchi* mid-quarter reports to go through and its inventory time and then another girl in assembly went missing last night.

CELESTINO: Another one?

SONIA: Third one this month. Too bad, this Blanca Rosario was good. Tough to replace, that's for sure.

CELESTINO: So what's this about a call?

SONIA: It came early this morning about eight thirty. I don't know how the call got routed.

CELESTINO: Who was it?

SONIA: You ever heard of Bustamante?

CELESTINO: No.

SONIA: That's the problem. Nobody has.

CELESTINO: So what did he want?

SONIA: She. It was a *pinchi* woman.

CELESTINO: The hell you say.

SONIA: She said she had a special shipment she wanted us to move for her. More *contrabanda* than you can dream in twenty years, she called it.

CELESTINO: What the hell does that mean?

SONIA: Nobody knows who this bitch is. Nobody has anything that big in the works.

CELESTINO: Then she's a crank.

SONIA: Not so fast, baby. This lady knows how we cut deals with the narcos, how we charge them a toll so that *pinchi* Frank and the INS look the other way at the *puente*.

CELESTINO: She knows this?

SONIA: And she knows they smuggle their shit in our trucks in TV boxes.

CELESTINO: *Cabrona*.

SONIA: She even offered to give us information on other local smuggling operations so Frank can bust their ass. Is this wild *o que*?

CELESTINO: Keep checking her out. If she's for real, we'll know it soon enough.

SONIA: This woman freaks me out, *mi amor*.

CELESTINO: Let me worry about her. There's more pressing *negocio* afoot.

SONIA: Now what?

CELESTINO: Sonia, between you and me, I don't understand Mexico anymore. Juarez disagrees with me. And this factory, you deal with it more than I do nowadays. You make this *maquila* hum.

SONIA: Damn right.

CELESTINO: You got good people skills—

SONIA: Fire and hire!

CELESTINO: You're bilingual—

SONIA: English and html.

CELESTINO: And you know how I like things.

SONIA: Eggs hardboiled, cars imported, women four-alarm. What's your point?

CELESTINO: I need your help with a young man.

SONIA: What kind of help? Who's the young man?

CELESTINO: It's complicated. My...my son is home after a long absence and he's going to need some help adjusting.

SONIA: Hold the phone. I thought you said he was stillborn.

CELESTINO: Only to the world. I'll explain it all later. Right now, I need your help.

SONIA: You mean, he needs a mother.

CELESTINO: There's a big change coming and I want you to be part of it. I looked at the charts and by the stars' conjunctions, you are there.

SONIA: What am I wearing?

CELESTINO: Silver, 16 million volts of flowing silver just above the knee, sandals, a brooch like a jaguar's eye, regal hair pinned back by regal hands.

SONIA: On my ring finger. Is the diamond one full carat?

CELESTINO: *(presenting her with a ring)* Two.

SONIA: Let's see the boy.

(*The Robles Estate. FRANK enters.*)

FRANK: That's not possible. I just had him washed and changed. He's sleeping it off.

CELESTINO: How is he?

FRANK: Sleeping it off. I guess you know the whole story.

SONIA: Oh yes. Maybe you should send the servants home till he gets better.

FRANK: Are you ordering me?

SONIA: Just a suggestion, Frank.

FRANK: I saw your bags in the hall. Does this mean you're moving in?

SONIA: Looks like it. Now you can spend more time with your family, I'm sure your wife misses you.

FRANK: Lady—

CELESTINO: Frank, Sonia is my wife now.

FRANK: Many happy returns.

SONIA: Gracias, Francis.

CELESTINO: We work as a team on our other enterprise. I expect us to work as a team here.

> (FRANK's cell phone rings. He answers.)

FRANK: Hello... Yeah? Who?... Hold on... You know a Bustamante?

SONIA: How did she get the number?

FRANK: Something about a shipment. Shit guaranteed to break your heart, her words.

CELESTINO: A poet.

FRANK: She's got some shit on a rival operation. Coming next week. She wants to rat these losers out as a sign of good faith.

CELESTINO: I don't talk with snitches. Take it, baby.

(SONIA takes the phone and notates as SETH and CARL enter.)

FRANK: Your hats, boys.

SETH: Mr. Robles.

CARL: Sir.

FRANK: What's the news, Carl?

CARL: Picked up a couple wets outside the city limits.

SETH: Young guys. Right off Highway 80.

FRANK: Any I.D. on them?

CARL: *Nada.* One of them's a retard but the other speaks English pretty good for a greaser.

CELESTINO: The term used in this house is Mexican.

CARL: Messican.

FRANK: Drive them to the station. We'll process them tonight.

CELESTINO: Wait. Bring them in, Frank. Let me see them.

FRANK: What for?

CELESTINO: I might need their services. Bring them in.

(SETH and CARL go.)

SONIA: (clicking the phone off) Done, *mi amor.* Time, place, tonnage, and caliber.

CELESTINO: Let's arrange a reception for these fuckers. No-one comes through my sector without my knowing. Or my fee.

FRANK: So you gonna tell me who this Bustamante is?

CELESTINO: In time, *compadre.*

> *(SETH and CARL bring in ALFONSO and PEPÍN.)*

SETH: This is them.

FRANK: Which one of you's the retard? (No response.) All right. Which one's the genius?

PEPÍN: Me, *señor.*

FRANK: How old are you?

PEPÍN: Many ages, *señor.* My feet are babies cause they came out last, my head's retired cause it came out first, my mouth's of drinking age, my hands old enough to drive, and my weenie is newborn every night.

FRANK: And you? You don't talk? That's a fine old hat. Where'd you get the hat, boy?

BLANCA: Hats R Us.

SETH: Musta stole it, this funny guy.

PEPÍN: *Oye*, I'm the funny! How many wetbacks does it take to screw in a lightbulb?

SETH: How many?

PEPÍN: I'm asking you, stupid.

(*PEPÍN roars with laughter.*)

SONIA: Where were you going?

BLANCA: Wherever they need pickers.

FRANK: What's this suitcase for, Jose?

BLANCA: It's Alfonso to you, *pendejo*!

PEPÍN: He don't have *chi-chis*.

CARL: (*striking him*) Shut up, retard!

BLANCA: *ORALE*, I TOLD YOU LEAVE HIM ALONE!

(*She jumps on CARL but FRANK grabs her.*)

FRANK: Boy, in case you ain't noticed, you're a *mojado* now, and in this state, *mojados* rate lower than dog. You understand?

BLANCA: I understand you're a *pinchi gringo* in a country fulla *pinchi gringos*, and I'd rather be dog than you any day!

> (*FRANK takes out his gun, aims it at her. CELESTINO places his hand on FRANK's gun and slowly lowers it.*)

CELESTINO: Willful boy.

FRANK: Nobody's ever talked to me like that before.

BLANCA: How come we're here? How come you don't send us back?

CELESTINO: I have need of a tutor. Say yes, you get bed, board, and documents. Say no, you go back.

BLANCA: What a country. Who am I tutoring?

CELESTINO: My son. Lazaro. I'll have sandwiches in the kitchen for you.

FRANK: Put the Jerry Lewis in the car--

PEPÍN: NO! NO! ALFONSO! *¡CARNAL!*

BLANCA: Wait, he don't go nowhere without me! He's my brother!

CELESTINO: I only need one of you.

BLANCA: He won't take up room. He'll eat off my plate. He'll sleep with me.

PEPÍN: How many wetbacks does it take to change a bed?

CELESTINO: You start now.

> *(CELESTINO and SONIA go.)*

CARL: Is he serious, Frank? Guy's one taco short of a combination plate.

FRANK: I'm sure you men will manage with him just fine.

SETH/CARL: WHUT! US? NO WAY!

PEPÍN: *¡Orale!*

> *(Lights change. DOLORES over the sleeping LAZARO.)*

DOLORES: Embryos inside embryos inside embryos. Your dream is your chrysalis, a flicker of the eyelid your wing, your waking a pinch of this skin.

> *(She pinches him and dances away. LAZARO stirs.)*

LAZARO: *Luz. Mas luz.* Too much *pinchi luz.*

> *(He takes in the newness. Feels his neck. Sees his arms.)*

No chain. No pain.

> (The fabric of his pajamas.)

Soft.

> (He twists around and checks the
> label of his pajama top.)

Pierre Cardin. *Chingao*, this **is** heaven.

> (CELESTINO steps forward.)

CELESTINO: Do you know me?

LAZARO: Are you God?

CELESTINO: I am your father.

LAZARO: ...father?

CELESTINO: You are my son. *Mi varon.* Born
under *Centauro*. You don't remember me? You
don't remember anything?

LAZARO: I remember being pissed about
something.

> (He feels CELESTINO's leather
> coat.)

Italian?

CELESTINO: Yes. Lazaro, *escuchame*. You've
been very sick. You had a rare condition. For
three weeks you've been sleeping.

LAZARO: Asleeping?

CELESTINO: Dreaming. You spoke of an island. And a chain. But there is no chain.

LAZARO: *¿Un sueño?*

CELESTINO: I missed you, boy. I missed you so much. A lifetime gone by.

LAZARO: No shit.

CELESTINO: I'll teach you. I'll make up for the lost time... *mijo.*

LAZARO: *Apa.*

> (SONIA *steps forward with her opened compact. She shows him his reflection.*)

SONIA: Lazaro. *Mira.* This face, this young man...

> (He is intrigued by the reflection. He sniffs the make-up.)

CELESTINO: This is Sonia, she's your--

SONIA: Mother. I'm your mother. Don't you know me?

LAZARO: I know Anne Klein. *(FRANK steps forward.)* Frank?

FRANK: Pilgrim.

LAZARO: You were in this dream. You were Tio Sugar who kept me chained. Shot me up with T-rex. Sent me on prickly death. You were a real fucker, Frank.

FRANK: Well, what can I tell you.

CELESTINO: Can you stand? Are you ready to see your house?

SONIA: It's real. Twenty-two rooms.

FRANK: Tino, I don't think it's a good idea. I don't think he's ready.

> (LAZARO suddenly turns and
> lunges at FRANK.)

LAZARO: *PINCHI* FRANK! *TU ME CHINGASTE, CABRON! TU!*

> (He latches onto FRANK's head and
> tears his ear off. CARL and SETH
> run in to separate them. LAZARO
> spits the ear out.)

SONIA: OH MY GOD!

CARL: JESUS H!

CELESTINO: LAZARO! Get him off! Stop it!

*(They tear LAZARO off FRANK,
who screams holding his bleeding
head. LAZARO spits the gory mass
on the floor.)*

LAZARO: I WANT MY CHAIN! *MIS* COVER
GIRLS! MY TV GUIDES! GO BACK! I
WANNA GO BACK!

*(He knocks SETH and CARL to the
floor and runs out.)*

SONIA: Oh my god! My god!

CELESTINO: He's an animal!

SONIA: What did you expect! He's been caged
all his life!

FRANK: Goddammit! Can we talk about this
later? Get me an ambulance!

CELESTINO: Get up and find him!

FRANK: He's going back, Tino! I'm putting
him back!

SONIA: NO! He's just scared and confused!

LAZARO: *(off)* WHERE IS *MI ISLA!*

CELESTINO: *¡MADRE DE DIOS!*

*(CELESTINO and SONIA rush
out.)*

FRANK: Lord... I'm passin out...

> (DOLORES enters with a jar
> bristling with herbs and
> wildflowers.)

DOLORES: *Ruda, romero,* passion flower,
yarrow. *Cascara sagrada, yerba buena.* yellow
shame. All my remedies crowd the river banks,
catching wind and drowsy bees on their buds.
If you doze off, they'll catch your daydreams
too.

FRANK: Dolores...

DOLORES:(as she rubs some herb extract on
his ear) Rub a little self-heal on and the
swelling will go down.

FRANK: I'm seein' things...

DOLORES: Me, too. I'm seeing that maybe if
the sun stays warm, I might be coaxed on the
grass and toward my girl's conception. It just
seems like the thing to do.

FRANK: No...

DOLORES: Now, while Pepín's dipping his
feet on the shore, digging up crayfish with his
toes. I could hike my dress up and fuck or just
keep picking *yerbas* all day.

FRANK: I never, never meant to...

(MAMA delicately picks up the ear.)

DOLORES: Here's a rare and pretty one. I'll save you for my birth pains.

FRANK: Whut? Birth pains? What do you mean...?

> *(She nimbly places it in her jar and seals it.)*

DOLORES: *Albacar*, bitterroot, y *linaza*. All these I'll save for the fevers of denial. Teas and *purgas* for the fevers of denial.

> *(She smiles on FRANK. Lights change. BLANCA and PEPÍN eating sandwiches in the kitchen.)*

PEPÍN: Mm. Good. *¿Y el tuyo?*

BLANCA: Good.

PEPÍN: I like baloney. Baloney is the best meat. You make baloney into many things. Baloney makes sun, baloney makes flower, baloney makes happy face...

BLANCA: Don't play with your food.

PEPÍN: What do you have?

BLANCA: Ham.

PEPÍN: You know, *carnal, hamon* is the best meat—

BLANCA: Pepín, that dream you had, the one before Ama died, you said you saw this man and a woman giving birth...

PEPÍN: *¡Mamasangre!*

BLANCA: You don't remember their faces?

PEPÍN: It's all a big darkmess. Only one face I dismember.

BLANCA: Who?

PEPÍN: He was dark and quivery--

BLANCA: Yeah?

PEPÍN: Scary and glary--

BLANCA: Like Sincero?

PEPÍN: No, baloney. He was a big bloody piece of baloney... WWWAAAHHH!

BLANCA: You mean, the baby.

PEPÍN: WWAAHHH! he went, like a monster without any chones!

BLANCA: Don't eat my sandwich. I'm gonna see if there's a way outa here.

(BLANCA goes. PEPÍN puts slices of baloney on his face and staggers around like a big monster.)

PEPÍN: AWWOORR! GRRR! OOGA BOOOGA!

(LAZARO enters. He takes the meat off his face and eats it.)

LAZARO: *Isla*. Where did *cabrones* put my island?

PEPÍN: I didn't take it.

LAZARO: *As if que si, as if que no,* they said a dream, but I don't believe it.

PEPÍN: *Oye, vato,* maybe you're a dream. My dream. Maybe I'm *mimis* and the baloney is making me see shit!

(LAZARO eats BLANCA's sandwich.)

Hey! That's not yours!

LAZARO: Hungry.

PEPÍN: *Mano,* you gonna get me in trouble! Blanca's gonna be mad cause she'll think I ate her samwich cause you won't be here cause I'll wake up!

LAZARO: And maybe if I wake up, you won't be here!

PEPÍN: ¿O si? (He leaps on Lazaro.) Get back in my dream, duermevato!

LAZARO: ¡Ya! Get off me!

>   (They wrestle as CARL and SETH enter.)

CARL: Easy, muchacho.

SETH: Lookee here, Lazaro. TV Guide.

LAZARO: TV guide...

CARL: Survivor...

SETH: 20-20...

>   (He reaches for it. They knock him out.)

CARL: Smackdown!

>   (They carry him off.)

PEPÍN: ¡Chingao! Duermevato fell outa my sleep and now he's got the shit-kicky outa him! I gotta get him back in!

>   (He runs off. Lights change. FRANK talks as CELESTINO scans his

charts and peers through his
telescope.)

FRANK: I'm telling you, it was her! I saw her right before I passed out. She was gatherin' flowers and weeds.

CELESTINO: There. Disturbance in the field of Centaur.

FRANK: She said something about conceiving a girl. My daughter.

CELESTINO: A collision of star systems. He's on fire.

FRANK: Do you register what I'm saying? I saw her! She looked like she always did. Like I remember her.

CELESTINO: You remember her too fondly, Frank.

FRANK: Only woman I ever washed my truck for. Look, maybe his coming's got something to do with this.

CELESTINO: I have to make things right, Francis.

FRANK: For who? For you? Cause it ain't for him. He don't know how to act, he don't know thing one about being human!

CELESTINO: He'll learn.

FRANK: He'll learn that you let his mother die!

> (FRANK's wound stings and
> thunder explodes. The lights change
> as DOLORES appears before him,
> her hands stained with blood.)

DOLORES: ¿Que paso, baby?

FRANK: Judas priest...

DOLORES: Why do you look at me like that?

FRANK: Dolores...

DOLORES: I did all I could, I swear.

CELESTINO: What's the matter with you? Vivian was your sister! That's her blood on her hands!

FRANK: I know, I know! JESUS!

CELESTINO: Pull your head out of your ass, fool! She's illegal! When are you going to tell your wife about her? When are you telling your blue-eyed babies? Does the agency know you're balling her every night?

FRANK: You wouldn't, Tino! You wouldn't!

DOLORES: ¿Que dicen?

FRANK: Hold on, honey. *Un momento.*

CELESTINO: She can't ever come back and you can't go looking for her.

DOLORES: *¿Que pasa?*

FRANK: Dolores, Tino here is gonna drive you home. I have to stay with the baby and...

DOLORES: *Perdoname.* I did all I could.

FRANK: I know. I know. I'll meet you there.

DOLORES: Will you, *querido*?

FRANK: Count on it.

DOLORES: I waited for you, my love, all those years ago, even as the current took me and my sweet Pepín I waited for you to save us. I waited for you. I'm waiting for you still.

FRANK: I don't go there. I never go there. You know that.

DOLORES: *"Amor eterno, E inolvidable*

> *Tarde o temprano estaré contigo*
> *Para segir, amándolos."*

> *(She fades away and the lights resume.)*

CELESTINO: Are you in love with a ghost, Frank?

FRANK: I hate you, as I hate him, as I hate all your goddamned race. And I reckon I'd despise her too if I didn't hate myself more.

> *(Lights change. LAZARO hog-tied on his bed. BLANCA in a separate area.)*

LAZARO: No memory of my hole, my chain, my isla. But this room. This bed. These ropes. They remember me.

BLANCA: Trying to run. Stay with my cause. *Sincero. Sangre.* But I can't. Against my will, I go this way.

LAZARO: Something here was

BLANCA: Compelled by the suit

LAZARO: Dreamt in blood

BLANCA: Compelled by his shoes

LAZARO: A tearing of membrane

BLANCA: Legs obeying trousers

LAZARO: A mother's cry

BLANCA: Up the marble staircase

LAZARO: A womb on fire

BLANCA: Hallways like uterine canals

LAZARO: Bleeding on this bed

BLANCA: Through a bone-colored door

LAZARO: Parting of the legs

BLANCA: Opens like an eyelid opens

LAZARO: Opening

BLANCA: Slowly

LAZARO: Now

> *(They see each other: a recognition.)*

BLANCA: Are you Lazaro?

LAZARO: Am I?

BLANCA: I'm Alfonso. I'm supposed to tutor you.

> *(They remain mesmerized by each other. So many recognitions.)*

LAZARO: C'mere. In the light. *(She approaches.)* I seen you before?

BLANCA: I don't know you, *vato*. This is my first time in this house.

LAZARO: Bitchin.

BLANCA: How are you supposed to learn anything tied up like that?

LAZARO: I can learn about knots....

BLANCA: Get up.

(She begins to undo the ropes.)

LAZARO: You sure we never met?

BLANCA: Positive.

LAZARO: I was on this *isla* where I saw the strangest *locos*. Came and went like vapors.

BLANCA: Uh-huh.

LAZARO: Anyway, this one covergirl came up my shore.

BLANCA: A covergirl, huh?

LAZARO: *Bonita*. She rose from the water *y me dijo*, she said, you're gonna be free soon. She said to wait for her.

BLANCA: Maybe you should have.

LAZARO: She was something else. *Oye*, can I ask you, which do you read, Elle or Esquire?

BLANCA: Me?

LAZARO: Elle or Esquire?

BLANCA: Motor Trend. How's that?

LAZARO: Better.

BLANCA: What's that smell, man? Did you crap on yourself?

LAZARO: I had to go.

BLANCA: Man, you are too much. I don't know about this.

LAZARO: *Mira*, Alfonso.

BLANCA: Look, maybe I'm not cut out—

> *(She starts out. He knocks her down and sits on top of her.)*

LAZARO: I'm all teeth today, *carnal*, clamp myself on that vein, make a red drape from your neck to the floor, *puto*!

BLANCA: Whatever, *vato*! Whatever!

LAZARO: Answer me one *cosa*!

BLANCA: Sure. Anything.

LAZARO: Am I *soniando*? Is this real?

BLANCA: It's real, brother.

LAZARO: Then okay. Teach me.

BLANCA: Get off.

(LAZARO gets off her. BLANCA gets up, turns around and grabs LAZARO by the balls.)

First lesson. When your body functions go, do not, I repeat, do not sit them on top of your tutor. It's a foul practice and it grosses me out. *¿Me oyes?*

LAZARO: I hear you.

BLANCA: Then okay. On to lesson two.

(She drags him off. Crossfade to SETH and CARL with flashlights trained on the ground.)

SETH: Now, tell me again, what's it look like?

CARL: Looks like a big ol' goddamned ear, Seth. Frank said it floated off so it floated off. Now hunt! Goddog!

(PEPÍN enters.)

PEPÍN: *Hey, migra!* Migra! Where is he? What did you do with him?

CARL: Fuck off, retard.

SETH: Hey, little guy.

PEPÍN: Where's my dreamvato, *ese*? *You* took him away!

SETH: What dreamvato?

CARL: Don't pay any attention to the retard, Seth! Git!

SETH: Hold on, Carl. Fella needs our assistance. I'm Seth and this is Carl.

PEPÍN: Thirst and Carol.

CARL: That's Carl. **Carl**.

SETH: You say he's the man of yer dreams?

PEPÍN: No, he fell out of my dreams. He was in my sueno but he got out!

SETH: Well, from the sound a things, I'd peg him for a illegal alien.

CARL: For crying Jesus!

SETH: He violated the borders of that territory, Carl! You just don't do that!

PEPÍN: That's right, *ese*! He's a dream *mojado*!

SETH: According to our mission statement, it's our duty to prevent unlawful entry, employment, or receipt of benefits by those who are not entitled to them.

PEPÍN: He ate my samwich!

SETH: And to apprehend and remove those aliens whose stay is not in the public interest.

PEPÍN: That sounds like him, Thirsty!

SETH: Brother, I suggest you enforce the departure of this individual as expeditiously as possible.

CARL: Retardo's a wet, too, in case you forgot.

SETH: Not if he's here to escape persecution. He can apply for asylum.

CARL: He looks like he already belongs in one.

PEPÍN: *¡Gracias, Carla!*

CARL: CARL!

SETH: I'll get a form I-589 from the car for you to fill out. In the meantime, buddy, raise your *mano*.

SETH: You pledge to uphold the Constitution of the United States of America and to obey its gun laws and such, and stand up for the National Anthem at ball games no matter who sings the damn thing? Say I do, *señor*.

PEPÍN: I do, *señor*.

SETH: You're now a citizen-patrol chief of the INS.

PEPÍN: *¡Hijola! ¡Un Americano!*

SETH: Now you're authorized to use whatever method it takes to nab your *mojado*. The method I recommend is D & D.

PEPÍN: D & D?

CARL: Detention and Deportation.

SETH: You gotta set your trap in order to **detain**, and once he's in custody, you **determine** his status and **deport** his ass back. Which kinda makes it D, D & D. Do you know the point of entry?

PEPÍN: The kitchen!

SETH: Then start the search there, chief. Cause that's where he's prob'ly stashed. You know what? I got something for you. Hold on.

> *(SETH runs off. CARL searches for the ear.)*

PEPÍN: Carol, how come you so ugly?

CARL: What are you talking about? This is just my stern face. I wear this out on the field for protection. It's seen me through a few close calls.

PEPÍN: *¿De veras?*

CARL: Seth won't mention it cause he's jealous, but for outstanding service in the line of fire, I have received the Golden Huarache Award.

PEPÍN: Damn, *ese*. You mean, if I catch me a *mojado*, I can get a Golden Huarache too?

CARL: In your dreams.

PEPÍN: *Esuper*! Maybe if I get two *mojados*, I can get a pair of Huaraches!

(SETH returns.)

SETH: Okay, chief. Here's your form to fill out. Remember, you're persecuted. Try these out. Night vision scopes. With these babies on, there's no way in hell he'll dodge you.

(PEPÍN tries them on.)

PEPÍN: *¡Suavecito!*

CARL: Have you gone batty?

SETH: It's all in fun, Carl. C'mon. The State Department's gotta surplus of these. Besides, he may turn out to be a fine border scout.

PEPÍN: *(striking a pose with the night vision glasses on)* I am *La Migra*!

CARL: Little boys.

SETH: Wait till dark, chief, let the critter make his move. When you see him, pile-drive him headfirst back into your waking dreams. You got that?

PEPÍN: I am *La Migra*! Don't move, *joven*, I am *La pinchi Migra*!

SETH: Thass it! Meaner!

PEPÍN: I AM *LA MIGRA, CABRONES!*

> *(Lights change. BLANCA ushers LAZARO in, with a set of clothes. He dresses.)*

BLANCA: I hear you been chewing on people's heads.

LAZARO: I was looking for something.

BLANCA: What kinda something?

LAZARO: Ideas. Ain't that where they come from?

BLANCA: Guys like you don't need ideas. You need a fucking leash.

LAZARO: 'nother chain.

BLANCA: A new chain, bro.

LAZARO: Still a chain.

BLANCA: Forged of new links, bro.

LAZARO: Chain's a chain.

BLANCA: Respect, charity, goodness, bro.

LAZARO: That ain't no chain, bro.

BLANCA: Love and faith and truth, bro.

LAZARO: Yeah right.

BLANCA: This is real shit, Laz, things that never change.

LAZARO: Only things that don't change are dead, bro.

BLANCA: Only if *la vida's* awol in your head, bro.

LAZARO: I don't wear truth around my neck, ese.

BLANCA: You wear it in your heart, or you're fucked. You wear it close to your soul or you die. Ground changes beneath you, people change their minds, but not truth. Keep it close, keep it tight, keep it shackled to your better sense.

LAZARO: My better self.

BLANCA: Fucking A. Chew my head, bite my ear off, rip my fuckin' heart to pieces. I'm all out of ideas.

LAZARO: But never never outa truth.

BLANCA: Right. On to Lesson three.

> (SONIA enters him with a small
> case.)

SONIA: Is he washed?

BLANCA: Yes.

SONIA: Good. Do it often and fastidiously, your body is unclean to those who misunderstand you. You are your pigment. You'll be reminded of and judged by it for the rest of your *pinchi* life.

> (She opens her case.)

My family was very poor living in the valley. There were eight of us *mocosos* in a little shanty, and being the youngest, I got all my sisters' old dresses. I was so second-hand in those rags, smelling of moth balls and rice. My hair thick in my face. And then one day I got a job selling--

(presents make-up supplies.)

....glamour.

LAZARO: Unbelievable!

SONIA: Check it out, baby. Eaus de toilettes--
Parfums--

LAZARO: Face scrubs, scented soaps, bath
oils--it's real...

SONIA: My articles of the Constitution. This is
how you become American.

> *(She applies cream to his hands and
> face.)*

I sold these over the counter at the mall. That's
where I met your father. He offered me a job
being manager at his maquiladora, his plant in
Juarez. I almost said no.

LAZARO: Ay. The natural yet sultry feel that
lasts and lasts.

> *(She applies hair gel.)*

SONIA: Working with this gave me power, I
could make new faces out of old, I could put
Hollywood on the eyes of the brownest girl!

LAZARO: *Mi sueño.*

SONIA: (daubing cologne on his face) These are the talismans of beauty, Lazaro. These make the world bearable.

> *(She puts on his coat as the crowning touch to his new look.)*

Remember, you're not a beast, a savage, a heathen, you are now fully Christian... Dior.

> *(SONIA smiles, gives him a gentle kiss, and goes.)*

LAZARO: How do I look?

BLANCA: *Bien guapo.*

LAZARO: *¿Guapo?*

BLANCA: Time for Lesson Four.

> *(Lights to black. A vision of the heavens appears. CELESTINO's voice blares.)*

CELESTINO: *Lazaro Robles. Hijo Bravo.* This is your dominion...

> *(He appears. A slide presentation only visible to LAZARO commences.)*

Up there our fates are inscribed. Up there, the gods of antiquity slam down shots of *Patron*

with the *dioses de mi* own mythology.
Everything moves for the good of the
Organism. There, the Great Bear, the Bull and
the Dow Jones arrow between them, and over
here Sun Microsystems. This is your *Mundo
Comerciante.*

SONIA: Crown your head with knowledge.
Everything a worldly man needs to know:

> *(LAZARO is fed data via
> headphones and reading material.)*

FRANK/SETH/CARL: Texas History, Texas
Monthly, Austin City Limits, Dallas Cowboys,
price of oil per barrel, EDS, Bill Moyers, Wall
Street Journal, Beemer 500 series.

SONIA: This is El Paso, gateway to the North,
city on the cusp of Time.

FRANK: And this Juarez, back door to the
Third World, to all parts Mexican.

CELESTINO: This is Rio Bravo, Rio Grande,
Rio Polluted...

SONIA: The river that separates and binds the
cities to el Organismo.

CELESTINO: And this is my grand enterprise,
the NexMex Maquiladora. Our fine addition to
the two-plant system of the US and
Mexiconomies.

SONIA: One factory in El Paso for assembling parts by robotics. One factory in Juarez for assembling parts by hand. Together these plants collaborate to bring to America its finest contribution:

CELESTINO: Television.

FRANK: This is the US Border Patrol, an arm of the Immigration and Naturalization Service, sovereign protector of America's boundaries, watching out for illicit goods and persons. This agency stems the flood of narcotics threatening the Great Organism.

CELESTINO: But to keep pace with *traficantes,* we bargain with the Devil. A number of select cartels find safe passage north for a special toll and secret information on rival groups.

SONIA: This fee is funnelled into the NexMex account where it is recycled as clean money.

CELESTINO: As for those whom the heavens do not favor:

> *(LAZARO is given night-vision specs. He puts them on, lights go black. The river at night. A handful of smugglers, masked and armed, dragging a small pontoon of packaged drugs. They stop when a*

large white light captures them and
they raise their arms in surrender.)

FRANK: *ALTO,* MOTHERFUCKERS!

CELESTINO: We tolerate some parasites and some we don't. Some lies valued as highly as truth, some truths dismissed as idle dreams, all for the sake of the Organism. These smugglers chose to keep the truth from me but I will not keep it from them. Say *fuego* and *fuego* comes.

LAZARO: Me?

CELESTINO: Say fire.

BLANCA: You can't cut them down like dogs. They're giving up!

LAZARO: I don't want to kill anyone, *Apa.*

CELESTINO: You're a Robles now. Say Fire!

BLANCA: You don't have to say anything.

LAZARO: WHAT DO I DO?

CELESTINO: Speak the truth! Say Fire!

BLANCA: Remember what I taught you!

LAZARO: This can't be real!

CELESTINO: THEN MAKE IT REAL!

(LAZARO struggles for a moment, then utters the cry.)

LAZARO: ¡FUEGO!

(Gunfire erupts. They are mowed down. SETH and CARL enter and drag the dead and their cargo off. LAZARO removes his specs.)

Who is the Organism?

CELESTINO: You.

(Everyone goes, except LAZARO and BLANCA. She angrily drops his lunch at his feet.)

BLANCA: Lunchtime.

(They sit.)

LAZARO: I'm sorry. This world is hard to learn.

BLANCA: You're learning quick. Time for your American History.

(As he eats, she produces various items.)

This is your father. This is you as a baby. The house you were born in. And you here at the ranch as a boy.

LAZARO: As a boy...

BLANCA: Here is your birth certificate. Your degree from SMU. Business Administration. Your membership into the El Paso Country Club.

LAZARO: Your hands are shaking.

> (BLANCA *pulls them away and continues.*)

BLANCA: This is your passport. Driver's license, platinum card, and social security.

LAZARO: What does it mean?

BLANCA: It means you're set for life.

LAZARO: But is it my life? Do these things make me real?

BLANCA: The shit you make happen, that's what you are.

LAZARO: I didn't want to kill those men.

BLANCA: Then why?

LAZARO: It's what men do. They kill.

BLANCA: Didn't I teach you? Didn't I give you something to hold onto?

LAZARO: Words. Like from my radio on the isla.

BLANCA: Eat.

(He eats.)

You gotta learn to front off the bullshit, lie for lie, like I taught you. Ride your truth home. Cause home is all we got.

LAZARO: Where's your home?

BLANCA: Gone. I used to live in the *colonia* with a sick mother and brain-damaged boy. Leaving her passed out drunk in our one-room shanty so I could work in your dad's *maquila* while Pepín's doing dog tricks for the tourists. Going to the bathroom between cars. You don't want to know about my home.

LAZARO: It's more real than this.

BLANCA: Juarez? Give me a break.

LAZARO: What?

BLANCA: Over there, beyond the border freeway is a big town full of people with more reality than they can take. They live eat sleep within dreaming distance of this theme park called America. It draws them across the river like moths to the marquee. Then it burns them and chucks them back. So there's poverty violence and despair so thick in that city that even Mexico can barely claim it. Still the people thrive. Still they make the best of it.

Playing and loving and dying in the shadow of this Dreamlandia.

(LAZARO gently kisses her.)

Whoa, vato. What are you doing?

LAZARO: I can make you American. I can keep you here with me.

BLANCA: Shit... *mira*, first of all, men are not supposed to kiss, *sabes*.

LAZARO: Why not?

BLANCA: 'Cause...'cause... it's just the way it is. I can't get involved in this right now...

LAZARO: In that long dream that seemed to last my whole life, you were there as a woman. But here you are a man. Either way, you're the only real thing to me!

BLANCA: That's fucked! Listen up. You gotta get away from your *jefe*. Get away from all this. Its not real, its all a LIE. Even me, none of us are what we say we are.

LAZARO: A lie? You?

BLANCA: This crap ain't yours! I don't know whose it is, but it ain't yours! And that lady ain't your mother, neither! Lazaro, you gotta go. Leave all these fucking *mentiras* behind!

LAZARO: What are you talking about?

BLANCA: The island! It's real! Go out there, about three miles south along the bank and you'll see it! We've all made a fool of you.

LAZARO: Where are you going?

BLANCA: I have to get away from here! I can't breathe! I can't think straight! Oh my god!

LAZARO: Alfonso, wait!

BLANCA: Let go a my arm.

LAZARO: Don't leave me! You always leave me!

BLANCA: I can't stay!

LAZARO: I'm not letting you get away again! No way!

BLANCA: Lazaro.

LAZARO: NOT AGAIN, DREAMFUCK!

> (He knocks her roughly on the
> ground and tries to kiss her.)

BLANCA: STOP IT LAZARO! DON'T TOUCH ME!

LAZARO: I WANT YOU! *¡SOMOS IGUALES!*

BLANCA: GET OFF!

(BLANCA scrambles to her feet and pulls out her knife. SETH and CARL rush in and grab her. CELESTINO enters behind them. He goes directly to LAZARO and violently grabs him.)

CELESTINO: New lesson. Beware the illegal. The most disposable. The most *invisible*. They slip in through our lawns, our kitchens, our *hoteles y restaurantes*. They lack identity so they abuse ours. America can't afford to be soft on them.

BLANCA: Fuck you! You're more of a wetback than we are!

CELESTINO: I'm not a wet.

(BLANCA spits on him.)

BLANCA: You are now.

CELESTINO: Save this little *puto* for me.

(SETH and CARL take BLANCA away.)

BLANCA:*(as she is dragged off)* It's real, Lazaro! Go there! See for yourself! See for yourself!

CELESTINO: *(to LAZARO)* Don't make me believe in curses again.

*(He goes. LAZARO remains. Lights
shift to the island. DOLORES
quietly waits by his hovel.)*

LAZARO: Real. My *isla.*

*(He drags his chain out and feels its
links. DOLORES strews the herbs
and flowers of her jar in a wide arc
around him.)*

No dream.

DOLORES: *Aqui. La hora de tu ser.*

LAZARO: What have I been living? *¿Y porque?*

DOLORES: *Eres cruzado, cruzando el rio, el cielo,
la tierra, y el Corazon.*

LAZARO: Less than a dog's life, a lie, a filthy
lie repeated day after day after *dia y dia y dia...*

*(LAZARO falls weeping.
DOLORES stands over him.)*

DOLORES: Now the son comes for his second
birth!

*(She takes his head and pulls. He
cries out.)*

LAZARO: No! I don't want it! I don't want to see!

DOLORES: We shed light as we shed blood.

LAZARO: I don't want this life!

DOLORES: ¡Ahora, maldicion, vas a dar luz!

LAZARO: NO! NOO!

DOLORES: I dug my nails in you once!

(LAZARO cries out.)

I dug my nails in your skull! You wear the marks like a crown of thorns!

LAZARO: NOOO!

DOLORES: Now I bring you in to be my fire!

(She stands him to his full abominable height.)

LAZARO: ¡CABRONES! ¡PINCHIS MENDIGOS! ¡Si asi es, asi es! So be fuckin it! You want me to live these lies, fine! I will manifest you by the book! Up the ass! You gonna see this Cover Boy shine! You gonna see this Cover Boy flame! You gonna see this Cover Boy BURN!

(BLACKOUT.)

End of Act One.

Act Two

> *(Darkness. PEPÍN wearing the*
> *night-vision goggles.)*

PEPÍN: I am *La Migra*.

I detain, determine, deport. Keep the *mojados al otro lado*. Don't put your brown on my ground, *vato*!

> *(Stillness. He grows apprehensive.)*

¡Trucha! Who's slimppin shadows by me? *¿Eres tu, sueño* man? You think it over, *hombre*, I got my googles on for *Yankeelandia!*

> *(Murmurs all around him.)*

Who's there! *¡Alto! ¡Manos arriba! ¡Le doy un* kick *en el* weenie!

> *(Shadowy figures emerge from the*
> *darkness.)*

Detain, determine, deport. Detain, determine, de...

> *(PEPÍN sees images of border-*
> *crossers creeping past him.)*

¡MIRA! Fantasmas, ghost crossers wading through the *rio*. Girls riding on the backs of men, old *rancheros* with their *botas* held high, young *chavalos* linking hands from one hell to the other, mothers with bundles held to their bosoms. Guided by the *lancheros* and the little stars reflected on the water, the desperate, the hungry, the hopeless, the dreams of the dead crossing.

> *(MAMA emerges from the group of ghost-crossers.)*

PEPÍN: *Mama.* What you doing with these spookies?

DOLORES: Looking for her, *mijo*. Belladonna hides in clumps along the shores.

PEPÍN: Belladonna?

DOLORES: Pretty lady with the kiss of death.

PEPÍN: Never kissed me, Ma.

DOLORES: But you kissed her, Pepín. Cupful of death, half a cup of madness. *Ah, mira. Here it is.*

PEPÍN: Leaves like angel wings.

DOLORES: I ground them to make a tea for myself. It was never meant for you. A cupful of death.

PEPÍN: Half a cuppa madness.

DOLORES: *(rubbing the leaf against his heart)* I'll brew more of this. Someone's heart will need the bracing of this herb.

PEPÍN: OOFAS! Lookit where you're standing, *Jefita*! Right on the *linea* between U.S. And U Lose. As a citizen escout of the Border Patrol, I demand your *papeles, Mami!*

DOLORES: Here.

> *(She places the ear in his hand and goes.)*

PEPÍN: Eerie.

> *(Noise from off.)*

Oofahs! *Otros* spooky *vatos!*

> *(He hides as SETH and CARL drag BLANCA on. FRANK behind.)*

BLANCA: Get your paws offa me! Does Robles own alla you dogs or do you think for yourselves sometimes?

CARL: Aw don't be so glum, Al, this is better for all a us.

SETH: Nothing personal, y'understand.

CARL: Mr. Robles just don't appreciate your teaching style.

SETH: So he hereby relieves you of your duties.

BLANCA: What you gonna do? Gun me down, leave me for the turkey hawks? Why don't you say something?

FRANK: *(produces the knife)* Where did you get this?

BLANCA: It's mine.

FRANK: WHERE DID YOU GET IT?

BLANCA: GO TO HELL, GRINGO!

FRANK: Mr. Robles asked that you be found right here in possession of this blade, this controlled substance and a couple Smith and Wesson slugs. Now, I might decide to skip the slugs if you come clean about the damn knife.

BLANCA: It belongs to Sincero.

FRANK: Sincero.

BLANCA: You know him?

FRANK: What's he to you? How do you know him? Spill the refrieds.

BLANCA: All these questions. He's supposed to be my *jefe*.

FRANK: Your father…

BLANCA: *Puro cabrón.* I got no stomach to see him, but I need to.

FRANK: Boy, you already have. This is my knife.

BLANCA: Wait a minute. You?

FRANK: Given to me when I joined the *Migra*.

BLANCA: You can't be Sincero.

FRANK: You can't be my son. But there you are saying it.

BLANCA: You're a gringo.

FRANK: You're a by-god wetback. How do I know you're not dicking with me? Playing up to my weakness.

BLANCA: My mother's name is Dolores.

FRANK: And she was my weakness.

BLANCA: How can you be him? I don't get it.

FRANK: Frank in Spanish is Sincero, you damn fool! Frank, sincere. Sincero. Your mama's idea of irony! Where is she?

219

BLANCA: Dead.

FRANK: Then Tino was right. Are you mine, then?

BLANCA: Oh shit, kill me! Shoot me! I don't wanna hear this!

FRANK: Is that idiot boy my Pepín?

BLANCA: Shoot me! God! Don't tell me any more!

SETH: Chief, what you gonna do? You got orders to cap yer own bloodkin.

CARL: And yer son's got cause to geld you, too.

FRANK: *(revealing her hair)* Except he ain't my son. You're my daughter.

SETH: Whut! No effin' way!

FRANK: You're my girl, ain't you?

BLANCA: *¡Gringa!* Everything I ever hated! *¡Soy pinchi gringa tambien!*

(She runs into the river.)

FRANK: WAIT! I WON'T HURT YOU! I JUST WANNA TALK!

BLANCA: Wash away, wash away!

FRANK: IT'S DARK OUT THERE. YOU'LL DROWN.

BLANCA: Drown this body, erase me! Suck the whiteness off!

FRANK: Get in there and find her.

CARL: I ain't goin' in there!

> (The waters sweep her away. PEPÍN leaps out in alarm.)

PEPÍN: ¡BLANCA!

FRANK: (catching him) Whoa, sonny! Did you call her Blanca? Is that her name? Answer me!

PEPÍN: Blanca…

> (He recognizes him.)

FRANK: I'll be damned. Is that her name? Blanca? Haul him back to the compound. And keep yer yaps shut about this till I talk with him!

> (SETH and CARL take him off. FRANK slashes the dark with the flashlight beam.)

COME BACK! I WANNA TALK! FER
CRYING JESUS, DOLORES, WHATTA YOU
DONE TO ME!

(*Lights change. CELESTINO and
SONIA enter.*)

CELESTINO: I can't believe it. My own son.

SONIA: Tino, I don't think you have the whole
picture—

CELESTINO: I give him everything he needs to
be my exemplary boy: education, money, stock
options, and what does he turn out to be?
Maricón.

SONIA: What do you expect? What experience
has he ever had with women? Fashion
magazines!

CELESTINO: My son is not a *maricón*!

SONIA: Baby, trust me. I know what he likes,
and it's not other men.

(*Her cell phone rings. She answers.*)

SONIA: *Diga.* Her again.

(*She passes the phone.*)

CELESTINO: Bustamante, you're a ball-buster.
(*pause*) Yes, your information was accurate. We

222

took care of them. But that won't make us bedfellows. *(pause)* And if I say no? *(pause)* Let's assume then I say yes. Where do we meet and when? There? You want to meet there?

> *(Pause. He shuts off the phone and hands it to SONIA.)*

SONIA: Well?

CELESTINO: The terms are decent.

SONIA: What did she hold over you, mi amor?

CELESTINO: The usual bullshit.

> *(LAZARO bursts in.)*

LAZARO: *Papá.* What have you done with Alfonso? Where is he?

CELESTINO: *¿Buenos dias, mijo, como estás?*

LAZARO: Where have you taken him?

SONIA: Good morning, Lazaro.

LAZARO: *Mama,* where is he? All his things are gone.

CELESTINO: He had to go, *hijo.* His Visa ran out.

LAZARO: You deported him, didn't you?

SONIA: He wanted to go home--

223

LAZARO: Lies! He said they were all lies!

CELESTINO: *¡Está bien!* The truth is he's dead. The truth is he was a *maricón*, and no-one turns my son into a *maricón*. I never would have brought you back from that-

SONIA: Tino…

CELESTINO: *(gripping him by the throat)* …I raised you to be a man! Be a man!

LAZARO: I like that. I like your hand on my throat. It feels like a chain. I wake up in the middle of the night missing the cold steel on my skin. But then I remember I have you. My great dad. I like your hand on my throat.

> *(SETH and CARL enter dragging PEPÍN in.)*

CARL: Shake a leg, retard!

SETH: Quit yer wiggling, chief!

PEPÍN: NO! You swored me in, you made me citizen chief, *la Migra!*

> *(PEPÍN collapses in a heap before them.)*

CELESTINO: *¡Chingao!* Didn't I say I wanted them both taken care of?

CARL: I know, sir, but Frank said to bring him.

224

SONIA: What for?

SETH: Just said bring and we brung.

PEPÍN: Please, Thirst, let me keep the googles! I haven't found my *duermevato* yet!

SETH: Sorry, chief.

PEPÍN: *¡Mira! ¡Duermevato!* Here at last! Now I'll get my Golden *Huarache*!

> *(PEPÍN goes for LAZARO. He gives him a vicious blow.)*

LAZARO: This is an illegal. A burden on this land. The most disposable. The most invisible.

> *(LAZARO grabs PEPÍN's leg and slowly twists it around.)*

LAZARO: These people are a world removed, *verdad, Papa*? Isn't that what you said?

> *(PEPÍN's leg snaps and he passes out. FRANK enters.)*

SETH: Jesus wept.

SONIA: That's enough, Lazaro.

FRANK: What's going on? What the hell have you done to him?

CELESTINO: I underestimated you.

225

SONIA: Get him out of here.

(*SETH and CARL carry PEPÍN off.
FRANK glares at LAZARO.*)

FRANK: You shit.

CELESTINO: Get over it, Frank. I need you
and Sonia in Juarez.

FRANK: Me?

CELESTINO: J-town, Francis. We have a date
with Doña Bustamante.

FRANK: Are you outa yer head? You know
damn well I don't go there.

CELESTINO: Better change the uniform.

FRANK: I don't go. You know I don't go. I
never go.

CELESTINO: Sonia will accompany you.

FRANK: I don't trust her.

SONIA: Ha!

LAZARO: Let me go.

FRANK: You?

LAZARO: I want to see the other side. Mexico
and the *maquila*.

FRANK: Are you kidding me?

SONIA: What can it hurt?

CELESTINO: *Mijo*, everything in my life has been for you. Will you be my centaur?

LAZARO: Whatever you want me to be, *Padre*.

SONIA: *It's settled:* Juarilandia!

> (*Lights change. BLANCA enters, putting on a white smock, white rubber shoes and gloves, hairnet, and surgical mask.*)

BLANCA: Races, *Ama*, these races, they grow fathers, mothers, daughters, sons and gods, these *raices* brown as book, white as bone, black as tar, they tell us who we are and punish what we're not. I'm brown, I'm *India*, then Spanish, then white, or half white which is worse than being all, I am all, Ama, all that I denied is me! What am I? What race dries up and another grows? I saw him, saw the blood with blood matched up and it was mine. I'm a white lie, lie of this Sincero, his half-truth, half-breed, half Blanca, all *desmadre*! My father with his *raza* stripped mine off and slipped me half of his and left me with no race at all.

In this *maquila*, rebuild yourself. Out of parts imported from the north, make yourself new. This time without the *raza*.

> *(She puts on her surgical mask.*
> *Lights shift. LAZARO, FRANK and*
> *SONIA enter.)*

LAZARO: The Threshold

FRANK: Border checkpoint

SONIA: To another world

LAZARO: Strange world

FRANK: Illegitimate culture

SONIA: *Ciudad Juarez, Chihuahua*

LAZARO: A city shaped like music

SONIA: Ground out of daily life

FRANK: Terrible, perilous music

LAZARO: Earthy, rich, spilling from cars and open doorways

FRANK: The smell of old meat, gasoline, piss

LAZARO: The smell of perseverance, of people, of business

SONIA: And the garish walls

LAZARO: Painted like parrots and iguanas in Benetton colors

FRANK: Random and flaking

LAZARO: Orgies of cars on the roads

SONIA: *Chavalitos* hawking *Chiclet*, cigarettes, rings of *plata*

LAZARO: Their dusty faces artifacts of me, burnt the brown of *centavos*

FRANK: Faces I have all expelled before

SONIA: And fruit stands and kiosks and vendors of ice

LAZARO: Churches with crumbling saints, Martin, Jose, Luis, Francisco

FRANK: Faces, swarms of faces, all of them sons and migrants

LAZARO: A messiness of living, a riot of language, old world in a new dream.

SONIA: I don't like it. Can we go to the hotel?

> *(Lights change. The silence of their hotel room. FRANK is anxious.)*

You have to watch your purse or they'll rob you blind. Don't drink the water, don't get in taxis, don't stay out past dark, and always haggle. Haggling and *la mordida*, the bribe, are the two laws of this country.

FRANK: So where is she?

SONIA: We just got here. She'll call. Relax.

FRANK: If I'm not in my room, I'm at the bar.

(*FRANK goes.*)

SONIA: It's hot. Open a window.

LAZARO: It's open.

SONIA: You want to take this room or the one next door?

LAZARO: Either one.

SONIA: When she calls, stay in your room. Don't come unless I say so.

LAZARO: (*his coat*) Feel this. Italian.

SONIA: You think you're pretty hot after that performance with PEPÍN, but these people are no idiots. If she's half like the fucks we deal with, she's watching us right now. You hear me?

LAZARO: In the town, *en el aire*, in the people, this ripeness. Everyone in heat. Even here, this table, two flies pinned together, oblivious to danger, passion too small to see. So dangerous, so blind to reality, two flies making fly-love.

SONIA: *Asi es la vida, Lazaro.*

> *(He slams his hand, smears it across the table top.)*

LAZARO: You think she saw this?

SONIA: *¿Que te pasa, mijo?*

LAZARO: I don't like you calling me *mijo*.

SONIA: *Pero sabes muy bien que tu eres--*

LAZARO: *Lazaro. Y tu eres Sonia.*

SONIA: I'll take the other room.

LAZARO: How old are you? Almost half as old as my father?

SONIA: Older than you.

LAZARO: Not by much. I see how you look at me. Not with a mother's attention but attention to other *cositas*.

SONIA: You flatter yourself.

LAZARO: Rub more of that cream on me. Run those hands down my back again.

SONIA: You're not playing fair.

LAZARO: I'm not playing.

SONIA: You're not the son I thought you were.

LAZARO: Lovers never are.

SONIA: I have a lover already.

LAZARO: Buy get one free.

SONIA: Sounds like a bargain--

LAZARO: You said I should haggle.

SONIA: For a haggler, you don't give an inch.

LAZARO: An inch is all I need.

> *(They kiss and he mounts her on the bed. CELESTINO and FRANK enter on either side of them with phones.)*

FRANK: There's no word from Bustamante.

CELESTINO: Be patient.

FRANK: What the hell are we doing here? Why are we dealing with some damn woman we never met?

CELESTINO: Think of it as a test, Frank.

FRANK: I see in the faces of all this teeming Mexico my verdict. The undocumented of all my life. Now their eyes document me, make me the alien.

CELESTINO: Tell Sonia to give you and Lazaro a tour of the plant. He should know it.

FRANK: They sure spend a lotta time together.

LAZARO: *(making love to her)* ¡ASI!

CELESTINO: Mindful of the time, Frank. Mindful. The skies are a whorehouse tonight, all constellations in thermonuclear heat, the Archer's arrow in Andromeda's mouth, Aries ramming the back end of Orion while his dogs do each other, and even my Centaur mounts the Lady, Frank, roaring into Virgo's crease, pounding away, disgusting: *las estrellas Francisco*, are brimming with betrayal!

> *(Lights shift. The Maquiladora.
> BLANCA at a table. Connecting
> colored wires to corresponding
> sockets. A voice on the speaker barks
> incomprehensible commands.)*

BLANCA: My new world order.

> *(SONIA leads LAZARO and
> FRANK through.)*

SONIA: My office is this way. Don't mind the workers.

*(LAZARO approaches the platform
where BLANCA works.)*

LAZARO: What are you doing?

BLANCA: *No hablo Ingles, señor.*

SONIA: *Mas respeto.* This is Sr. Robles.

(BLANCA nods deferentially.)

FRANK: Can we move on? It's warm in here.

LAZARO: What's she's working on?

SONIA: Television circuit boards.

LAZARO: How much is she paid?

SONIA: Well enough.

BLANCA: Five dollars.

FRANK: You do speak English.

LAZARO: Five dollars an hour?

BLANCA: A day.

LAZARO: Take off that thing.

BLANCA: I can't, *señor.* Regulations.

LAZARO: How do you like your work?

BLANCA: *Oh, señor,* putting wires into sockets
ten hours a day, very exciting.

LAZARO: Maybe you should get a raise.

BLANCA: Oh no. A raise is what unions want, but when *la policia* shoots its leaders and makes everyone sign retractions, it becomes clear: we don't need a raise. Everything is *suave*.

LAZARO: Is my father aware of this?

SONIA: He mobilized the police.

BLANCA: I like making TVs, *Sr.* Robles, make no mistake. Dreams shine in these boxes, American dreams *para gente importante* like you. I make it possible to bring into your house *el* Bugs Bunny.

LAZARO: You have one?

BLANCA: No, *señor*. But the extra cardboard boxes they come in make fine insulation for my house.

FRANK: Have I seen you before?

BLANCA: Not likely. I've lived in *La Colonia Insurgentes* all my life.

SONIA: One of the cardboard settlements of *la cuidad*.

FRANK: You do look familiar....

BLANCA: We all look the same, *patron. Con su permiso.*

(She goes back to work.)

SONIA: We employ about two thousand women, but there's a large turnover. A lot of these girls go missing.

LAZARO: How?

SONIA: Rape. Murder. They work late hours, walk long miles across barren desert *lotes.* Many for the last time.

LAZARO: Serial killer?

SONIA: Serial machismo.

(They go. FRANK returns to BLANCA, slowly removing her mask.)

FRANK: I been seeing things all day. So I know it can't be you. But maybe pity lives in the delusions of a crazed old man. I don't shun what I got coming. I compromised my badge, my heart, and my sister's life for Lazaro. Your cousin. I'm a craven fuck. I know that. But I never meant your mama harm. I loved her. A dose of mercy might could ease my load. But if

you're not so inclined, you might do what I'm
too coward to administer myself.

> *(He gives her the knife. A moment.*
> *She puts the knife down.)*

Sorry, miss. I mistook you. You look like
someone I never knew.

> *(He goes out a different way. She*
> *grabs the knife.)*

BLANCA: *Ama*, where is it! Where is the *coraje*,
the need to hurt! Where is it! Why should I pity
this man? His confession? His repentance?
What makes white men repent their whiteness!
God, that touch, that look in his eye, they erase
everything, they form this need in me for
father. For the first time... *padre...*

> *(She runs. Lights shift to the Estate.*
> *SETH and CARL with PEPÍN. He*
> *lies with his head buried in his*
> *arms.)*

SETH: Talk to him, Carl.

CARL: You talk to him.

SETH: How's your leg, chief? Lissen, little
buddy. I know what we said, but you gotta
unnerstand, we were only funnin'.

CARL: We got no power to make you one of us. Only power we got is to make you one of them.

SETH: You're gonna have to go back now.

CARL: Back to Mexico.

SETH: We'll give you a ride, though. In our SUV. Whattaya say?

PEPÍN: Can I keep the googles?

CARL: No way. No way, Seth.

SETH: It's for his own pertection, Carl. Nighttimes out there in Mexico are fulla evil hazards, mark my words!

CARL: Hazards like whut?

SETH: The *chupacabra*.

CARL: *Chupa-whut*?

SETH: A wicked creature born of industrial pollution and the evil spell of *Santería*.

CARL: You kiddin', right?

SETH: The thing about this *chupacabra* is it sucks the blood of goats without spilling a drop. Once, I swear to God, one time it jumped a Texas Ranger while he was on patrol.

Drained the body of blood. Looked like the husk of a two-week old *tamale*.

> *(CELESTINO enters.)*

CELESTINO: Leave us.

> *(SETH and CARL go.)*

I know you. It took a while but I remember. You're the *bruja*'s son. You were there the night she delivered Lazaro. How is your *mama*? You wanna call her on the phone?

> *(He takes out his celphone. Pretends to dial.)*

Pi-pa-pi-pa-pa-pa-pi-pi-pa-pa-pi.

Bueno. Sra. Dolores Midwife? I have your little *payasito* right here. You wanna have a word?

> *(He gives the phone to PEPÍN. He speaks in falsetto.)*

Alló, Pepín. How your leg? Brusha your teeth. Say your *Padre Nuestros* and make the man happy. *Adios mijo. Cleeck.*

> *(He puts the phone down.)*

CELESTINO: *Mama* dead.

PEPÍN: *Muerta?*

CELESTINO: It's up to me to care for you. But you have to help me. Who's that young man Alfonso? Why did he come?

PEPÍN: *No puedo.*

CELESTINO: What? *No pedo? No pedo?*

> *(CELESTINO lifts his leg and makes a farting noise.)*

Prrt. *Si Pedo.*

PEPÍN: *Huh?*

CELESTINO: BPLLFFT! *(PEPÍN snickers.)* PPPPPPPPRRRRFFTTT! *(The fart propels him to his feet.)* ¡*Pedo Americano!* You try.

PEPÍN: *(raising a hip)* psssst.....

CELESTINO: ¡*PEDORRO!*

PEPÍN/CELESTINO: PRRTTTT! PRRRRT! PRRRT! PRRRRRT!

> *(They parade around arm in arm until PEPÍN falls in pain.)*

PEPÍN: AAAY-AYY-AYY-AYYY!

CELESTINO: Sorry, sorry, sorry. Can I tell you a secret? When I was a *chavo*, I was like you. I used to dress up like a clown and do silly tricks for *centavos*. Juggle. Magic. Breathe fire with real gasoline. It ruined my lungs.

PEPÍN: You?

CELESTINO: Humiliation is standing between lanes of cars aimed toward the US, while all the clean Anglo faces pass by me and my stupid tricks.

PEPÍN: *Chiste.*

CELESTINO: I might have killed myself on solvents and glue, except an old white couple swept me into their car and smuggled me past Immigration. That's my secret, Pepín: I no American.

PEPÍN: *You a Mexicano?*

CELESTINO: That's what Bustamante called me over the phone. "Mexicano, you murdered your own wife. To hide your roots, she died." Specious accusation. But how did she know?

PEPÍN: *¿Eres mojado?* Like me?

CELESTINO: *Pedo* is a fine Spanish word, meaning gas to some, drunkenness to others, bullshit to yet other people. But the translation for *pedo* I prefer is **trouble.** *(Gripping his throat)* *VA VER **PEDO** SI NO ME DICES DE ALFONSO.* I see how Frank looks at you! He

241

brought you back for a reason. Something lives between all you fuckers. Now talk!

PEPÍN: Don't hurt me! Please! ¡No Pedo! Alfonso the mister....

CELESTINO: Yes?

PEPÍN: Is really my sister.

> *(Lights change. The Board room.*
> *SONIA and LAZARO.)*

SONIA: So where the hell is she? And where did Frank wander off to?

LAZARO: We don't need him.

SONIA: Fuck. Everyone's running on Chicano time.

LAZARO: How long have you and my father been together?

SONIA: A few years.

LAZARO: Did you know he had me put away? I've seen the island, the chain.

SONIA: I didn't know anything. I didn't know your father could be like that, and to his own kid. It's like I never knew him.

LAZARO: You played along with the lies.

SONIA: So have you. We all play along or else how could we live? We make ourselves believe its not so till it's not.

(*BUSTAMANTE enters.*)

BUSTAMANTE: *Buenas noches.*

LAZARO: Doña Bustamante.

BUSTAMANTE: In the flesh, *cabrones.*

SONIA: About time.

BUSTAMANTE: Okay. You're the midlevel bitch, so you must be the *Patron. Sr.* Robles the badass magnate. Kinda young to be fucking around with the *toros, no?*

LAZARO: *Lazaro Robles.* I come on my father's behalf.

SONIA: No, he doesn't. You deal with me.

BUSTAMANTE: But I like the smell of young Robles.

SONIA: We keep him out of this or we don't deal at all.

BUSTAMANTE: *(pulling a gun)* Then deal with this, *babosa.*

SONIA: That won't solve a damn thing and you know it.

BUSTAMANTE: Maybe not over there, *pocha,* but over here, it solves everything.

LAZARO: You've made your point. Put it away.

BUSTAMANTE: But I haven't made my point.

LAZARO: Then maybe you should. We're on a schedule.

BUSTAMANTE: *Tambien yo, Robles. Tambien yo.*

> *(She tosses the gun to LAZARO.*
> *Takes out her cell phone.)*

This is my third ear. It connects me to all of Mexico. Direct to a satellite called *Solidaridad.* Solidarity. An electronic Quetzalquatl soaring over its people. Big saucer-shaped eyes transmitting images and cries of *los Mexicanos.* Calls to action, to prayer, to the harvest of this fucking crop called *coca,* they all come here via Solidarity. Can you take my world, Robles, or are you pussy-gringofied?

LAZARO: *Dale* gas.

> *(BUSTAMANTE dials her phone.*
> *LAZARO's cell phone rings. He*
> *answers.)*

LAZARO: Noise.

BUSTAMANTE: That's right.

LAZARO: Corruption.

BUSTAMANTE: Go on.

LAZARO: Pops and wheezes.

BUSTAMANTE: Sounds of hunger.

LAZARO: Despair.

BUSTAMANTE: Slaughter.

LAZARO: Call-waiting.

BUSTAMANTE: Wait no more. Listen. Listen.

LAZARO: I hear…insurgence.

BUSTAMANTE: Yes.

LAZARO : Coming on a wide bandwidth.

BUSTAMANTE: Digital aliens.

LAZARO: A million people of indeterminate flesh.

BUSTAMANTE: Roaring into your ear.

LAZARO: My brain, my heart.

BUSTAMANTE: Busting through your walls, fences, surveillance towers.

LAZARO: Overrunning me.

BUSTAMANTE: Sucking up your light, your strength, your water.

LAZARO: Taking over me.

BUSTAMANTE: The totems of the new culture: the corrupt leaders, presidents, generals, police, college deans, narco bosses--

LAZARO: Los CEO's de multinational corpse and Citibank executives on Telemundo, a silicon breast in each hand--

BUSTAMANTE: *¡Asi mero!*

LAZARO: All of them calling the shots.

BUSTAMANTE: And what else!

LAZARO: Real life day of the dead *calacas* begging for dog food

BUSTAMANTE: *¿Y que mas?*

LAZARO: Poor children trading ATM cards for coca

BUSTAMANTE: *¡Y que Mas!*

LAZARO: Cops moonlighting as narco bodyguards!

BUSTAMANTE: *¡Y QUE MAS!*

LAZARO: *La Virgen de Guadalupe* whoring herself for a fix!

BUSTAMANTE: Now you got it!

LAZARO: Money, narcotics, crime, industrial waste, human cargo!

BUSTAMANTE: HA HA!

LAZARO: All of them laughing, laughing at the drug war, the legislation, the just-say-nos, the Founding Fathers of the DEA—

BUSTAMANTE: HAHAHA!

LAZARO: Laughing like skulls at the Privilege which spawned it all and now pray for it to stop, as if the bleeding ever stops, as if the music ever stops—

BUSTAMANTE: It's a dance, *machoman*, with a technobeat between two countries posing in the mirror

LAZARO: Only which is the real

BUSTAMANTE; Which the *sueño*

LAZARO: As if *que si*

BUSTAMANTE: As if *que no*

LAZARO: Are you mah bitch?

BUSTAMANTE: No, you mah bitch now!

LAZARO: Yes!

BUSTAMANTE: We the best export, the true ambassadors.

LAZARO: The real Zapatistas of these twisted times.

BUSTAMANTE: 'Cause the real narcotic is **hope**, smuggled in body cavities they will NEVER reach, muthafukkah.

LAZARO: And one awesome apoca-lipstick day

BUSTAMANTE: All the cell phones, yours and mine

LAZARO: Gonna wail on the very same line.

BUSTAMANTE: Solidarity.

> (*LAZARO clicks the cell phones off. Silence.*)

SONIA: (*dryly*) AY. *Que* sexy.

BUSTAMANTE: Now are you made.

LAZARO: What is it you want?

BUSTAMANTE: Give me Celestino. I give you the keys to the kingdom.

LAZARO: As if you can.

BUSTAMANTE: The *carteles* put a price on his head. With him gone, you are your own man. Everything is yours. The plant, the house, finances, this whore, *todo*. Grant my cargo passage. Leave the rest to me.

LAZARO: He is my father.

> (*BUSTAMANTE takes a packet and slits it open. LAZARO takes a nailful of powder and runs it along his gum. A recognition.*)

BUSTAMANTE: Do you know this, Robles? Do you remember?

LAZARO: T-rex.

BUSTAMANTE: He raised you on this.

LAZARO: When do we start.

BUSTAMANTE: I'll let you know. Leave your cell phone on.

> (*She goes.*)

SONIA: I AM NOT A WHORE, *PUTA*!

> (*Lights change. PEPÍN hobbles in. He is severely beaten.*)

PEPÍN: *Va ver pedo.* Gonna be some big gas trouble. Cause a me telling the *Big Queso* everything. My sister *es mi brotha,* my mama is mama is midwife *tambien* to the baby I seen. And how we come lookin' for the lost *Sincero,* I told him! How in my sleepies I see *Dreamlandia* calling all of us home.

(*FRANK enters, in another area.*)

FRANK: This theme park, this Mexico, *circo de* hell. Goddamn Lazaro was right. I go the vertigo. Everywhere I turn I see my girl, And Dolores a thousand times over nailin' me with her looks. *¡Yo estar mucho borracho!*

PEPÍN: I know! I'll call my *San Francisco!* (*PEPÍN takes out the ear, keys into it like a cellphone.*) Pi pa pi pa pa pa pi.

FRANK: The world's gone tequila, Tino! I hope that poor boy eviscerates you!...

(*PEPÍN calls into the ear.*)

PEPÍN: Hallooo!

(*FRANK reacts.*)

FRANK: OW!

PEPÍN: Halloo!

FRANK: What the...?

PEPÍN: Knock knock.

FRANK: Who's there?

PEPÍN: Cara...

FRANK: Cara who?

PEPÍN: Cara lotta wax in this thing, *vato*!

> *(PEPÍN shoves his finger in.*
> *FRANK writhes in pain.)*

FRANK: AAARGH!

PEPÍN: There. Better. Reception clear!

FRANK: I'm losin' it! Holy God!

PEPÍN: Ain't no god here. Only *San Pedo*, the patron saint of human *piñatas* and porky rinds from heaven! Say *Amen*!

FRANK: I'm losing my fuckin' wits!

> *(FRANK starts to go but PEPÍN's*
> *voice yanks him back.)*

PEPÍN: Get your honky butt back, *jefe*! I told yoos to say amen!

FRANK: AMEN!

PEPÍN: That's more like it.

FRANK: I see how it is. Them people, the poor wetbacks that I wet back to die, they're angels, right! Yer an *angelito*! Alla heaven is a holding pen fulla Mexicans! Lined up in Judgment! The Lord *habla Español*!

PEPÍN: That's right.

FRANK: Only manly thing to do.

PEPÍN: What?

FRANK: Mosey across *La Avenida de las Americas*. Step in front of a big rig.

PEPÍN: *Pero por* why?

FRANK: I can't live with this.

PEPÍN: Hell, we do!

FRANK: You don't unnerstand. Here's where I drove my own bloodkin. I see them everywhere. A common girl in a factory turns into my daughter! I see my woman in the faces of the poor! I can't take it!

> (*FRANK takes a step. The honks and screeches of cars.*)

PEPÍN: BUT SHE NEEDS YOU, SINCERO!

> (*FRANK steps back.*)

FRANK: What...who, who needs me?

PEPÍN: *Lo sabes bien, Papo.*

FRANK: Blanca.

PEPÍN: I had a dream. With all of us in it. *Duermevato*, you, me, Blanca and Mami Dolores. I know the place. She's there for you. Follow the voice in your hole and I'll take you to her. Follow. Follow.

> (*PEPÍN and FRANK go. Lights change. LAZARO and SONIA undressed in the hotel room. A bacchanalia of coke.*)

SONIA: Looka me! Looka Sonia del Valle now, motherfuckahs! She rams herself splat against the pane of three am and morning shatters to pieces at her feet of *puro* silk! She got a new body on, wider hips, glamor lips, fine lookin babe, feeling loosy goosy wearing danger like a fang! No more of that plant, trade my *maquila* for a shotta tequila, see ya girls, I'm done with your *chile, chiquitas*! And no more old man, taking his damn astrology charts to bed like they're gonna help! Ha! Miss Thing is leaving your moon, *viejo*.

LAZARO: Cover girl roar, cover girl hot!

SONIA: And to think I coulda been your mother! Vivian!

LAZARO: Wait. You knew her?

SONIA: One nasty cokehead, according to Tino. He couldn't let nobody know he was in deep with the cartels. So when time came for you to show your pretty head, he wouldn't take her to the hospital and—

LAZARO: She died giving *luz*.

SONIA: She was Frank's sister, too! Frank's your uncle! Junior, you're a therapist's goldmine!

LAZARO: I guess I am.

SONIA: Tell me again! When do we get rich?

LAZARO: Soon as Bustamante calls, I send my attorney to expose the shameful scandal of my father. The DEA find his ass to pay, hey, I'm a son of the USA, then its *tu y yo* in St Tropez.

SONIA: Wicked boy! How did you ever come up with this plot?

LAZARO: I read the synopsis in TV Guide.

> (*She laughs. They kiss.*
> *CELESTINO, SETH, and CARL*
> *walk in.*)

SONIA: Shit.

CELESTINO: A long time ago, a *partera* told me that my wife would bear me a terrible son. That he would bring ruin on my head, usurp the love of my woman, and devour my life. Mandated by the stars, she said.

LAZARO: What took you so long?

SONIA: Celestino... I can explain...

CELESTINO: Please, Sonia, there is nothing to explain. You were the unfortunate wedge between fate and free will.

LAZARO: Do what you want with me. Just leave her alone.

SONIA: You... you knew he was coming?

CELESTINO: She made her choices.

LAZARO: And I made mine. But she has nothing to do with this. Let her go.

SONIA: Tino, you have to believe me--

CELESTINO: Quiet, Sonia.

LAZARO: You and me, *Papá*.

(*Lazaro's cell phone rings.*)

CELESTINO: Go on. Pick it up.

(As LAZARO reaches for the phone, CELESTINO slam his head to the table and knocks him out. SETH and CARL grab him as TINO answers the phone.)

CELESTINO: Yes. Yes. Good.

(He hangs up. As LAZARO is taken out, SONIA gathers her clothes.)

SONIA: Tino, he he he coerced me, he got me high, he made made made me take it, I swear, I didn't I didn't I love you...

CELESTINO: Let's get us some air, *querida*. Go for a drive.

(Lights change.)

SONIA: Where are you taking me?

CELESTINO: *Mira.* Dots of dead ice. We study these sad flecks to understand how we started, to measure something of our future in them. We assign weight and substance to these insubstantial echoes of light. But if we're observing the light of stars long ago put out, then what do **they** see, but the light of our sun already millions of light years dead? What does that make us? *¿Como damos luz?*

SONIA: I'm sorry. I was... overwhelmed.

CELESTINO: My wife died of this shit. It's an unpardonable practice.

SONIA: What are you going to do?

CELESTINO: I'm setting you free, Sonia. Go. Follow the stars home, stay off the street. Some of my employees have met a rough end here.

(He goes.)

SONIA: CELESTINO! YOU CAN'T LEAVE ME HERE! FOR THE LOVE OF GOD!

(Shadowy PRESENCES gather around her, skulking.)

SONIA: Oh no...oh no... señores... guapos... please...

(They stand at a distance.)

They found her half-buried in the desert.

(They edge closer.)

Sonia with a new body. It was her scent that drew them to her. Not Estee Lauder. Not Mirabella. Not even Calvin Klein. The essence of Sonia. Soñar. To dream. Sueños sueños son.

(Darkness sweeps her up. Lights change. BLANCA sits before the

opened suitcase of her mother.
DOLORES enters.)

DOLORES: *¿Que, mija?*

BLANCA: I was in him. Inside the man feeling his bones and muscles, the gone-to-shit dreams of *gringo*-hood, guiding me from one shore to the other. The whole time I thought it was him.

DOLORES: It was you, *mija*. Always you.

BLANCA: I am my father's daughter.

DOLORES: But where was Sincero? Why was he deaf to me that night?

> *(DOLORES holds up the coat and BLANCA places her arm through the sleeve. Her hand emerges from the cuff as Frank's and it gently touches DOLORES' face.)*

BLANCA: I was there. On the levee. Hiding from myself.

DOLORES: Sincero…

BLANCA: All my bones turned to shame.

DOLORES: Why didn't you come?

BLANCA: I couldn't. He woulda killed you. He woulda shot you in the water if I tried to save you.

DOLORES: Better dead than so unloved.

BLANCA: I loved you always, my love never failed you.

DOLORES: <u>You</u> did. Will you fail Blanca too?

BLANCA: My girl. Pretty, bold and true as her mother. I wish I'd known her.

DOLORES: Do you?

BLANCA: I'm sorry for lots of things in my life, but not her.

> *(DOLORES kisses her hand as it slips back into the sleeve and BLANCA removes the coat.)*

That was him that spoke, Ama, but it was me, too.

DOLORES: *(taking one of the jars from the case)* For you, I've made a special tea. How much you drink will kill you, steal your wits, or make you face the devil.

*(BLANCA drinks. Gags. Feels
herself change. Then she turns
toward the river with resolve.)*

BLANCA: I was born here, but decided there.
It's there I have to go.

> *(BLANCA closes the case, and
> charges with it into the water.
> Thunder. Lights change. The island.
> CELESTINO surveys the skies as
> SETH and CARL carry LAZARO
> on in his old rags. They shackle him
> to his chain.)*

SETH: Hurry. He's wakin' up, Carl.

LAZARO: *Ay....*

CARL: Hey, pilgrim...

LAZARO: Sonia?

CARL: No, buddy. It's me. How you feelin'?

> *(Thunder overhead.)*

CELESTINO: *Desmadre* is the forecast in the
skies tonight.

LAZARO: Where am I?

CELESTINO: I feel it. The constellations crashing to earth.

LAZARO: Oh no…

CELESTINO: Bearing down like gods toward the border.

LAZARO: Not again.

CARL: It was all a bad dream, Laz. You been passed out since you drank this Extra-strength T-rex-inna-thermos, remember? Remember?

LAZARO: *¿Solo un sueño?*

CELESTINO: *Igual como la vida, hijo.*

SETH: It must've been a good dream, chief. I hope you got laid.

> *(A storm commences with loud claps of thunder and lightning.)*

LAZARO: As if *que si*. As if *que no*. As if this life dreamt that life which dreamt this and which is real and which is just wish, wish, wish them back, no fuck that! No way no way NO WAY!

CELESTINO: Consider it a dream. It was too short, too violent, too senseless to have been anything else. This is the only world you know.

LAZARO: I was Lazaro Robles.

CELESTINO: And I was your father. But we all gotta wake up some time.

> (SETH and CARL draw their
> weapons.)

LAZARO: What…what are you doing?

CELESTINO: One final piece of business. Doña Bustamante designated this checkpoint for her shipment. Your *isla* is our beach head.

SETH: There! I see something there!

CELESTINO: Do you hear me, *vieja*! I'm ready! *(They see BLANCA rise out of the water toward him.)* You.

LAZARO: Cover girl.

BLANCA: I said I'd come back to free you.

CELESTINO: What are you doing here?

BLANCA: I am your *contrabanda*, Celestino.

Distilled by time and my mother's tears, the last narcotic to cross your *frontera*. The years you barricaded yourself with an empire of shit. Look at him! He's your son! No-one caused her to die but you, you proud sick *pendejo*. Hear your woman's truth as my mother sealed it in a jar-

> *(She opens a jar and a long cry sails over them. SETH and CARL cower in fear. She then takes the ropes from the case.)*

Remember these? These cords bear witness, these ropes know what he's owed, not just in light, breath, blood, and time, but in Love. LOVE.

CELESTINO: No.

BLANCA: The key.

> *(SETH gives her the key and she advances toward LAZARO. CELESTINO aims the gun.)*

One kilo of the truth, *patron*. Tell your son why his mother died.

> *(She waits for a moment, then unshackles him.)*

LAZARO: Tell me, Apa.

CELESTINO: It was not my fault. It was hers. Dolores. *Curandera maldita,* you set the stars against me.

(Loud clap of thunder.)

Mojada, you're dead! *Una sombra!* As *if que si!*
As if *que la chingada!* I make the border! I make
the countries! I make the chain! I am *el mero*
skin of God, *puta!*

CARL: Put the gun down, Mr. Robles.

CELESTINO: *¡Mira! Espantos, fantasmas,*
wading in the *rio.* Crying for the homeblood.
The blood is *voz.* The *voz* has mouth. Mouth
has wound. Wound is...

> *(He fires. A shrill piercing cry*
> *merges with thunder.)*

FRANK: *(off)* Don't shoot! Hold yer damn fire!
Goddammit! GODDAM-ALMIGHTY!

SETH: That's the chief!

> *(FRANK lurches on with the limp*
> *bleeding body of PEPÍN.)*

BLANCA: PEPÍN!

FRANK: Lookit what you done! Bastards!
Lookit what you done to my SON!

CELESTINO: Did you see her, Frank? Your
woman's out on the water again!

FRANK: You're all right, boy. You'll be fine.

PEPÍN: Blanca, you're back. *Hola*, Thirst. Don't need googles nomore.

SETH: We gotta get you a doctor, little guy.

FRANK: Go! Now!

(*SETH and CARL run off.*)

BLANCA: Oh my god, Pepín! You're bleeding!

FRANK: I'm sorry! I tried not to let this happen! But he said to come because there was this—

PEPÍN: ¡*Alli!* I see it! LOOK!

(*He breaks away and wraps his eyes around his vision.*)

Mi gran sueño! The dream that dreamed me first. Look through the hole in my chest at the gold of *Dreamlandia, vatos.*

(*As they begin to move toward a threshold, the lights change and the storm abates, and they see what PEPÍN sees.*)

Ghostcrossers in a Spanish play played many nights before, before the before. Strangers passing through each others' *corazones*. I see them. A King. A Prince. A Royal Lady. An old Duke. But where's the Fool? Gotta have a Fool.

> (*As they move slowly through another space, they step toward each other.*)

Ahh. Now I see these shadows tip heaven on its side, not the other way around.

> (*CELESTINO faces LAZARO; BLANCA faces FRANK.*)

CELESTINO: If stars keep their word, then so must I; do with me what you will.

LAZARO: There was no verdict but that you passed on yourself. *Senor, levanta, dame tu mano.*

> (*LAZARO takes his hand.*)

FRANK: You are my daughter and that's enough to live for.

BLANCA: My mother was good; she deserved a better death.

FRANK: I'll honor her with my own for your sake.

BLANCA: *Padre, me daz luz otra vez.*

(He kisses her hand.)

PEPÍN: *Suave. Pero* where's the Fool? *Yo no veo el* Fool.

LAZARO: *(to FRANK AND BLANCA)* To you both I grant all the mercy you desire. To my father, forgiveness.

BLANCA: This is it.

CELESTINO: This is how we conquer fate.

FRANK: In story. Old dramas long ago played out.

> *(PEPÍN dies. The lights change back. The sound of a light rain on the water. They seem to wake from the dream. Embarrassment and helplessness.)*

BLANCA: Can't we pretend, can't we make everything from before…

FRANK: No.

CELESTINO: No.

LAZARO: ...no.

(*She goes to PEPÍN.*)

BLANCA: He's dead. (*weeping over his broken body*) How do we wake up from this dream, this nightmare?

FRANK: Maybe we don't.

CELESTINO: Maybe he just did.

(*LAZARO takes to the shackle and holds it up to CELESTINO.*)

LAZARO: Why did you let her die?

(*CELESTINO takes it, feels the weight of the chain in his hands, and then slowly brings the shackle up to LAZARO's face.*)

CELESTINO: To save you.

(*CELESTINO drops the shackle and creeps into LAZARO's hovel.*)

LAZARO: *Si asi es, asi es.*

BLANCA: Apa.

FRANK: I can't be your father. I don't know how. I don't...

> *(DOLORES appears as a faint image over water.)*

DOLORES: Sincero.

FRANK: Dolores?

BLANCA: It's her.

DOLORES: *¡Sincero!*

FRANK: Over here! Dolores, I got our boy!

DOLORES: *Cuidado, mi amor.* It's deep and cold.

FRANK: *(taking PEPÍN in his arms)* I ain't afraid. I'm comin'. *(turning to BLANCA)* I wish in some world we coulda been... well...

DOLORES: *Yo he sufrido tanto por tu ausencia*
          Desde ese dia hasta hoy, no soy feliz--

(FRANK wades with PEPÍN into the river toward DOLORES.)

FRANK: I'm comin', Dolores, I'm comin'…

(They vanish in the current.)

BLANCA: It's over, cuz.

LAZARO: You and me. *¿Somos familia?*

BLANCA: All that's left of it.

LAZARO: And Alfonso?

BLANCA: He's still around.

LAZARO: We better go before one of us wakes up. But where? Which side?

(BLANCA takes his hand and slowly guides him into the water with her. Step by step.)

BLANCA: We just go, Lazaro, *tu y yo*, we step into the flux of our world, this river, we go in, eyes opened, hearts bent toward the land that needs us most; we go in breathing and let the water decide.

(They walk the water and exit.
CELESTINO alone. BLACKOUT.)

End Of Play

BETHLEHEM

a river play by Octavio Solis

Characters:

Lee Rosenblum (Leandro Guerra)

Mateo Buenaventura

Mrs. Buenaventura (Ama)

Mrs. Miranda Dewey

Dru

Shannon Trimble

Sonia

Barry's Voice

Medical Examiner

(Shannon and Sonia are played by the same actor. The part of the Medical Examiner can be played by Dru or a disembodied recorded voice. Barry's voice should be recorded using the voice of the actor playing Mateo.)

The time is the present. The play takes place in El Paso.

Mateo's backyard patio and front yard. Lee's motel room. The action flows smoothly from one location to the other, and from one time to the other.

Bethelem was originally produced by Campo Santo and Intersection for the Arts in San Francisco, California and premiered at Intersection for the Arts (Deborah Cullinan, Executive Director) as an Equity approved project on July 10, 2003 under the direction of Octavio Solis with the following cast and creative team:

Mrs. Dewey: Margo Hall

Lee Rosenblum/Leandro Guerra: Sean San Jose

Mrs. Buenaventura/Ama: Catherine Castellanos

Mateo Buenaventura: Luis Saguar

Dru: Marcelina Willis

Shannon/Sonia: Anna Maria Luera

Understudy for Mrs. Dewey: Selana Allen

Lighting Design: Jim Cave

Properties: Katherine Covell

Set Design: James Faerron

Sound design: Drew Yerys

Original Music: Abel Sanchez

Stage Manager: Nancy Mancias

Fight Choreography: L. Peter Callender

Sound Operator: Lena Monje

Production team: Melyssa Jo Kelly & Athena
Osborn & Sarah Sherwood

Researcher: Adam Palafox

Assistant Director: Kenn Watt

Bethlehem was originally conceived and
developed by the American Conservatory
Theatre, San Francisco (Carey Perloff-Artistic
Director, Heather Kitchen-Managing Director)
and received support through a Rockefeller
Foundation grant.

This play is for Jeanne.

Act One

(Against the desert mountain background of West Texas, in an old El Paso neighborhood, the sun rises on the BUENAVENTURA house. MRS. DEWEY, a stern woman of middle age, enters mournfully singing a gospel tune as she carries a suitcase marked with crosses and handwritten scripture. She kneels before the house and opens the suitcase, revealing an ornate shrine to her young daughter. She takes her Bible out and erupts in a shouted prayer.)

MRS. DEWEY: Come, oh Lord. Come forcibly here, come irresistible to my side, impel the fury, rouse it from its shell and impel yourself in it; pay it back, this crime dipped in God's blood; send my darkened angel to impel the justice from hell's own drum and strike this world down strike this world down strike this world down for me!

(LEE, in his mid 20s, wearing requisite Dockers and sports coat,

appears silhouetted in the dim light of early morning. He carries a small recorder in one hand and a small white paper bag in the other. Severely jet-lagged.)

LEE: Cool southwest Texas morning mist. Crisp blue desert peaks behind me. El Paso ready to go into dog heat. I am right on the cusp between past and past.

MRS. DEWEY: Strike all time and place for me, Lord!

LEE: I don't believe in premonitions because they never amount to much. But I feel like this story is meant for me.

MRS. DEWEY: And send me your Wingéd Wrath!

LEE: It is, after all, my first story.

MRS. DEWEY: Are you him? Are you my angel?

LEE: Angel? Me?

MRS. DEWEY: Are you not summoned?

LEE: Ma'am, I'm Jewish. But can I ask what you're doing out here?

MRS. DEWEY: Go away.

LEE: Are you praying for him? Ma'am, are you praying for Mateo Buenaventura?

MRS. DEWEY: Don't say his name to me! You don't know the demon!

LEE: I read the pertinent facts on the plane.

MRS. DEWEY: Then you know him even less!

LEE: Tell me, then.

MRS. DEWEY: I know what he did to her. I know what he did to her pertinent facts. He came upon her innocence and thrust his hand in and pulled out--.

> *(She thrusts her hand inside his coat and takes his wallet out.)*

LEE: Hey!

> *(She takes his driver's license out, examines the back facing, and throws it back to him.)*

MRS. DEWEY: You haven't signed. Still in possession of your organs if not your wits. Hallelujah, thank you, Jesus.

> *(LEE grabs his wallet back. AMA, an old woman with old world ways, a steel bun on her head, steps out*

with a broom toward MRS.
DEWEY.)

AMA: You again! GET OFF! Get off my yard!

MRS. DEWEY: There is no truth in his mouth,
his eyes are pits for vipers--

AMA: He's done nothing to you! Nothing!
Leave us alone!

MRS. DEWEY: His mouth is a wide open
grave, his tongue seduces--

AMA: Get away from us! SHOO! *¡ANDALE,*
VIEJA CABRONA! ¡MALDICION!

MRS. DEWEY: YOU ARE MALEDICTION!
YOU BESHAT HIM INTO THIS WORLD!

AMA: *¡YA!*

> *(She drives MRS. DEWEY away.)*

MRS. DEWEY: *(as she runs off)* God shall
avenge, oh yes, hallelujah, Lord! Etc.

LEE: Are you Mrs. Buenventura?

AMA: He won't see you.

LEE: Ma'am. If I could take a moment to
explain--

AMA: He won't see nobody.

LEE: Is that what he says or what you say?

AMA: Don't be so smart with me. I know what you are. The grass dies where you stand.

LEE: *(handing her his card)* Lee Rosenblum. This is our magazine.

AMA: *(spitting on it and tossing it aside)* Smut.

LEE: Ma'am, please. I think you and your son deserve a fair hearing--

AMA: Get off!

> *(She swipes him with her broom on the face. Bread spills out of the bag all over the ground.)*

LEE: Ow! Fuck!

AMA: Idiot! You shouldna ducked! I was gonna miss you anyways!

LEE: My tooth.

AMA: Don't be faking. I'll know if you're faking. Good grief.

LEE: Jesus, I only brought some sweet bread.

AMA: Good grief almighty.

LEE: God, I'm bleeding...

(A man appears in the back.
Shrouded in shadow. He is more
shape than substance.)

MATEO: Ama.

AMA: I told him.

MATEO: Did you hurt him, Ama?

LEE: Mateo?

AMA: I was trying to scare him off.

LEE: Sir, could I have a glass of water, please?
And some tissue.

MATEO: Get him in the house.

AMA: He's a liar and a weasel.

MATEO: Pick up his bread and get him in the
house right now.

(The man edges away. AMA helps
LEE pick up the bread and they go
inside as MRS. DEWEY steps
forward and picks up the calling
card.)

MRS. DEWEY: Already blood on the front
steps. Blessed are the wise, blessed are the true,
the upright and innocent, but woe to him who
bleeds at the Devil's door.

(The shady arbor of the backyard patio rises out of the background. Old Mexican tile on the ground, wrought iron furniture, and stone benches. LEE enters across from an ominous-looking terra cotta figure of some Aztec deity.)

LEE: A dark entry into a darker living room and then she leads me to this patio. Ice pack for the swelling. My Rockports on his turf. Small Pre-Columbian ceramic figurine, looking at me like I'm Cortez. Too late. You lost.

(AMA enters with a cup of herbal tea.)

AMA: Here.

LEE: What is it?

AMA: *Yerba buena* to dull the pain. But I ain't sorry, in case you're thinking.

LEE: Who's the holy roller?

AMA: Don't pay her no mind. Damn freak. *Está loca.* When *mijo* came after his release, there was a whole group of people making a *mitote.* Saying get him out, he'll murder our children and what-not. Neighbors who used to say hello, spitting in my face. And the news people. Lotsa cameras and trucks *y que nada.*

Seeing my house on TV, hearing the news lady call me names. But two weeks pass and look: only her. Regular as the sun.

LEE: She's sure mad about something.

AMA: Mateo won't discuss her. So don't.

>   *(She goes. MATEO enters, unseen,*
>   *eating the sweet bread. LEE glances*
>   *again at the ceramic figurine, almost*
>   *touches it.)*

MATEO: *Pan sagrado para la pena del diablo.*

LEE: Excuse me?

MATEO: My old man used to go out and get bread for us when I was a *chavo*. His way of making peace. *(MATEO offers him a piece. LEE takes it.)* How's your jaw?

LEE: I'll live.

MATEO: My mother, *sabes*, gets overprotective sometimes.

LEE: She packs a good swing.

MATEO: Her house is the only place on earth I'm welcome.

LEE: Am I?

MATEO: Depends. How much you know about me?

LEE: Not nearly enough. Mostly stuff about the "incident". Court papers, news clippings. A little about your odd jobs, fleabags, drinking binges. Nobody really knows you.

MATEO: Is that you're after, Mr. Rosenblum? The Mateo no-one knows?

LEE: If you'll let me. We want to do an in-depth for the magazine. A couple hours a day for a couple days. Get to know you, your life, your version of things. Larsen, my editor, would offer remuneration but it's not our policy.

MATEO: I don't care about no damn money. I wanna be left alone. I'm not what they think, you know. I was innocent of that crime.

LEE: Then say it for me. Let me do a spread on you and show people your side of things. A real human, with feelings and memories, more than a criminal act and a news story, but more like us, like real *gente*, Mateo.

MATEO: Real what?

LEE: People. Real people.

(He approaches LEE.)

MATEO: Are you Mexican?

LEE: Me? No... I....

MATEO: Waitaminnit.

> (With his finger, MATEO delicately
> pulls down the skin under his eye.)

MATEO: I look in your eye. That red tomato edge in your eye and it look Mexican to me. It got that shredded Mexican pride in it still. Overripe. Sore to the touch. Sleepless. The pride that never sleeps, but waits. Waits for something just outa reach of this world. Your clothes are a mask. Your name is a mask. That makes you white. But what makes you Mexican like me is your soul itself is a mask.

LEE: I'm Lee Rosenblum.

MATEO: That's what your card says.

LEE: I'm from New York.

MATEO: Your complexion is from New York.

LEE: Look, am I doing this story?

MATEO: Tell me your given name. *Tu nombre santo.* Or no interview.

LEE: I told you my name.

> (*MATEO gives LEE something in a hanky and goes. The patio recedes into the background as MRS. DEWEY steps forward on the front yard.*)

MRS. DEWEY: Look what's come from the belly of the beast. What's he given you, Mr. Rosenblum?

LEE: My tooth.

MRS. DEWEY: Will you give him good press and put him on your cover? Make him a household name? Scant consolation to the people he's hurt. None at all for Shannon Trimble.

LEE: Who are you? What's with this vigil? Are you related to Shannon?

MRS. DEWEY: What do you care? You only come to know the devil. Not his victims. Whore yourself, do your spread.

LEE: There's no spread. I'm not doing it.

MRS. DEWEY: Too late, Mr. Rosenblum. The Beast has struck his deal with you. Hallelujah.

> *(She goes, singing to herself, as an austere seedy motel room emerges. There's a bed and a nightstand. LEE violently opens his briefcase, spilling all over the bed photos of the crime scene.)*

LEE: He doesn't know me. He doesn't know me. He doesn't know me. He doesn't know me. He doesn't know me. Fuck him. He's doesn't know shit about me! I don't need this fucking interview.

> *(He takes a quart of bourbon from his brief and almost downs a swig when he realizes something about the room. He takes it in.)*

LEE: Motel room. Twin sized bed. 19" TV. Remote screwed into the table. My eyes screwed to the grisly pictures of high school death. Blood on the carpet. Smears on the drapes. A twin bed soaked in gore.

> *(He picks up one of the photos on the bed.)*

Tell me, Shannon Trimble. Do I need this story?

(SHANNON, a pretty Texas teen, sultry and a little drunk, slinks in from the shadows.)

SHANNON: Does the story need you?

LEE: Intelligent, pretty, all of 17.

SHANNON: I got me ID that says 21.

LEE: Popular at school, especially with the boys.

SHANNON: But I like mine with experience.

LEE: A penchant for older college guys, some even older.

(The deep brutish voice of BARRY, bellows from off:)

BARRY: *(off)* SHANNON!

SHANNON: SHADDUP, BUTTHOLE! *(To LEE)* Barry's such a goon.

LEE: What do I do, Shannon? I can't lose this spread.

SHANNON: Watch that hootch, big guy. I might want me a shot later.

LEE: I walk away now and blow my first assignment and Larsen won't like it. He'll never give me a better one.

SHANNON: I need a dollar for the juke box.

LEE: That lady thinks I don't care about you. I do. If I believed in God, I'd want to know what the hell He was thinking letting someone as young as you end up on a coroner's slab.

SHANNON: Mister, God ain't got nothin' to do with it. Desire bereft of body, that midnight car with the headlights off, and all the darkness to spare...

> *(He starts to follow SHANNON as she drifts away. A blinding flash out of the darkness. DRU enters with a camera. A worldly-wise photographer, she moves like the world is her studio.)*

LEE: Dru!

DRU: Howdy, Rosenblum.

LEE: What are you doing here? I thought you were in Israel or wherever.

DRU: Well, somebody's gotta bust your balls. Can I have a whiff of your breath freshener?

LEE: Let me get you a glass.

DRU: *(tossing him a small film roll container)* Here.

(LEE pours her some.)

LEE: Jesus, it's good to see you. When did you get in?

DRU: Just this afternoon. Is this the best you could do? Motel 666?

LEE: I was looking for something that would approximate the place she died in.

DRU: Method Journalism. Up yours. *(drinks)*

LEE: How the hell did you find me?

DRU: Larsen. He thought it'd be a real laugh to pair us up again. *(seeing the photos on the bed)* Whoa. Jesus. He really filleted her, didn't he?

LEE: Don't look at them. They'll give you nightmares.

DRU: I've seen worse. I got first-hand experience with monsters all over this planet.

LEE: Dru, seriously. What are you doing here? Because--

DRU: Relax, I'm here to take his picture. You should be grateful. I'm the one who got you this job, remember.

LEE: It's just that, you know, stuff between us—

DRU: I learn my lessons. I'm actually over you, Rosenblum. And I'm engaged.

LEE: Really?

DRU: No. Ha! But I could be. I got friends in the press corps, you know.

LEE: I don't doubt it.

DRU: So tell me about this creep. How soon can I set up a shoot?

LEE: It's not happening.

DRU: Wait a minute, wait a minute, hold the phone.

LEE: I'm not doing it. The fucker started playing head games with me and I just said no way.

DRU: What kinda head games?

LEE: Riding me for information, turning talk around to me, getting personal.

DRU: Is that it?

LEE: I do a serious interview, Dru. I don't involve my personal life.

DRU: What serious interview? Jesus, you work for a nudie magazine. And personal life, give me a break. You never sit still long enough to have one. Six months in bed with you and all I got to know was your bed.

LEE: I have a rule about professional distance.

DRU: *(aiming the camera at him)* Me too. It's called depth of field.

LEE: Dru...

DRU: *(advancing toward him)* We never really officially broke up. Technically we're still in the game. As a journalistic team, I mean.

LEE: You're saying I should do this.

DRU: Only way to get the close-up is to get up close.

LEE: Something about him, though. He gets you in this space. He takes the doors and windows out.

DRU: I'll keep mine open for you then. Rm 216. I better go unpack. I want to be ready for this perv.

LEE: Let me soften him up. In the meantime, I got someone else you should check out.

*(Lights change. MRS. DEWEY
enters. DRU takes out her camera
and snaps away as LEE recedes with
the motel room.)*

MRS. DEWEY: O Lord, praised be your name, I
pray for deliverance from trouble and fear! —

DRU: Great! Do that again!

MRS. DEWEY: My King and my God, the
wicked will perish as you so command —

DRU: Arms in the air, eyes to God!

MRS. DEWEY: Providence shall make it so.

DRU: That's it!

MRS. DEWEY: Providence shall see it done.

DRU: Good!

> *(MRS. DEWEY stops and turns her
> steely gaze to DRU.)*

MRS. DEWEY: The Word is made Flesh and
the Flesh shall be commanded home.

> *(MRS. DEWEY takes her charm and
> places it around DRU's neck. She
> goes. DRU follows her as AMA
> appears with LEE in the patio.)*

AMA: *¿Otra vez?*

LEE: Tell him… Leandro is here.

(MATEO enters.)

MATEO: Leandro who.

LEE: Leandro Guerra. I was born in Fabens, just a few miles from here.

MATEO: Bring Leandro some *horchata*, Ama. *(AMA goes.)* You've had *horchata*, no?

LEE: Do we have a deal?

MATEO: How the hell did you end up a Rosenblum?

LEE: My parents split up. Mom took me to New York and remarried. She died within the year and my stepdad raised me.

MATEO: That's some trick. Tradin' off skins just like that. Didn't yer old man have a say in it?

LEE: I don't know. He disappeared into Mexico with my little…

MATEO: Yeah?

LEE: Listen, all the credentials you need are in this folder.

MATEO: Shit on your credentials. I'll never talk to a Jew reporter.

(LEE moves to take up his folder. MATEO places his hand over it.)

MATEO: But I *will* talk with a Mexican.

(They smile at each other and LEE prepares his tape player.)

LEE: You and your Mom seem pretty close.

MATEO: Nobody closer. Greatest woman I ever known. Ain't nothin' in the world I wouldn't do for her.

LEE: Buenaventura Tape 1. 9 am.

MATEO: Do I need to talk loud or what?

LEE: Don't worry. This'll pick you up. So she's a great cook, huh?

MATEO: The old country way. None of this microwave stuff. She uses old cast-iron *ollas* handed down from her *nana*. She gets everything from the market in Juarez.

(AMA returns with a tray of food, horchata and whiskey.)

MATEO: ¿*Que no, Ama?*

AMA: Try it. *Sabe rico.*

LEE: Mmm. This is good.

AMA: Put some *chile de arbol*. Better when it's spicy.

MATEO: One of the delicacies I missed in the ward.

AMA: *Sopa de lengua.*

MATEO: Tongue.

LEE: Thanks. Really good.

> *(AMA plants a kiss on his forehead and goes.)*

MATEO: She's made me this *caldo* since I was a little boy. My dreams swirl in this soup.

LEE: Before we start…can I ask you?…who's the woman out there?

> *(MATEO drops his spoon into his bowl and glowers at LEE.)*

MATEO: Do I have to answer for every little pissant bitch on this earth? Am I to explain the logic of idiots? *Esa pinche vieja es una puta! PUTA!* I ain't been allowed to live my own life. I ain't been alone in the presence of a woman other than my mother in more'n TWELVE years! You know what that does to a man? People like that make me wish I was back in the psych-ward.

LEE: So you don't know who she is...

MATEO: No. *(He enunciates into his recorder.)* Fuck No.

LEE: Did the treatment help?

MATEO: *(taking his whiskey)* Oh yeah, big help. I'm a rehab wonder. My personality disorder's diagnosed, addressed, and redressed. I'm a fully medicated citizen.

LEE: You sound bitter.

MATEO: It wasn't my idea to declare me loony-tunes. That was my lawyers.

LEE: You didn't want the insanity plea?

MATEO: The whole shebang made no sense to me, but damn if the jury didn't buy it. Suckers'll believe anything. I got drawer fulls of bullshit medication I'm supposed to be taking. *(MATEO raises his glass.)* This is all the sedation I need. Wild Turkey! No way am I sick and no way did I touch that girl.

LEE: I may have my facts wrong, but didn't your semen place you in the room?

MATEO: I don't deny some consensual messin' around. I just don't recall when or how or what.

LEE: You blanked out.

MATEO: Blinded by the Turkey. Slipped in the gap. The interstice, doctors called it.

LEE: Are you an alcoholic?

MATEO: Uh-uh.

LEE: Do you have nightmares?

MATEO: No.

LEE: Did you ever torture cats, dogs?

MATEO: Never.

LEE: Into self-mutilation?

MATEO: No.

LEE: What about compulsive masturbation?

MATEO: Get outa here!

LEE: Enuresis?

MATEO: Oh for cryin' Jesus!

LEE: What about your father?

MATEO: What about him?

LEE: Well, I read that he was in and out a lot. Always on the move. But there's no mention in the trial transcripts of any past abuse.

MATEO: I like that word. Abuse. Good fucking clinical word.

LEE: Did he whup ass on you?

MATEO: He applied discipline.

LEE: I can guess how severe that was.

MATEO: Well…. guess.

> (LEE pauses as he is taken aback by
> the reversal.)

LEE: He slapped you around some. Knocked a few teeth out. Whipped your bare ass with the buckle end of the belt.

MATEO: Colorful.

LEE: Left you bleeding on the floor sometimes. Without food. Your mom probably tried to stop it, but a man's home is his dungeon. And yours is his buckle. Am I right?

MATEO: And the buckle?

LEE: Something with his name probably. Big and silver and… cold.

MATEO: You guess pretty good.

LEE: Did he mess with you in other ways? (MATEO snorts.) What's so funny? If you don't want to tell me, cool. If you can't remember,

I'm cool with that too. But sometimes, Mateo, after discipline, there's a need to comfort, a need to love again.

MATEO: Seein' him undo that buckle could only mean one of two things and I hated both of them.

LEE: Did he do these things in Spanish or in English?

MATEO: What the hell difference does it make?

LEE: What if his beating words were English and his loving words were Spanish. 'Cause what does a boy understand, and what stays in his head as strange language? Words of another world raping you all your fucking life.

MATEO: How do you know my shit so well? Are all our old men so alike?

(LEE hesitates for a moment.)

LEE: My father was a man with a grudge. He resented having to live in a country that resented him. He was one of those large impenetrable men who walked around like they're in a bullring.

MATEO: Yeah.

LEE: On nights after he'd spray my sheets with discipline, I'd get up, inch slowly down the hall, cross the long line between me and my baby sister's room. Crawl in her bed and stay there all night.

MATEO: Watching for him?

LEE: Lying beside her, counting out the little embroidered roses on her pillowcase. You're not getting her, I kept saying.

MATEO: You saved her.

LEE: I wish. He ran off to Mexico with her. Haven't heard a word since. I've never told anyone. That I remember it at all is... *(LEE shuts off the tape player.)* I'm supposed to be asking the questions.

MATEO: Can I ask you one more? What's that word, enuresis?

LEE: Bedwetting.

MATEO: That one I did! I pissed them sheets till I was fifteen.

> *(MATEO bursts out laughing as he goes. The motel room appears with SHANNON waiting by the bed, dressed in the white smock of a forensic psychiatrist with a stack of files.)*

SHANNON: *(throwing files on the floor as she speaks)* On more than one occasion, he was able to subvert the process of analysis to his ends.

LEE: No shit.

SHANNON: He likes the company of other patients but only insofar as they serve his needs.

LEE: Why does he make me talk about myself like that? My sister and all that...

SHANNON: He suffers from a superiority complex. He cannot tolerate those who think him inadequate, antisocial, or unclean. So he levels the psychological playing field.

LEE: He can't be that cunning. He's a lowlife.

SHANNON: A mendacious individual who blurs the lines between conjecture and fact, truth and insinuation.

LEE: Why is he even talking to me?

SHANNON: He likes the attention. In all my years on the ward, I never saw anyone so enjoy his incarceration and treatment.

LEE: He thinks he's innocent.

> *(DRU enters distractedly, her gaze caught on something off.)*

DRU: Lee...

SHANNON: Exculpation through denial. Denial of his crime, denial of his past, denial of his denial.

> *(BARRY'S voice bellows from off.)*

BARRY: *(off)* SHANNON!!!

SHANNON: Later, sugar.

> *(SHANNON rushes off into the shadows. DRU turns.)*

LEE: I'm going to have to play hardball with you, sir.

DRU: Lee.

LEE: Hey.

DRU: You okay?

LEE: I think we're getting somewhere. He gave me *sopa de lengua.*

DRU: What's that?

LEE: Tongue.

DRU: Gross.

LEE: I'm going to transcribe the interview off the tape.

DRU: I can do it for you if you want.

LEE: No, it's fine. I'll do it. *(He notices her agitation.)* Are you okay?

DRU: You told me to see that lady on the vigil. So I did.

LEE: What happened?

DRU: Well…you know, I watched her pray and sing Jesus to herself for a while and got a few good shots. Then just like that, she gave me this charm, blew her candle out, and locked herself in her van. I left a note with my phone number saying I needed her to sign a release and then came back to my room to jump in the shower and when I came out…

> *(MRS. DEWEY appears standing by the bed. LEE watches the exchange.)*

MRS. DEWEY: Miss Dru? Is that your name?

DRU: How did you get in?

MRS. DEWEY: I came to sign that form.

DRU: Yes. Let me get that for you.

MRS. DEWEY: I'm sorry I was in such a state. When I have the Holy Spirit, all the world is a blur to me.

DRU: You were fine. *(reading her name on the form)* Mrs. Dewey.

MRS. DEWEY: Your friend seems fascinated with the butcher. He's not interested in anything I have to say.

DRU: He's always been a little self-absorbed.

MRS. DEWEY: You, on the other hand, pretend to understand my situation.

DRU: I understand you're in some kind of pain. You act like you're the mother of the girl he killed but they moved to Canada years ago. So who are you?

MRS. DEWEY: Some years ago, the Lord called my daughter Chelsea home. She was in a freak automobile accident. For two weeks, she remained in a coma and my husband and I prayed for her deliverance. When she was declared brain dead, sweet Christ spoke to me to let her go. So I had the plug pulled on my baby. The heart was removed, shipped to a hospital in Dallas, and transplanted--

DRU: I'm sorry about that, but what does that have to do…

MRS. DEWEY: …transplanted into Mateo Buenaventura.

DRU: Oh… my god.

MRS. DEWEY: My Chelsea saved that man. He had an obligation to live well and serve others and stand as an example of God's grace. He received a miracle, a gift, a second chance at life, and what did he do just months after receiving my daughter's organ? Murdered a girl exactly her age. The soul of my Chelsea in him and he commits this butchery. How can she rest as long as a part of her lives in that monster? He entered into a covenant with God and he shat all over it! They said in court that it was her heart that made him crazy! He blamed my Chelsea for the murder! So I sit in front of his house every day to remind him that he's living on my daughter's time.

DRU: What for? What good can it do her now?

(MRS. DEWEY places her hand against DRU's chest.)

MRS. DEWEY: Whose heart beats here, Miss Dru? Do you know that every heartbeat has its own signature? God forbid you should come that close, but if you do, listen to that demon's heart and see if don't you hear my Chelsea calling. Crying to be rid of that filthy man.

DRU: What do you want from me?

MRS. DEWEY: Don't take his picture. Mateo's an unholy and dangerous man and he knows his time is nigh.

DRU: Nigh?

MRS. DEWEY: God is my surgeon, Miss Dru.

> *(She goes. LEE reads the name on the form.)*

LEE: Miranda Dewey. That's why she checked my donor status.

DRU: My heart is still pounding.

LEE: Come here.

DRU: I'm getting a double-lock on that door, I swear... *(LEE draws her close.)* I pride myself on knowing my subjects. I tell myself this is what I do. But what my camera knows and what I know are not the same. They're not the same.

LEE: Do you want to spend the night here?

DRU: Just tonight. Just…you know…

> *(She kisses him, tentatively. As he speaks, LEE holds DRU, then guides her toward the bed. She unbuttons her blouse and lies on it facing him.)*

LEE: I tell myself we're just trying to ward off this encroaching darkness. But something else is happening. She feels good. Warm. She lets me feel things I haven't allowed myself in a long time. Both of us, we're lonely as hell and we count on each other's detachment, but this evening, we make real love and lie in each other's arms desperately feigning sleep, filled with this vague sense of shame.

> *(He takes a large canvas bag from under the bed and the room recedes. MATEO enters, bringing with him his patio.)*

MATEO: Guilt and agitation. I bring out the best in people. I wouldn't worry. This shame grows into this wonderful fucked-up thing we call conscience.

LEE: Did you pick that up in the psych-ward?

MATEO: No, I learned that in church. So she wants pictures of me?

LEE: Just a couple shots. Candid. Dru wouldn't take but twenty minutes. She'll improve on those old prison mugs everyone's seen.

MATEO: I'm not sure a chick in my house is a good idea right now.

LEE: She's not a chick, she's the best in the biz. She'll capture your essence.

MATEO: Is that what you got in the bag? Some essence?

> *(AMA enters with a plate of food.)*

AMA: *Mijo, aqui te traigo tantita comida para que no te canses.*

MATEO: *Ay, Ama. Mira.* You did all this today?

AMA: *Andale, a comer, mijito.*

MATEO: *Gracias.*

> *(She kisses him tenderly on the forehead and goes, casting a malevolent eye on LEE.)*

MATEO: *Ama* never had a chance to be good at nothing in her life but being *Ama*. But what's an only son for?

> *(LEE unzips the bag and takes out some 8x10's, which he lays before MATEO.)*

LEE: I think you know Shannon Trimble.

MATEO: Sweet Jesus.

LEE: Let's see: deep purplish contusions along the neck area, bruising on the hands and wrists, numerous violent hacks to the torso, a deep vertical gash one centimeter left of the sternum, with the heart violently taken out of its chamber.

MATEO: Please take them away.

LEE: Trauma throughout.

MATEO: I don't doubt it. I hope the poor girl died quick.

LEE: The poor girl's name is--

MATEO: I know her name! I seen the pictures! And I'm sorry, that was Evil, an altar for pure Evil, that poor body was not a body but a sacrament to hell!

LEE: When the maid found her, all her teen spirit had soaked the mattress. How's your lunch?

MATEO: Fine.

LEE: They never found her heart. Not a trace. Where'd you put it?

MATEO: Nowhere. I had nothin' to do with nothin'.

> (*LEE takes tools from the bag. Cutting shears. A small hatchet. A crude boxcutter. He ceremonially sets them on the ground before him.*)

LEE: Prima facie.

MATEO: God almighty.

LEE: Evidence rendered at first view.

MATEO: Where did you get those?

LEE: The hatchet and the boxcutter came from a woodworking shop. The cutting shears I bought at a hardware store. They're not the actual weapons you used but they never found those, either.

MATEO: *Madre Santa.*

LEE: Talismans of death, Mateo. These are for the science of pain.

> (*MATEO feels the tools with a mixture of awe and terror. He recalls.*)

MATEO: I was at *Los Tres Aces* drinking myself blue. Exchanging slurs with other drunks and losers. Trying to make the words out in those Patsy Cline songs on the jukebox. Funny how all the petty grievances you got with life just swarm all over you when you're fucked up on Wild Turkey. You think if you keep perfectly still hunched over the bar, they'll ignore you and overrun the poor slob in the Ryder cap next to you. But no. They smell the booze and the self-pity and press theirselves on you like nobody's business. So I left. I got in my pickup and drove.

LEE: Where to?

MATEO: I just drove. The last I recall was me trying to put the broken knob back on the radio. Next thing I know it's six in the morning and I'm standing naked on the shallow end of this icy pond off the Interstate. Shakin' all over like the palsy. The rest is public record.

LEE: You don't remember the hatchet? Or the other tools?

MATEO: I kept them in the toolbox in the bed of my truck. But I didn't use them, and toolbox got stole.

LEE: Shannon had had a fight with her boyfriend. She forced him to pull over and she jumped out of his car. Some truckers remembered seeing her bearing north just a mile from her parent's house.

> (From the surrounding dark,
> SHANNON strolls drunkenly on
> and stands in her own space.)

MATEO: It's always that close.

LEE: Did you see her, Mateo?

MATEO: No.

LEE: While you were reeling in the cab of your truck grumbling about the shitty hand life dealt you and the radio fulla static and the little knob in your hand, did you look up and see this beautiful young thing on the roadside?

313

(MATEO slowly turns and sees her standing in the cold.)

MATEO: Maybe I pulled over.

LEE: I woulda. I woulda eased to the shoulder and lowered the window on her side and said:

MATEO: Can I get you out of this cold, miss?

SHANNON: No thanks.

LEE: I wouldna taken no for an answer.

SHANNON: Why not?

MATEO: 'Cause, hell, I got some good dope in here that I don't know if I want to smoke all by myself.

SHANNON: I'm almost home, anyways. I should go on.

MATEO: I'll drive you to your boyfriend's and we'll all get high. We'll party up.

SHANNON: I don't think he wants me around right now.

MATEO: Whut? You mean he let you walk all alone at this time a night?

SHANNON: Kinda.

MATEO: Well, hell with him. C'mon. I'll take you home.

(She sits next to MATEO.)

LEE: Wasn't that the way it happened?

MATEO: What was her name?

SHANNON: Shannon.

MATEO: Are you as potted as I think you are, Shannon?

SHANNON: No, not really. Hey, that's my house you just passed.

LEE: Where did you take her, Mateo?

MATEO: Let's not go home right away. I'm really in need a company.

SHANNON: But I really have to get home.

MATEO: I'm really in need of some company, Shannon.

SHANNON: But I'm about to pee.

LEE: Did you take her to your motel room? Is that where you went?

MATEO: Right through that door. I'll get my stash and papers.

> *(They enter the motel room. SHANNON sprawls on the bed and watches.)*

LEE: While she went to the bathroom, did you go out to your truck? Did you get the tools? What grabbed at you so tightly that you had to use a hatchet to make it let go?

MATEO: I wasn't hardly there.

LEE: What did it feel like? Did it feel like the devil, Mateo?

MATEO: I was driving. Patsy Cline in my head. I fall to pieces. Road all pitch black and the headlights ahead making me blind. I was blind....!

LEE: Look at her, Mateo.

> (MATEO turns to SHANNON, smiling blithely at him. He studies her.)

MATEO: I'm looking for traces of him on you. For signs of his correction. Did he beat you? Did he whup you with plastic conduit too? Did he run his filthy mouth along the curve of your shoulder and the arc of your neck and the inside of your thigh? Like fathers do.

LEE: Who are you talking to? Is this Shannon Trimble?

MATEO: I'll take you away if you want. I know how he is. Will you come with me?

LEE: Who is this, Mateo?

SHANNON: *(turning to LEE)* Desire bereft of body.

MATEO: Nobody.

LEE: What does your old man have to do with her?

MATEO: Nothing. Shannon Trimble is nothing.

SHANNON: So where's this awesome dope?

MATEO: None of this happened. This is all in your head!

SHANNON: I could use a big ol' doobie to settle my stomach.

LEE: Tell me, Mateo!

SHANNON: Hey, hold on. Are you...are you crying?

LEE: MATEO!

> *(MATEO roars with rage and charges the girl. He stops. The hatchet suspended. He turns and plants the handle of the hatchet in LEE's hand.)*

MATEO: You do it.

(LEE looks at SHANNON, who sits up and smiles.)

MATEO: Look in her face. If you can't ruin that, then I never did!

(SHANNON stands and collects the tools and the 8x10s.)

SHANNON: Local Girl Found Murdered! Grisly Discovery in Motel Room! Drifter Arrested in Downey Slaying! Brutal Murder Shocks Residents!

(SHANNON takes the hatchet from LEE.)

Murder Weapon Found on Writer. Slain Girl's Smile Haunts Journalist. Search for Missing Heart Continues.

(SHANNON goes.)

MATEO: I loved her.

(MATEO goes. Lights change as LEE speaks into his recorder.)

LEE: All day restless all day trying to make sense of things see past the face of Shannon see that other face the face that loves him back not Shannon someone else inside her calling him to his evil. Who. Who. All day asking who till the sun peels back the sky to show me night.

(The motel room. DRU is lying on the bed, asleep.)

The motel. Dru in bed. Her own mystery.

(DRU lifts her head, in the spell of some dream. Her eyes open.)

DRU: I hear it.

LEE: What.

DRU: In my sleep. The heart.

LEE: Whose heart.

DRU: The girl.

LEE: In Mateo.

DRU: Beating against his chest. Beating to get out.

LEE: Does it get out?

DRU: He's lying on the roof of his house. Flat on his back. Naked.

LEE: His chest bared.

DRU: And it comes out. I see the Dewey lady with the Ginsu knife carve open his chest and pull it out.

LEE: Her daughter's heart. The Dewey heart.

DRU: No. No. Not her heart. Not his heart. Mine. I'm lying on my back looking at my own heart. Oh my god. Oh my god. LEE!

(LEE shakes her and she wakes with a start.)

LEE: It's a dream. A nightmare. None of it's real.

DRU: I still hear it beating.

LEE: It's nothing. The ceiling fan.

DRU: What's wrong with me?

LEE: Nothing. Listen. Do you remember the times we went out, the movies we saw, the talks we had in bed with the light out? Do you remember that?

DRU: Sure I do. Don't you?

LEE: Hardly. I remember it mostly like the details of someone else's life, but not mine. I remember wishing I could say I loved you.

DRU: You didn't. But you didn't have to. That wasn't the game.

LEE: I need you tonight, Dru. I can't be alone.

(LEE kisses her.)

DRU: Why are we here, Rosenblum?

LEE: To get the story.

DRU: Fuck that. Maybe we're the story.

LEE: I mean his story.

DRU: Then get it. I want to go home. Don't you want to go home?

> (*Crossfade to MATEO's house. MATEO enters with a tray carrying a bottle and a pair of shot glasses.*)

MATEO: Hell, we all want to go home.

LEE: What is it?

MATEO: Mescal. Some tribes in Mexico used it for the visions it produced. *Un tragito.*

> (*LEE reluctantly takes a glass. They raise the shots and then down them.*)

MATEO: I didn't make much hay with the other inmates in the Ward. Kept to myself, resisted friendship with the doctors 'cause what are they really after, am I right? These mornings, lately, I been getting up earlier than usual and moping around the house, waiting for you to come. You make me see things, now maybe I return the favor.

LEE: What do you want me to see?

(MATEO pauses for a moment. LEE turns on the tape.)

MATEO: Hot summers stealing pomegranates from the neighbor's yard as a kid. Riding my old bike around the school. Cotton fields thick enough to hide in. Can you see them?

LEE: Acres of them. And a Mexican accordion crackling out of some old radio somewhere. Those dangling clumps of red *chiles* on the porch...

MATEO: *(as he pours another set of shots)* Ristras.

LEE: And sitting at the window in Yosemite Sam pajamas watching the dust devils outside.

(They down the next round.)

MATEO: There's a cigar box under my bed filled with mementos, little matchbox car, a couple marbles, a picture of my mom, and this crystal from Carlsbad Caverns...

LEE: I remember Carlsbad Caverns. We all went to Carlsbad Caverns. We all peed in Carlsbad Caverns.

MATEO: *(as he pours another set)* Oh hell, sure we did, after all the Fanta Orange Cola we drank on the way, what'd ya expect?

LEE: Here's to pissin' in the Cavern!

LEE/MATEO: Pissing in the Cavern!

> *(They toast and drink and laugh awhile. MATEO pours another set.)*

MATEO: Different generations, you and me, but the things we did in this town don't change.

LEE: I wonder how I ended up the way I am. How quickly those dust devils swept me up and took me east. If I'd stayed here, chances are I'd probably live out the pattern of my old man's life.

> *(LEE pours another round.)*

MATEO: *Watch-ale.* You gettin' to the worm.

LEE: It's just like sushi, man. *(They drink.)* You know, in love you can't harbor secrets, you can't hold anything back, not if it's real, not if you really expect to share your lives. That's what love is, and I don't know if I ever knew that, but this girl, she doesn't give up...I could be messing up her life while she makes me feel a little like... shit... what was I saying?

MATEO: That a little love justifies the blazes of hell.

LEE: That's not what I was saying.

MATEO: It's what you meant. You ain't the only one with a sister gone.

LEE: Wait. Wait. You? (*MATEO shakes his head.*) You have a sister, Mateo?

> (*MATEO gets up to make sure they're alone.*)

MATEO: My mother doesn't know.

LEE: What are you talking about?

MATEO: Keep your voice down! My father had another woman, *en Mexico.* He was gone for weeks, nobody knew where. If Ama asked, he answered her with silence. But one day I said to myself...

LEE: Follow the fucker.

MATEO: We can't talk anymore about this. *No mas.*

LEE: Mateo, you have to tell me--

MATEO: My mother, goddammit!

LEE: You mention that you got a half-sister living in Mexico for the first time, it's not in any of the court transcripts, it's not mentioned anywhere!

MATEO: It ain't relevant!

LEE: I want to get to the truth, Mateo, but you gotta help me.

> *(A dare is exchanged. LEE drinks the worm. A threshold is crossed.)*

MATEO: Belen. I stole me a car and followed him across the border. To a dusty pueblo called Belen.

LEE: And you saw her.

MATEO: The other woman was older, poorer. But he seemed to treat her better than he treated my mom.

LEE: And he had a daughter.

MATEO: *Toda mi pinche vida*, I felt her presence. In everything I did, a craving for someone. On those rough nights, sitting in my room alone, I used to imagine holding her. My secret sister.

> *(SONIA steps into the light carrying a large bundle. A young dark beautiful girl of 16 with black hair, dressed in a simple cotton dress. She sets her bundle down, unwraps it and starts to display various folk dresses on the sacking. LEE does not see her.)*

LEE: She was living under the same roof with that bastard, wasn't she?

MATEO: Over the next couple weeks, I made some trips down. I studied her. The more I watched her, the more I learned about myself. Innocence, love, shit beaten out of me long ago. Unbearable, yes, but it was hope. Only now...

LEE: He was there.

MATEO: Only a matter of time. I had to get her away.

LEE: So you went to her. You told her who you were.

MATEO: No...It was she who came to me.

SONIA: (*hardly looking up to see them*) *Oye joven. ¿Que haces aqui en el sol? Ya te apareces como un Hershey.*

(*LEE turns and sees her.*)

LEE: Oh my god...

SONIA: *¿Sabes lo que te digo?*

MATEO: Like you, I was struck dumb.

SONIA: What's the matter? You want me to talk English?

MATEO: She's waiting.

(LEE slowly walks toward her and he is transported to an ancient village plaza, blazing with sun. He seems younger in this space.)

LEE: Yes.

SONIA: Okay. Why you wanna look like a Hershey? Move to the shade. There's lots of shade in Belen.

MATEO: I freeze up with a kind of terror I never felt before.

LEE: I like it here. I wanna get browner.

SONIA: *Americano.* What are you doing?

LEE: What do you mean?

SONIA: I seen you. Sitting in the car across the street. Walking around the *Ayuntamiento. La tienda.* Sitting here in the *zócalo.* Like a Hershey.

LEE: So?

SONIA: So you're spying on me.

LEE: I'm not spying on you.

SONIA: Then what are you doing in Belen?

LEE: What do I say?

MATEO: You're waiting for a friend.

SONIA: Who's this friend?

LEE: No-one you know. He's coming up from *la Capital* and we're going to take off to California.

SONIA: Big Hershey lies. Help me with these.

> (*LEE helps her unpack and spread across the floor several long beautiful skirts of brilliant colors. Lacey frills. Colorful folk embroidery.*)

SONIA: Right about now all the *turistas* are suppose to come out of the *mesónes* into the square. To buy their colorful *curios* and gifts to take back across. Look around. You see any *turistas*?

LEE: No.

SONIA: I see one.

MATEO: Look at the dresses, fool.

LEE: They're beautiful.

SONIA: *Ama y yo*, we make them in our house. The fabric comes from Jalisco but the embroidery is all ours. The lace here. I did that.

LEE: It's very nice.

SONIA: All by hand. Those little purple roses are not easy.

LEE: Have you been doing this for a long time?

SONIA: Long enough. Just sewing for one night is a long time.

LEE: Do you have one of your own?

SONIA: Me? What good is a dress like this to me? Where am I going to go wearing these *rositas*? It's very poor in this *pueblo, chavo*. I don't want to look haughty.

LEE: I think you'd look like a princess.

SONIA: Okay. Who are you? Why are you following me?

LEE: My name is... Mateo. I'm from El Paso. I didn't mean to scare you.

SONIA: I'm not scared. It's just been a while since a boy took any notice. In so obvious a way, I mean.

LEE: Was I obvious?

SONIA: *¡Chale!* Sometimes it's like I don't even have to look up. I can feel your eyes all over me. I catch myself doing things. Like stretching in front of the window. Wearing my good shoes to the store. Stealing Ama's make-up.

(LEE looks down in embarrassment.)

SONIA: The way these tourists haggle. I better lower prices to half.

> *(She turns the sign around. Price cut to half.)*

MATEO: Sitting in the sun, with the mockingbirds' squawk above the empty square and a few bees drunk on nectar buzzing over the dresses, I form a word out of the urge to cry.

LEE: Sonia.

SONIA: How do you know my name?

MATEO: How…?

LEE: Sonia, do you miss having someone to share secrets with? Someone you don't even have to talk, you know he feels what you feel--

MATEO: He senses things inside you--

LEE: --he lives that other part of you.

SONIA: I don't know if I understand…

LEE: Look. One dress is so different from the other. The sleeves are different--

MATEO: --the embroidery--

LEE: --the patterns. But they share the same material.

MATEO: The same fabric--

LEE: --They breathe the same.

SONIA: They do.

LEE: I breathe the same. You and I. The same air. Am I wrong? Don't you feel it?

SONIA: Like this?

(She kisses him.)

LEE: No. No. Sonia. No.

SONIA: *¿Que pasa? ¿Que no te gustó?*

LEE: Yes, I liked it but...

MATEO: This is what evil means.

(LEE walks away, leaving her alone with her dresses, still in the memory.)

LEE: You feel like a traitor to your own best cause. All your itinerant heroism turns to shit. You like it. You like her tongue in your mouth. You realize all along, this girl you're stalking, you're compromising her soul.

MATEO: I wasn't stalking her. *(to SONIA)* Was I?

(SONIA gathers her wares and vanishes into the blackness. AMA returns.)

Wasn't I just following little roses on a dress?

AMA: I have the water running in the bath.

(He goes. AMA gives LEE a look. He is still in a daze.)

AMA: Call before you come over. He sleeps in on Wednesdays.

LEE: *Sra.* Buenaventura, would you be open to some questions? Off the record?

AMA: Mateo says nothing we say is off the record. So nothing we say.

(They exchange a look and she goes. MRS. DEWEY appears on the front lawn.)

MRS. DEWEY: Here he comes. The left hand of death. What excuse does the monster give you now, Mr. Rosenblum?

LEE: Stay away from my photographer, Mrs. Dewey.

(LEE moves on.)

MRS. DEWEY: You feel compassion for him already, don't you? Don't you?

LEE: You don't know him. You don't know anything but your own pain. His story is deeper than your pain.

MRS. DEWEY: Will you follow it then? Will you follow the deed to its bed of straw, its first breath, its suckle of human blood? Will you draw from the same swollen tit?

LEE: The days of gods and devils are long gone, Mrs. Dewey. And you're beginning to realize that. Or your prayers might have been answered by now.

> (LEE goes. MRS. DEWEY cries
> after him.)

MRS. DEWEY: He'll answer them! He will! But He moves according to his own time! Isn't that right, Lord! Ain't it so, Father! *(singing)* He Keeps his Promises!... *(She stops and then lets the doubts wash over her.)* Why dost thou stand afar off? Why dost thou hide thyself in my time of trouble? Answer me, Lord... speak to me, Lord...

> (She goes in a cloud of doubt. The
> motel room. DRU enters.)

DRU: Lee?

*(She sees the laptop near the bed. She
opens it and turns it on. She starts
up the program on the computer.
LEE enters, startling her.)*

LEE: What are you doing?

DRU: I was hoping to read what you've
written so far--

LEE: Turn it off.

DRU: C'mon, I need to know what angle
you're taking on him.

LEE: Sorry, Dru. That material is confidential,
between me and him, noone else.

*(He shuts the laptop off and tucks it
under the bed.)*

DRU: Are you forgetting this confidential
material is going in a magazine?

LEE: I don't care what happens after I turn it
in. Till then, hands off.

DRU: What is it with you?

LEE: I told you, Dru. Professional distance. I
think I need some time by myself tonight,
okay?

DRU: Jesus, Lee.

LEE: No, Dru, I'm sorry. We can't do this.

DRU: What's going on?

LEE: I need my key back.

DRU: Why are you being like this? This isn't you.

(No response.)

DRU: It's him, isn't it? What's he telling you? What are you telling him? Oh no. You haven't told him about us, have you? Have you?

LEE: I know what I'm doing.

DRU: I'm not so sure.

LEE: He's just a story, Dru. The key.

DRU: (tossing him the key) Fuck! I'm still getting my shoot.

> (DRU turns and starts setting lighting equipment, tripods, etc. in MATEO's house as SHANNON enters, taking out some bloodied pictures.)

SHANNON: Here's pictures of me and my brothers that we took at Ruidoso. Snow all around and them laughing. That's Sal. And big brother Brent trying on his new skis. My daddy never smiles 'cause of his teeth. But Momma always looks like a movie star. And here's me. Making a snow angel.

(She shows a photo of her reddened corpse sprawled on a white sheet.)

BARRY: (OFF) SHANNON!!!

(SHANNON goes. DRU checks her equipment. LEE preps his recorder.)

LEE: Remember, do what you normally do, let me handle the chitchat, play it cool and he'll be cool.

DRU: I know what I'm doing, too, Rosenblum.

(DRU plugs in a cord. Lights come on.)

LEE: Dru… last night I wasn't myself, I was--

DRU: Forget it. Just let's get this done so I can beat the hell out of here.

(MATEO enters with his glass of whiskey.)

LEE: Mateo, buenos dias. This is the shooter I told you about. Ms. Suffolk.

(As MATEO turns to see her, she snaps a Polaroid of him.)

DRU: Call me Dru. Hope you don't mind all this gear.

MATEO: *(eyeing her warily)* No, I don't mind…

DRU: Promise, I won't break anything. Give me a minute to get all plugged in.

LEE: The way this thing'll go is you sit there and we'll talk like usual, and she'll work around us. Just be natural, she'll find the best shots.

MATEO: *Está bien.*

> *(MATEO sits.)*

LEE: Is something on your mind?

MATEO: No.

LEE: Are you sure? What's up?

MATEO: Nothing.

> *(Lights flood the area, forcing MATEO to cover his face.)*

DRU: Sorry!

MATEO: Do we really need all these lights?

DRU: Won't know till I get a light reading.

LEE: Your eyes will get used to it. Just relax. I need my recorder.

(He goes and whispers to DRU as MATEO uncomfortably takes his seat.)

LEE: Jesus Christ, Dru. What the hell are you doing?

DRU: You don't hear it? That beating?

LEE: Hear what? What are you talking about?

DRU: Forget it. Just stay outa my way.

MATEO: Is something the matter?

LEE: No. Buenaventura Tape 14. 9 am. Photo session. Testing, testing...

MATEO: She seems tense.

LEE: She's not. She's a pro.

(DRU comes right up to him with a light meter.)

DRU: Shit. I'm barely getting a reading. Can you move your hand, sir?

(MATEO lowers the hand from his face.)

You eat up a lotta light, Mr. Buenaventura.

(She adjusts a lamp and takes another reading.)

LEE: So what do you want people to think when they read this article about you?

MATEO: They can think what they like.

LEE: What if they still think you're guilty of that crime?

MATEO: Then you haven't done your job.

> *(DRU starts snapping MATEO with her Nikon.)*

DRU: Don't mind me.

LEE: This is what we mean by candid. This is how she works. Right, Dru?

DRU: Move out of the frame, Rosenblum.

> *(DRU proceeds to snap a series.)*

MATEO: Does she have to get that close?

LEE: Dru?

DRU: Nice.

MATEO: I ain't accustomed to people being in my face.

DRU: Eyes here. Chin up. Good. Good.

MATEO: Especially members of the opposing sex.

DRU: Don't move. Excellent. Nice. Good.

MATEO: Are we done?

LEE: I think we're done.

DRU: Wait. One more thing. May we unbutton the shirt?

MATEO: My shirt?

DRU: Right. Could we open it up, please?

MATEO: What for.

LEE: Dru, is this appropriate?

DRU: I got a little more left on the roll. If we could just get the shirt open. Please.

MATEO: You didn't mention this.

LEE: You don't have to do it.

> (MATEO unbuttons his shirt. A
> long ugly scar down the middle of
> his chest is exposed.)

DRU: Like that. Like that. Hold it open. Beautiful.

> (She starts snapping.)

MATEO: You like this?

DRU: Yes sir. It's lovely.

MATEO: A real sight to behold?

DRU: Oh yeah, really something.

MATEO: You want me to touch it? You want me to lay my hand on it?

DRU: Sure.

> (He does. She continues snapping away.)

LEE: I think that's enough, Dru.

MATEO: I got this from an operation.

DRU: Yes, I know.

MATEO: A heart transplant.

DRU: I know.

LEE: Dru, back off.

MATEO: I got a young lady's ticker inside me.

DRU: Uh-huh.

MATEO: Sometimes it talks to me, you know? It does. It says things.

DRU: I bet it does.

LEE: Stop it.

MATEO: It's saying something now. You wanna know what it's saying?

DRU: What is it saying?

MATEO: It's sayin'…. *(suddenly grabbing DRU by the throat.)* MAKE SURE YOUR FACE IS THE LAST GODDAMN THING THIS BITCH EVER SEES!

LEE: MATEO! NO!

MATEO: FUCKING CAMERA! FUCKING BITCH WITH HER FUCKING LIGHTS!

DRU: Okay…

LEE: Let her go…

MATEO: *¡Ya me cansé de tus pendejadas, pinchi puta cabrona!*

> *(He turns her camera toward her face and snaps the shutter.)*

LEE: Okay, Mateo! Cut the bullshit, okay, okay?

> *(He releases her. DRU sinks to the floor, gagging and gasping for air.)*

MATEO: Photo session over. Get this cow out of my house.

(MATEO rips the cords out of the wall. The lights go out. DRU gets up. As she goes, she turns and aims her camera.)

DRU: Hey, asshole.

(MATEO turns. She snaps one and staggers out. He starts after her in a fury then turns to LEE.)

MATEO: What is this! Did you tell that cunt about my operation!

LEE: I'm sorry, okay! Jesus! Calm down!

MATEO: What was that damn thing she kept putting against me? Was that some radar thing or what?

LEE: It's a light meter! She needs it for her f-stops.

MATEO: What the hell are f-stops?

LEE: F-stops are.... shit, I don't know! It has to do with the camera!

MATEO: We're done. Give me that tape. *(LEE hands over the tape from his deck.)* This heart was given me fair and square. If you think I ain't thankful, you're wrong. But it's my life now. I don't owe a thing to nobody.

LEE: Mrs. Dewey think you're evidence of the Devil.

MATEO: Dewey out there can KISS MY HAIRY BROWN ASS! YOU WANT IT, LADY, YOU WANT IT BACK, GO AHEAD, TAKE IT!

(MATEO rips off his shirt, baring his scar to the world.)

MATEO: RIP IT OUT OF MY FUCKING CHEST! I DON'T GIVE A SHIT! THINK I NEED YOUR GODDAMN CHARITY TO LIVE, THINK AGAIN! TAKE BACK THE DAMN HEART AND GET THE HELL OFF MY BACK! PUSSY, THAT'S WHAT YOU ARE! A PUSSY!

(MATEO falls to his knees in exhaustion. LEE keeps still.)

MATEO: I don't know about the Devil, but I got evidence of God. Coming out of the operation, I saw my ticker in this pan beside me. Really pathetic ruined looking sorta thing. I got this sudden perverted impulse to touch it. Don't know why. Maybe to be sure it was real. I reached across and sank my finger into it. It felt like meat.

LEE: Please. We're close. I can feel her. Sonia.

(MATEO sits up and begins his story. The lights change.)

MATEO: She waits outside the door of her house at night.

(SONIA enters into the light, cutting a sharp silhouette. She is quietly but ardently searching.)

MATEO: Looking for me. Standing like a cut-out with the porch light behind her. Three nights in a row, I sit out there under an old mesquite and wonder how that paper doll shape would feel against me. During the day, I sleep in this run-down *Plaza de Toros* closed for the season. But the nights I sit awake watching her, trying desperately to strip away the parts that are not my sister.

(SONIA calls softly for him.)

SONIA: Mateo...

MATEO: Summons me on the third night.

SONIA: Mateo...

MATEO: She knows I'm there. She knows I will come.

SONIA: Mateo...

*(LEE moves irresistibly toward her.
She offers an old blanket.)*

SONIA: I brought you this for the cold.

LEE : I'm not cold.

SONIA: We can sit here and talk for a while.
They're asleep. *Sientate.*

> *(LEE spreads the blanket for her and
> they sit.)*

SONIA: You're a strange boy. You go away but
you don't go away.

LEE: Quit calling me boy. I'm older than you
think.

SONIA: You feel so familiar. Like I've met you
before. Why did you turn away when I kissed
you?

LEE: I wasn't expecting it. Girls in Mexico, I
heard you move fast.

SONIA: We just like to pick our fruit early.

LEE: What do your parents say about this?

SONIA: *Pos, mi amá es muy estricta.* She thinks
I'm too young to see boys. Still, she likes to sit
in the *placita* and watch the courting rituals
with me.

LEE: What's your father like?

SONIA: He's there. Except when he's not. He works in *Tejas*. *Apa*'s a very serious man. Always a lot of things on his mind. He drinks.

LEE: How is he... with you?

SONIA: He loves me. In a world of black and white, I'm the only one he sees in color, so he says. He's gone a lot, but every time he comes home, he brings me bolts of fabric from *el Norte.* The best Pima cotton. What's your father like?

LEE: Very different. In his world of color, I'm the only black and white.

SONIA: Is he mean to you?

LEE: Mean I prefer to indifferent. My father also goes away for long stretches.

SONIA: Do you know where?

LEE: No.

SONIA: We live such different lives. How can we be so alike?

> (*They kiss. SONIA rises and takes his hand.*)

LEE: No, Sonia.

347

SONIA: In your car. No-one will know. What's wrong?

LEE: I want you so much.

SONIA: Is that bad?

LEE: Yes.

SONIA: Then I don't care.

> (*LEE rises as SONIA disappears into the darkness.*)

MATEO: In the back seat of that old car. Stricken with something we thought would kill us. Stuck together like dragonflies.

LEE: Is this it? Is this where it starts?

MATEO: You tell me.

LEE: This is your story, Mateo.

MATEO: You so fuckin' interested, why don't you finish it?

> (*He drops the tapes in his whiskey glass and goes. LEE slowly retrieves the tape from the whiskey glass and plays it back on his recorder.*)

LEE: Sonia... (*Nothing.*) Sonia...

> (*Silence. Then...on the recorder...*)

SONIA'S VOICE: *Aqui... aqui te espero, mi amor...*

LEE: Sonia...

SONIA'S VOICE: *Aqui...*

> *(LEE turns and sees her rise out of the dark.)*

SONIA: The same air, you said. Right from each other's lips.

> *(LEE goes to her and kisses her.)*

LEE: In me I feel your heart.

SONIA: And yours beats in me.

> *(They kiss. MATEO appears. LEE and SONIA begin making love. Over them, the presence of the masked MEDICAL EXAMINER, who may be played by DRU. Over the following sequence, SONIA slips out of being and LEE plays out the perverse fantasy alone.)*

MATEO: She's mine. My secret now. I kiss her face.

MEDICAL EXAMINER: Massive swelling of the tongue due to strangulation.

MATEO: I kiss her neck.

MEDICAL EXAMINER: Singular purplish contusions circling the upper neck.

MATEO: I run my tongue like a razor along the seam of her skin.

MEDICAL EXAMINER: Deep incisions from the base of the xiphoid process of the sternum to the base of the neck.

MATEO: I kiss her lovely breasts.

MEDICAL EXAMINER: Lateral incision across the upper chest cavity.

LEE: Oh god....

MATEO: I draw myself inside her.

MEDICAL EXAMINER: Severe damage to the chest plate and rib cage.

MATEO: Tear through the membrane of her sex.

MEDICAL EXAMINER: Massive tearing of the pericardial sac.

LEE: No! Please!

MRS. DEWEY/DRU: Massive blood loss.

MATEO: She is mine!

MEDICAL EXAMINER: Pulmonary artery transected.

LEE: Sonia...!

MATEO: *¡Alma mia!*

MEDICAL EXAMINER: Heart dislodged from abdomen.

SONIA's VOICE: *¡Leandro!*

> *(LEE achieves climax and remains suspended in his ecstasy.)*

MEDICAL EXAMINER: Traces of semen detected in the uterine canal and throughout the vaginal area.

> *(Lights go to black. A single light reveals SHANNON, her throat blue, her torso a gaping bloody mess. She smiles at LEE through bloodied teeth.)*

SHANNON: So... where's that doobie you were gonna roll us, lonely boy?

> *Tableau. Blackout.*

End of Act One.

Act Two

> *(The arid desert explodes into view.*
> *Heat and creosote. DRU enters,*
> *gagging fiercely.)*

DRU: Air. Air.

I come out of that house with his hand still on
my throat. His fingers sorting through the
scraps of my breath, scream, wail, gasp. Fuck.

I toss my guts at the curb. What was I
thinking? Why did I fall apart like that?

> *(MRS. DEWEY enters and stands*
> *apart.)*

DRU: I see her. Seeing me. Giving me this look.

MRS. DEWEY: Like the Rapture's nigh but not
for me.

DRU: I should go back and pack my camera
and take the first flight back to New York. I
should resign this assignment and forget this
woman and you and that noxious prick. But
I'm groping for air and following her.

MRS. DEWEY: Walking.

DRU: Three shadow-lengths behind.

MRS. DEWEY: Then the bus.

DRU: Which takes us to the farthest stop out of town and into the desert we go and even though she never once looks back--

MRS. DEWEY: You're there.

DRU: We stand in the crazy heat among the sage and creosote. Holding my Nikon like a lung. For what seems like hours. Then...

>   (MRS. DEWEY crumbles to her
>   knees and sobs openly.)

MRS. DEWEY: LIAR! YOU LIAR! Call yourself a just God! But you're nothing but a LIE! YOU LIE!

DRU: Mrs. Dewey ...please...

MRS. DEWEY: He told me he would punish that demon! Look at what that monster's done to you! He'll kill you next time!

DRU: I won't let him. Please stop.

MRS. DEWEY: I abjure you! I *renounce* you on this day! *OHH!(collapsing)* My baby... I want my baby back. Chelsea...

>   (DRU strips her camera off and
>   rushes to MRS. DEWEY, who
>   collapses in tears on the ground.
>   They hold each other and weep)

DRU: Okay. I'm here… I'm here.

MRS. DEWEY: Chelsea…

DRU: I know, Miranda, I'm very sorry…

MRS. DEWEY: Oh god. How long since I heard that spoke.

DRU: What?

MRS. DEWEY: My name. Miranda. All the things I made forfeit in my life. The man I was married to for twenty years. The Girl Scout cookies every year. The PTA meetings. All gone since Chelsea.

DRU: She must have been really something.

MRS. DEWEY: Oh she was nothing special. Girl wouldn't do her homework, always boys boys boys, and I had to ground her a few times. But that just meant she was in the house laughing. We played with our little dog Patsy that she adored as all get-out. All her children's books piled up in my closet that I was saving for her children. Reading to her at night, kisses on her cheek, night-night rituals of mom and girl.

DRU: God, I wish I'd had someone like you growing up.

MRS. DEWEY: All forfeit now. That life is a mystery to me.

DRU: It's still your life. You have so much to cherish. What do I have? What good is my life? What am I living for? When that animal grabbed my throat, all I could think was I can't die yet. I haven't loved yet. Jesus, I have to fall in love once before I die.

(MRS. DEWEY rises to her feet.)

MRS. DEWEY: If you care for Mr. Rosenblum, take him away from here. Mateo is infecting him. You're his only hope. For some of us, the past is past and there's no recourse but wrath.

(MRS. DEWEY leaves.)

DRU: I turn around and head back to the main road and catch the bus, and sit as it takes the long route home. Every step I take to this motel, I tell myself I won't come to your room. I won't tell you. You won't listen, anyway, right?

(LEE appears in his room.)

Right?

LEE: I would never have let you do this if I knew you'd be in danger.

DRU: My question to you is what do you plan to do.

LEE: I'm going to finish the interview.

DRU: About us, Lee. What are you going to do about us?

LEE: Jesus, Dru...

DRU: I thought we had a chance. That last night I felt a part of you so brittle, so in need of mercy, you held me like you needed me...

LEE: Oh god, don't--

DRU: YOU NEEDED ME! I'm gonna level with you, Rosenblum. At the shoot, I thought it was his heart I was hearing. But it was mine. My heart. I'm really hearing it for the first time.

LEE: I have to work on the story now.

DRU: What story, Lee? What fucking story? I've seen your laptop. There's not a single word written anywhere in there! Just a title.

LEE: You had no right--

DRU: **Mateo Buenaventura**! That's all that you've written! Nothing but his name!

LEE: What do you want from me!

DRU: You! I want you! I want us to fall in love. We're like savages. Living day to day. Eating other people's lives. It's not enough for me anymore. I don't give a shit about the story or the magazine or Larsen! I want to see the real you.

LEE: I'M LEE ROSENBLUM! THAT'S ALL! THERE'S NOTHING INSIDE! NO SECRETS! NO SURPRISES! JUST LEE ROSENBLUM!

DRU: And I'm gone.

(DRU *turns to go.*)

LEE: You're leaving?

DRU: The first bird to New York. You want pictures, take them yourself. You wanna stick with this brute, knock yourself out. Frankly, you make a great couple.

LEE: Dru…

(DRU *goes.*)

I'll do it myself then.

(MRS. DEWEY *enters.*)

MRS. DEWEY: Will you?

LEE: Ma'am, I told you once, please leave my photographer in peace.

MRS. DEWEY: It wasn't me who hurt her.

LEE: Lady, I'm really sorry about your daughter, I'm sorry he had to have her heart to live, and I'm sorry for Shannon Trimble too. But you can't be playing God whenever you feel like it.

MRS. DEWEY: *(taking a large kitchen knife out of her bag)* Not even when God deserts us?

LEE: I'm not getting into this.

> *(He starts to walk away, then stops and turns.)*

Give me the knife.

MRS. DEWEY: Is that why that devil is still alive and my Chelsea dead? Would more faith ever change that? Or is it up to us make things right?

LEE: Hand over the knife, Mrs. Dewey.

MRS. DEWEY: I can't!

LEE: You're not going through with this. Nothing is going to happen to him.

MRS. DEWEY: Why are you protecting him? I don't understand.

LEE: I'm protecting you.

MRS. DEWEY: Listen to your Dru. She loves you. Get away from this man.

LEE: I can't.

MRS. DEWEY: How can you go there? How can you choose him over her?

LEE: Give me the knife, Mrs. Dewey.

MRS. DEWEY: She made me see. She made me see who I was, what I sacrificed to believe in the Lord, in justice and righteousness, and now what? When it all fails, what is there left to believe in?

LEE: Maybe the only thing we believe in is Buenaventura.

(*LEE takes the knife from her.*)

MRS. DEWEY: I am in such pain....

LEE: Go home. I'll take care of him.

(*MRS. DEWEY goes, moaning loudly, almost reaching song. MATEO enters with his bottle of whiskey.*)

MATEO: A little Turkey? (*LEE shakes his head.*) She's pretty agitated out there. Baying like *la llorona*. Gnawing on her tongue. That kinda restlessness breeds murder.

LEE: How would you know?

MATEO: What?

LEE: What do you know about murder? You haven't killed anyone.

MATEO: I've wanted to. Haven't you?

(LEE drops the knife on the table.)

MATEO: I'm gonna file a restraining order on that cow. How's your lady friend?

LEE: Don't talk about her.

MATEO: I hope I didn't hurt her.

LEE: Don't talk about her.

MATEO: She's a beautiful woman.

LEE: I'm not going to tell you again.

MATEO: What happened? Did you and the purty lady have a falling out?

LEE: It's none of your business.

MATEO: I kinda had a sense about that, you know. I got a nose for that kinda thing.

LEE: What are you talking about?

MATEO: Well, you know, don't you?

LEE: What?

MATEO: You don't know?

LEE: You're fulla shit.

MATEO: You're so goddamn smart, I figured you'da put *dos y dos* together by now.

LEE: What?

MATEO: She loves you.

LEE: You're outta your mind.

MATEO: She loves you but now she's packing her bags and heading off for greener enchiladas.

 LEE: You're such a sham, it's incredible.

MATEO: It's all right. It's in the service of our story. I don't know why, I don't know how, but I do believe your Dru is here for a reason. I do believe that, at some cost to her soul and yours, she's gonna get you the cover.

LEE: Where do you come up with this?

MATEO: Where else? Belen.

LEE: What did you do with Sonia? Did you rape her? Did you kill her? Did you cut her open like Shannon Trimble? Did you tell her you were her brother?

MATEO: I hate to bust your chops, but shit's already come down, *carnal*.

LEE: I want to loathe you, Mateo Buenaventura, I want to be morally repulsed by you. But all I feel is pity. I pity your sorry ass. I wish I knew why.

MATEO: Come to Belen. You'll see why. Come.

> *(LEE resists for a moment, then turns around and calls in desperation.)*

LEE: Sonia! Sonia!

MATEO: Waiting in the bullring. All night. Still musky with sex. Still reeling with love. Sisters are the sweetest fruits.

LEE: SONIA!

> *(SONIA darts out of the dark into his arms, clasping him tightly. She wears the white dress with the little roses.)*

MATEO: The sweetest.

LEE: Oh god!

SONIA: I'm sorry, I'm sorry! I came as quick as I could!

LEE: I was afraid...I thought something had happened.

SONIA: What? Nothing happens in this *pueblito*.

LEE: What are you wearing? Is this the same one from the *zocalo*?

SONIA: Do you like it? Do I look like a princess? That's what you said.

LEE: Yes.

SONIA: Finally, someone to wear it for.

(*They kiss.*)

MATEO: Last night I was terrified. I didn't know I could be like that.

SONIA: Me neither. It's like there's this other person that comes out. Who is this? Is this me? Are these my hands? My legs? How do they know what to do? How does that place know how to love?

LEE: It's crazy. I hardly remember what happened. I could have done anything to you and not known. I felt so out of time, so blind. Even after you left, there was this...this--

MATEO: Violence.

SONIA: What do you mean?

LEE: I was losing control, losing myself, it was like being in pain.

MATEO: Causin' it.

SONIA: I would never hurt you, lonely boy.

LEE: What did you call me?

SONIA: Lonely boy.

MATEO: She'd learned that phrase from an American song. Some damn pop tune that poked fun at heartbreak.

LEE: Sonia.

SONIA: Yes.

LEE: I want you to come with me.

SONIA: Come with you? Where?

LEE: Away from this. Back to the States. We can go anywhere. Right now.

SONIA: Now? *¿Estás loco o que?* I can't just take off like that.

MATEO: Don't let her get away!

LEE: Come with me. We'll get you some clothes in El Paso. Hurry.

SONIA: What about *mis papás*?

LEE: Forget them. It's just you and me from now on. *Vente conmigo,* Sonia.

SONIA: I can't. I'm still in school. My mother needs me. My father.

MATEO/LEE: FUCK HIM!

LEE: You don't need that bastard! You don't need to put up with his shit anymore!

SONIA: What are you talking about?

LEE: Poor Sonia. All this time, all those nights, dealing with him. Son of a bitch! He won't get you now.

SONIA: *¿Que dices?*

LEE: I came to save you. Don't you get it? I came to take you away from that fuck. I know what he'll do to you! I know his ways, Sonia!

SONIA: You're crazy!

LEE: He'll come into your room! He'll think he's entitled. You won't be able to stop him! I know!

SONIA: How! How do you come by this filth!

MATEO: Yes. How.

LEE: *Ven*, Sonia. Before he ruins you.

> (*LEE holds his hand out to her.*)

SONIA: I don't know who you're talking about. My father is good.

LEE: No.

SONIA: He brings me presents and fine Pima cotton, he adores me--

LEE: No...

SONIA: I can't. I can't go. *Lo siento.*

> (*Pause. MATEO calls in a booming voice we recognize as BARRY's.*)

MATEO: (*as the father*) *¡Sonia!*

SONIA: *¡SI, PAPI!*

LEE: I see. I see. You fucking whore. *Puta.* He's already had you.

SONIA: *No lo digas.*

LEE: Go on. Go to him. You want to stay with him, stay with him. GO YOU SLUT!

SONIA: *¡Leandro, no!*

LEE: Jesus, I should have known! You're his *puta*, the *puta* of Belen, La *Puta* Sonia What a laugh! I come to rescue a whore!

SONIA: Why am I listening to these lies!

LEE: *¡Gracias por todo, Puta de Belen!* Go to that pimp of yours and tell him Leandro Buenaventura appreciates the time with his...the time with his own...

       (LEE collapses in tears.)

SONIA: Who are you?

LEE: *¡VETE! ¡LARGATE DE AQUI! SONIA, POR FAVOR!*

SONIA: *No...Dios Mio....no puede ser...*

LEE: GET FUCKING LOST! BITCH! YOU BITCH! GO BACK TO MY FATHER! LET HIM GIVE IT TO YOU! WHORE!

       (SONIA runs in horror. LEE
       collapses, asphyxiated on his own
       sobs.)

MATEO: This is it. Where all things rise from, all sin and redemption, all pain and *pinche* delight, this seed, this cradle, this bethlehem, this town in heat. Your black hole. Sucking up the hopes of the sickest most contemptible sonofabitch of all: you.

*(MATEO takes the weeping LEE
into his arms.)*

MATEO: All the blindness of before, the blank
spaces, the check-out times, they were echoes
of this, the biggest blank, the lapse in time
spent with this little whore!

(MATEO raises LEE's face to his.)

MATEO: And the gall! The gall of the girl to
prefer him to you! You! What you sacrificed!
What you exposed! The heart, Sonia, took its
disbelief and made it faith for you, for you,
sister, lover, whore, devil! You could have
saved her, but she went with him and made
you nothing! Nothing, boy! The whole time
you were with her, you might as well have
been with yer old man! You know whut I
mean? Do you, Leandro?

LEE : I DO!

MATEO: Before what was in your soul could
find its way to her throat, you run. You run to
the car, then drive out of Belen, into the desert,
it don't matter where.

But she ain't gone, boy. She's here, in this
chest, beating like a crazy bell. You want her?
You wanna tell her what's really on your
mind? If you feel what I feel, and I think you
do, you'll go for it. You'll open me up and find

368

her! *Dale, Leandro!* TAKE THE GODDAMN
HEART, YOU WORM!

> *(LEE charges MATEO and slams his
> open hand into his chest repeatedly.
> Finally, he feels the long ugly scar on
> his chest and kisses it. He collapses
> in tears as MATEO leaves. Silence
> as Night descends. Then MRS.
> DEWEY enters separately, finds a
> place to set down and open her
> shrine.)*

MRS. DEWEY: Lord, I offer up this wretched
life to you. *(taking a small knife from her shrine)*
Make Chelsea see the great sin it is to die this
way, but greater yet to live so bitter.

> *(She places the blade against her
> throat and tries to slash it, but she
> cannot. MATEO enters with the
> duffel bag of tools and starts to cross
> past her. They see each other.)*

MRS. DEWEY: Devil. *(He pauses, then continues.
She stands in his way.)* Devil.

MATEO: Move outa my way, lady.

MRS. DEWEY: I'm not scared of you. Skulking
out the back way, like a tapeworm.

MATEO: I done nothing to cross you.

MRS. DEWEY: Like a parasite.

MATEO: Say whatever you want to me. I got rights.

> *(She spits at him. He takes a step toward her.)*

MRS. DEWEY: Come, demon. Come into the light. Oh, yes, thank you, Lord, Praise God.

MATEO: About your child. I'm sorry they put her heart in me. I had no choice in the matter.

MRS. DEWEY: The vilest creature I ever laid eyes on. Viler still close up. The lies gather on the corners of your mouth.

MATEO: I don't mean nobody harm.

MRS. DEWEY: What do you call yourself when you're alone with your conscience? What do the cries of that innocent girl call you at night?

MATEO: You don't unnerstand.

MRS. DEWEY: How is it possible to misunderstand hell?

MATEO: You say I killed a girl. Well, Miss high-and-mighty, you commit your little murders, too.

MRS. DEWEY: Liar.

MATEO: Think about it.

> (*MATEO reaches into her shrine and grabs a photograph of her daughter.*)

MATEO: Who pulled the plug on your daughter? Who decided she was ready to die?

MRS. DEWEY: FIEND!

MATEO: How much are you responsible? Put it in whatever words you want, it's still the same thing. It ain't like unplugging a table lamp, neither! That was her death.

MRS. DEWEY: Lord Jesus, smite this man.

MATEO: Thass right. Pray, lady.

> (*He turns to go as she raises the knife. MATEO stops, falls to his knees in pain and calls in another voice.*)

MATEO: Mama... (*She stops.*) Mama, it's me.

MRS. DEWEY: Who...

MATEO: It's me.

MRS. DEWEY: Chelsea...?

MATEO: Mama.

MRS. DEWEY: This... can't be some trick...

MATEO: No, Mama, please. Don't walk away from me. I'm here.

(*MATEO comes to his knees.*)

MRS. DEWEY: Child.

MATEO: Remember, Mama, all the things we did together? How we played with Patsy...

MRS. DEWEY: Patsy?

MATEO: Our little dog Patsy. Remember? Remember?

MRS. DEWEY: It's you!

(*She embraces MATEO with motherly fondness.*)

MATEO: It's been so lonely, Mama. Being here. Inside.

MRS. DEWEY: Darlin', I'm sorry.

MATEO: Don't worry, Mama. I've felt your closeness all these years, through this skin and gristle, I've felt your love. So true and constant.

(*MRS. DEWEY weeps convulsively.*)

MATEO: Don't cry. I have me a purpose now. I do. In this kinda sleep, the blood of this man passes through me, and you know somethin', Mama? I cleanse it for him, I give it air and light and newness, and I purify him daily, Mama, so he won't hurt nobody. I fix him pint by pint.

MRS. DEWEY: It's great, baby.

MATEO: I seen him when he's ugly, and truly, Mama, he's unforgivable, but somehow, my heart forgives him. Pint by pint.

MRS. DEWEY: I wish I could do the same, Chelsea.

MATEO: Try, Mama. You have to try. Or else my death's for nothin'.

> (MATEO lays his hand gently on
> her head.)

MRS. DEWEY: Dear Jesus.

MATEO: Whatever befalls him, befalls me. Sinking now. My words falling back in the mouth of this pitiful man. I'm not hardly a whisper, Mama.

MRS. DEWY: Baby...

MATEO: Not hardly a murmur...

(*MATEO grips his chest and staggers.*)

MRS. DEWEY: Chelsea?

MATEO: (*in his own gruff voice*) What you lookin' at? Spare me your pity.

> (*He grabs the duffel bag and rushes out.*)

MRS. DEWEY: Chelsea, baby? Chelsea...

> (*MRS. DEWEY goes to heraltar and closes it. She signs through her tears the first strains of a new song as she follows MATEO out.*)

MRS. DEWEY: Walk in the light... the beautiful light...

> (*Lights up on LEE lying on the ground, asleep. AMA enters and places a cup of soup by him. LEE stirs with a groan.*)

LEE: How long have I been out?

AMA: A few hours. I brought you some *caldito*. Go back to sleep if you want. I can reheat it.

LEE: *Gracias.* I'll take it. Is there some water?

AMA: Here.

(AMA pours him a glass.)

LEE: This smells good. *Es... lengua?*

> *(She shakes her head. LEE drinks the water down.)*

AMA: You better eat. You look pale.

LEE: *Gracias, señora.*

AMA: I used to make that soup for Mateo when he would come home from those long nights out. Drunk and sad. Face like a closed book. Only sixteen and so lonely.

LEE: You still see him that way, don't you?

AMA: He's my boy. Whatever happens, this fact does not change. The world can detest him, God can forsake him but his *Ama* never leaves his side.

LEE: You don't believe him anymore.

AMA: We all have our *desgracias*. Our shames. When yours are revealed and you're called to Judgment, better pray your mother has a broom.

LEE: Well said. Can I quote you?

AMA: Yes, Mr. Rosenblum. You can quote me. What are you doing in this business anyway? Do you like this work?

LEE: I wanted to be a writer. But I guess I just wasn't any good at putting down my stories. So I took a job telling other people's stories. I just never figured they would resemble my own.

AMA: You mean this story?

LEE: Your life here, this house, its flaking paint. The way mimosa trees bloom in the summer, the smell of my mother's cooking. It all used to be mine. Except this old figurine. What does it represent?

AMA: *Xipe Totec*. His father brought it a long time ago. Our Lord the Flayed One. A god of renewal.

LEE: Is that a mask he's wearing?

AMA: The skin of his victim. After a sacrifice, the Aztec priest put on the flayed skin of his "volunteer" and became the God. Seeing through the eyeholes of death, one appreciates life in a terrible new way.

LEE: I guess that's true.

AMA: Tell me about your mother. *¿Era buena gente?*

LEE: Yes. She was good people. But she always seemed a little inside herself. I think she married my stepfather, a Jew who never left

Manhattan, to help her forget, to get away from what we had here.

AMA: What did you need to get away from?

LEE: *(shrugs)* All I know is the yearning never goes away.

AMA: Where is your real father?

LEE: Somewhere in here, I carry the best and worst of him. The best I'm oblivious to. It's the worst I keep holding on to.

AMA: Then that's what you'll remember.

LEE: I guess we all have our Belen.

AMA: Belen? What do you mean?

LEE: Well... I guess sooner or later you'll know...

AMA: Know what?

LEE: About Mateo's half-sister. By your husband. He had another family in Mexico.

AMA: That's not true.

LEE: He said he tracked his father down to Belen, a small village where he met his sister.

AMA: Belen? Belen is the name of the junior high school he went to.

LEE: Hold on...

AMA: His father never went to Mexico. He hated it. He'd go for weeks to the racetrack in Albuquerque and get drunk there, but never Mexico. If he went, they'd never let him back across. He was an illegal.

LEE: But he said he met Sonia--

AMA: Sonia? Who's that? What has Mateo been telling you?

LEE: Where is he?

AMA: He's out.

LEE: Out? Where out?

AMA: He went out the back way. He said he was going to pick up some pictures.

LEE: WHAT?

AMA: What have you been listening to?

LEE: Oh my god. Oh my god.

> (LEE runs out, with AMA close
> behind. The motel room. DRU is
> packing her things. Her photographs
> lay displayed all over the bed.
> MATEO pushes the maid's cleaning
> cart in, the duffel bag resting atop
> it.)

MATEO: *¿Permiso entrar, señorita?*

DRU: What are you doing here?

MATEO: This room looks kinda familiar.

> *(DRU tries to escape but he shuts off her route with the cart.)*

MATEO: This where you and him been sleepin'?

DRU: What do you want?

MATEO: Well, first. I have a burning question on my mind only you can answer.

DRU: What's that?

MATEO: What the hell's an F-stop?

DRU: It's an aperture setting. For determining how much light gets through. And how much of the image stays in darkness. Something like that.

MATEO: Hm. I wanna apologize for hurting you the other day. I'm not keen on all them photographic lights. Oh, you got them already. Can I see?

> *(He scrupulously scans the array of shots.)*

Looka that. Damn. You know, I don't take too many pictures 'cause I'm vain and I tend to come unglued when I see bad ones of me showed around. So it's a fortunate thing that you're so good. You gotta eye for detail.

DRU: Get out.

MATEO: Which one do you like best?

DRU: I don't like any of them.

MATEO: But which one captures my essence? Your boyfriend says you're tops at doing that.

DRU: None of them. They're no good. I'm no good. I'm quitting this job.

MATEO: Too bad. I kinda fancy them. I look kinda smart in that one.

DRU: Maybe you are. Where's Rosenblum?

MATEO: Rosenblum's dead. Leandro Guerra is resting up at my house. He's been working real hard. Digging into territory he don't know much about. Him and that little recorder. Have you known him long?

DRU: What's it to you?

MATEO: Do you love him?

DRU: Get the fuck out of my room, Mr. Buenaventura.

MATEO: DO YOU LOVE HIM.

DRU: WHAT'S IT TO YOU? WHY SHOULD I TELL YOU ANYTHING?

MATEO: Then don't.

DRU: What does this Leandro person have to do with Lee?

MATEO: He hasn't told you? Thass his real name. Leandro. He's a Mexican down to his roots. I helped him come to terms with his culture. He been lying to you?

DRU: We don't lie.

MATEO: Oh, we're all in the business of falsehood, Miss Dru. So much deceit, the lies are like pollen, all over the air, landing in people's mouths, generatin' theirselves everywhere. See? All these Mateo Buenaventuras on your bed, all of them lies ready to take to the air. People will see this and believe it.

DRU: What the hell do you want?

MATEO: If you love him, you'll give me all your pictures, the negatives, too, and get him out of here. Go back to New York. Print another lie. Not this one.

DRU: Are you serious?

MATEO: I don't want these pictures out.

DRU: What about your vanity?

MATEO: Don't give me no guff. Life's too short for guff.

DRU: What if I don't let you have them?

> (He takes the cutting shear out of the bag and admires its lethal edges.)

MATEO: Draw your own conclusions, bitch. I'd just as soon leave here with your eye for detail in my pocket than without. But I'm leaving with the pictures.

DRU: I'm not afraid of you. You can't hurt me. You're the chickenshit here.

> (MATEO draws himself inward for a moment. Then he moves toward her with the shears.)

MATEO: Only in the madness of our dreams do we get this chance. Only when the waste of years is washed down with Turkey and Coke and our hand jerks away at some imitation of love, do we make such goddamn fools of ourselves. But sometimes we roll a seven. Get a second chance. Make up for the past. For lapses in judgment. And love.

DRU: Love?

MATEO: The creases in my heart these last twelve years have been caulked with blood cum tears and rot. A woman like you would heal what needs healin'.

> (He almost slips his hand inside her blouse, over her heart. DRU quickly slides out from beneath him and darts to the photos and negatives and takes them to the maid's cart, where she dumps them into a bucket and pours floor cleaner into it.)

MATEO: The tapes.

> (DRU gets the tapes from Lee's computer bag and gives them to him.)

MATEO: And that computer?

DRU: Not a single word in there about you. But don't believe me. Take it if you want.

MATEO: *Señorita* Dru, forgive me for hurting you. You gotta realize I'm as flawed as the next man.

DRU: You don't fool me. I've seen you butchers before. You're all the same. You think you win, you think you're entitled to be predators, in your sick heads you expect someone will say the magic word and make everything swell. Well, not me. You don't know shit about forgiveness. You don't understand mercy. Or else you would have shown some to Shannon Trimble. It's just all a convenient excuse for you. You're right, these pictures, they're all lies.

> *(She reaches in her pocket for a set of dog-eared snapshots.)*

These you took after you clamped your paws on my throat. It's me. Like I've never seen myself. Scared shitless. Like I'm going to die. This is as close as we get to evil. Because it's in what you do! It's in the pain you make! These pictures I'm keeping.

> *(MATEO glowers darkly and starts toward her. LEE calls from a distance.)*

LEE: *(off)* Dru! Dru!

MATEO: Ask him about his sister. Ask him to introduce you to Sonia.

> *(LEE bursts into the room.)*

LEE: Mateo, stand back! Stand your ass back! Okay. What's happened?

MATEO: Nothing's happened.

> *(MATEO leaves.)*

LEE: Dru? Are you all right?

DRU: I'm through. I'm going home.

LEE: Wait, wait. What did he come for? Where are the pictures?

DRU: They're in there. Help yourself.

LEE: What the hell? Did he do this?

DRU: I did it.

LEE: You? Are you out of your mind?

DRU: I'll save you a seat on the plane, Lee. I'm out.

LEE: You ruined them! You fucking ruined them! Jesus Christ!

DRU: You should do the same with your story.

LEE: What did he tell you? What did he say?

DRU: Those interviews are shit, Lee. You can't use them. He's a liar.

LEE: I don't believe this. What do you mean I can't use them? Where's my tapes?

DRU: I'm going.

LEE: Where are my tapes?

DRU: Who cares anymore--

LEE: WHERE ARE MY TAPES!

DRU: THEY'RE GONE, LEE! THE TAPES, THE PICTURES, THE STORY, ALL GONE! HE'S GOT THEM!

LEE: ARE YOU CRAZY! WHAT HAVE YOU DONE!

DRU: THEY'RE LIES! NOTHING BUT SICK LIES! THAT MAN FED YOU GRADE A BULLSHIT AND YOU FELL FOR IT!

LEE: IT'S NOT BULLSHIT! THIS IS MY STORY! THIS IS MY LIFE, DRU!

DRU: Tell me, baby. Are you Leandro? He says that's who you really are. Is that true?

LEE: That fuck.

DRU: Lee, is that really who you are?

LEE: He's a liar.

DRU: And who is Sonia?

LEE: Sonia?

DRU: He said to ask you. Something about your sister. But you don't have a sister, do you?

LEE: My sister?

DRU: What's going on? What've you told this animal?

LEE: Oh no. Oh no.

DRU: Who is this sister, Lee? Who is Sonia? What do these names have to do with the tapes? Why didn't you mention any of this before?

LEE: They're all lies. LIES, DRU! FUCKING LIES LIES LIES LIES LIES!

>*(He throws her on the bed and commences strangling her.)*

DRU: LEE! STOP! STOP!

>*(He chokes her until she is still. Lights change. LEE feels himself in the interstice. The terrible power. MATEO appears in his patio. He mutters the parenthetical text.)*

LEE/(**MATEO**): Prima facie

in the evidence rendered

the time recovered, (**time unfelt**)

in the corroboration of events, (**the witness statements**)

I begin to see her (**begin to put together**)

the victimology (**pristine**) undisturbed, (**uncorrupted**) hardly even here, I am hardly even here, prima facie bears me out, I'm not even here, (**I'm gone**) dissolved like emulsion (**no evidence**) no time recovered (**nothing corroborated**)

> *(LEE picks up the bag of tools and turns to MATEO.)*

LEE: Belen. Belen Jr. High. You never had a sister. Or did you? Are you going to say something?

There's no Belen. No Sonia. No pictures. No interviews. No Evil.

What have you made me do, Mateo?

MATEO: I made you remember. It only seemed like my life.

LEE: But you said Sonia--

MATEO: I never said Sonia. You did. She's your sister, ain't she?

LEE: Oh my god.

> *(LEE starts to retch. Awful dry heaves.)*

MATEO: You gave me the details and I put them in my soup. Your sis and the rose embroidery on her pillow. Your old man and his bullring walk. The nights you watched over her. The fearsomeness of Mexico. All in your *Sopa de Lengua*. It's your story.

LEE: Oh my god.

MATEO: How your daddy had his way with you but left her alone. How you slipped into your baby sister's bed out of a perverted sense of pertection and then of punishment. How you lost her, anyhoo, when your old man took her away. Brother, you can disown the memory. But it's the memory that owns you.

LEE: Then Belen--

MATEO: --is real if you want it. It's a dirt town in Mexico and it's a little girl's bedroom in Fabens. A border that's both a river and a dark hallway you gotta cross for her. There's only one Sonia, and, buddy, she was yours, but you know what? She's mine now. I own your story like I own her, in this heart, *para siempre*.

LEE: Oh god.

MATEO: See, I learned psychology at that hospital. I picked you like you picked me. It was stamped into your face. This is a lover of sisters. A lover of death.

LEE: No.

MATEO: But damn. I'm starting to wonder if your old man diddled you at all. Maybe that's somethin' you perjected on him to keep from facing up to your filth. *Alomejor* he took her to Mexico to get her away from **you**!

LEE: STOP IT!

MATEO: Now you know something about evil. Now you know Leandro Guerra. You still don't know jack about me, though. Never.

So... is she dead? Did you carve up your sweet Dru?

> *(LEE gathers himself and stands.)*

LEE: You want me to tell you? *¿Quieres ver lo que pasó?*

> *(The lights change as LEE reenacts MATEO's crime.)*

LEE: In a bar. Out by Midland. I sit there drinking, remembering, stewing, quietly feeling the same old dirty things with this new heart of mine. Then two people come in. Barry Stokes... And Shannon Trimble.

> *(SHANNON, tipsy, enters and stands in the spotlight.)*

Look at her. Look at her! *(MATEO does. LEE shouts for her.)* SHANNON!!

SHANNON: Over here! No need to bellow at me!

LEE: They dance. I watch them dance.

> *(SHANNON dances with her arms around the space her boyfriend fills.)*

LEE: I see that big burly man twice that girl's age kissing on her neck and her ear and put his hand on her ass and maybe even try to slip it up her skirt....

SHANNON: Quit! I said, quit!

LEE: And that calls some darkness up. Rage, betrayal, the resentment of years before. Something goes off in that cerebral annex I call a dick.

SHANNON: Quit, I said! Barry, take me home!

LEE: We just got here!

SHANNON: Take me home now! Dammit!

LEE: *(as BARRY)* Don't pitch a fit on me here, girl! I'll slap you upside the head!

SHANNON: That's it! Home!

*(SHANNON breaks away and
staggers in a new space.)*

LEE: So when they go, it's a relief. Seeing those
big hands all over her pale young skin. Who
knows what I feel now. Last Call! But I stay
awhile and drink some more and finally off I
go. Back to that skanky room I call home. And
I'm driving. And I see her. Just as I'm fiddling
with my radio. I Fall to Pieces.

SHANNON: How about a lift home, mister?

LEE: And she's in beside you. Smell of beer
and Estee Lauder. *(SHANNON stands beside
LEE.)* I'm not even thinking now. Not an evil
thought in my head. But something is stirring.
Something I haven't felt good about in years.
So I tell her I got some high-class dope in my
room and would she like to smoke it. And she
says--

SHANNON: Sure.

LEE: So I take her there.

> *(They go to the motel room. MATEO
> watches from his seat in the patio.)*

SHANNON: So this is your party palace!

LEE: I tell her to make herself comfy.

SHANNON: Honey, I'm always comfy. But I need to pee.

LEE: Right in there.

SHANNON: And as she sashays across the room to the toilet, you watch her move in slow motion, you take in every sway of her hips, every lilt of her youthful head, the bounce of lissome highschool hair beckoning life and joy and ruinous abandon.

LEE: I am getting laid tonight.

SHANNON: Get your rolling papers, Pancho!

> *(SHANNON starts to go but stops with her back turned.)*

LEE: Suddenly, with her absence I start to feel Absence, desire bereft of body--

MATEO: --this ain't what happened.

LEE: This is **my** story now.

MATEO: I wasn't there.

LEE: I AM! I am sitting in your skin feeling this crazy numbness strangle me. Then I know. I understand. Right there. In the interstice, right on the fucking f-stop. What you need is Sonia. But there is no Sonia. There never was any Sonia in your life to show you love, no matter how depraved. You don't know how to love, Mateo. You don't know how to feel. This numbness you only know as Belen, that's what you are. Not even this new transplanted heart can make you feel love.

SHANNON: I'll be right out, mister!

LEE: But maybe hers can. So I break the glass inside my legs and go to the door and open it and go to my truck and reach in the bed for my toolbox and I lift it and carry it back to the room.

> *(He drops the bag of tools on the floor.)*

LEE: And here's what I overlooked. What you refused to see. The victimology. Her story.

> *(SHANNON turns and stands poised between MATEO and LEE.)*

SHANNON: Unaware of the change in the man, I come back.

LEE: The girl from the bar.

SHANNON: Eager to get stoned.

LEE: Shannon Trimble.

SHANNON: I wanna get stoned.

LEE: Standing in the accident of time.

SHANNON: I wanna get stoned now!

LEE: Prima facie.

SHANNON: And I look around. No papers, no dope, no nothin'. Only an old Messican fool with this beatific look on his face and a toolbox at his feet.

LEE: I am hardly even here.

> *(LEE plays out the instructions SHANNON gives over the still body of DRU.)*

SHANNON: First he comes to me and kisses me on the lips. Like so, like he's short of breath and I let him.

LEE: I am hardly even here.

SHANNON: Then his hands rise up to my throat and start to press upon it. Then I get scared and I don't let him.

LEE: I am hardly even here.

SHANNON: I kick this way and that but he only tightens his grip and I scream but the scream frays where it meets the air and I know I am going to die.

LEE: Hardly even here.

SHANNON: I cry for my mother and my father and then for Barry that son of a bitch and terror like nothing I have ever felt before fills my brain and it crashes and I pass out and then die I die I am dead all my senses locked in this cold unfair unwished-for iron-wrought death.

LEE: I am hardly even here.

SHANNON: He places me gently on the carpet like a suit he just bought.

LEE: I am hardly even here.

SHANNON: He strokes the bruise petals on my neck, the little black roses of death.

LEE: I am hardly even here.

SHANNON: Then he turns to his toolbox. Oh, how I wish I had the breath to curse you.

> (LEE goes to the bag. He takes out the shears, the hatchet, the boxcutter.)

SHANNON: He brings them to my body and lays them down. Then my hands are placed above me, fingers reaching out like rays of light.

LEE: *(straddling the body of DRU)* No more a whore, no more.

SHANNON: According to his own inscrutable cause.

LEE: I am hardly even here.

SHANNON: He undoes my blouse and regards my tits in their dead calm.

LEE: I am hardly even here.

SHANNON: Then he takes the boxcutter and cuts along a seam down my throat to my chest.

LEE: *(painfully etching a seam in the air)* My bouquet, my roses.

SHANNON: The oozing blood comes warm and consolating to his hands. Then the hatchet arches up and--

> (*LEE takes the axe and swings it upward. The disembodied sound of a deafening WHACK.*)

SHANNON: -- he thrusts into my chest the edge, jabs it hard, then again-- *(Swings it down past DRU. Another WHACK.)* --putting all his body weight into my breastbone until it cracks the seal of bodily containment and out comes more blood and fluid.

LEE: The body guiding my hand, leading me in.

SHANNON: He takes the cutting shears and crunches through skin, bone, cartilage, and time and opens up the vault where all my feelings all my memories and tastes and aims and dreams and songs and fears and secrets all come steaming out right into his face.

LEE: *(the shears in his hand carving out the space before him)* I am hardly even here.

SHANNON: I WAS ALIVE, MOTHERFUCKER! I WAS MY PARENTS' PRIDE!

He gingerly slips the boxcutter into the fruitbowl of organs and cuts away the membranes and aortic gung, and with his other hand plucks off my heart and brings it up for air, which it vainly tries to pump.

LEE: Hardly even here.

SHANNON: More his than mine now, the heart sits in his hands and he almost cries for joy. The kinda joy I never expressed but at pep rallies.

LEE: *Mio.*

SHANNON: He holds it in his hands like the catch of the day and sees himself reflected in the teeming gore. Something, a mystery, a miracle of evil, makes my heart vanish from the earth and NOW he is free to love.

LEE: I am hardly even here.

SHANNON: He undoes his pants raises my skirt and pulls my legs up to him.

MATEO/LEE: Hardly even here.

SHANNON: And he enters.

MATEO: Hardly.

SHANNON: Not the body of Shannon Trimble who is gone forever now, not the girl who almost signed up for Cosmetology College this summer.

MATEO: Hardly even here.

SHANNON: He enters another time, a faraway place, an altar, full of strange faces and languages--

MATEO: Hardly even here.

SHANNON: He enters the body of a young girl, a shadow of himself, a love denied--

MATEO: Hardly even here.

SHANNON: And he feels the release of all his shame the heat the searing youth return he feels good--

MATEO: Hardly.

SHANNON: He feels good--

MATEO: Hardly.

SHANNON: He feels so good!

MATEO: Hardly!

LEE: ¡PAPAAA!

SHANNON: Till he dissolves in his own cleansing, in his own fluids, in the acid of pure memory, Mateo Buenaventura is hardly even here.

MATEO: Not even here.

SHANNON: He sees with mounting sadness the torso of his love opened like a flower and buttoning himself up, gathering his strength, he takes my body up and places it on the bed. But my body is not Peace.

IT IS ALL OPEN ANGER.

> (SHANNON steps off into the darkness.)

LEE: The tools go in the toolbox and the toolbox goes in some canyon and I go back to the day-to-day. Standing naked, in the man-made lake off the road, dazed, bedraggled, but somehow spared.

(He stands before MATEO, both of them caught, accused, angry.)

LEE: Prima facie. Your own black eden. Darkest Belen. Our Belen.

MATEO: *Chingao.*

LEE: You killed her. Do you see that now? Do you see what you are?

MATEO: I see.

LEE: But the heart, the girl's heart, I thought I had it. But I lost it. I lost it.

MATEO: You know where it is. It's with Sonia. Waiting.

LEE: You twisted old man.

MATEO: Finish the story, Leandro. I ain't scared. Are you?

(MATEO takes up the bag of tools and they walk off together. MRS. DEWEY enters singing with a renewed hope in he voice.)

MRS. DEWEY: Walk in the light, the beautiful light, walk in the light with Jesus beside…

(She sets up her shrine before the house as in the beginning.)

MRS. DEWEY: *Bendito* be my God. *Bendito* to forgive. *Bendito* a world where even the sweetest good can live on in the darkest soul. Mateo, I release you so that I may lay my child to rest.

> *(In the motel, DRU suddenly awakens, coughing and gagging on the bed.)*

DRU: Lee. Lee. You can't believe him. Please don't believe him... Lee...

> *(She passes out. Mrs. Dewey kisses the picture of her Chelsea and seals it in the suitcase.)*

MRS. DEWEY: *Bendito.*

> *(A cry. AMA bursts forth in a frenzy.)*

AMA: *¡AAAYYYY! ¡AYYY! ¡SANGRE EN MI CASA! ¡SANGRE!*

MRS. DEWEY: What is it? Oh God. What's happened?

AMA: *¡AY, HIJO MIO! ¡HIJO MIO, QUE HORROR!*

MRS. DEWEY: Has he killed again? Has Mateo killed again?

AMA: NO! NOOO! MY BOY SLAUGHTERED! HE'S BEEN MURDERED! *¡ASESINO!*

> *(LEE enters, soaked in blood, carrying a white paper bag, shivering madly. AMA flees in terror.)*

AMA: *¡EL DEMONIO! ¡AGGGHH!*

MRS. DEWEY: Oh Lord.

LEE: Mrs. Dewey.

MRS. DEWEY: You poor man. What have you done? Oh my heavens.

LEE: I've been there, Mrs. Dewey. I've gone down to that darkness and sought the wicked out.

MRS. DEWEY: I told you to get away! I told you nothing good would come of this!

LEE: I have stood where killers stood and put my hand on death.

MRS. DEWEY: Curse the day! Curse the day, O Lord!

LEE: Rejoice, ma'am. God's on the cover again.

MRS. DEWEY: I don't know what you mean.

LEE: Balance. We're all trying to find balance. How do we get back to Belen?

MRS. DEWEY: We pray.

LEE: We could do that too. Anyway, your prayers have come to pass.

> (*LEE offers her the white paper sack. The swelling red stain of blood weighs it down.*)

LEE: He fought me hard for it. But I got it for you.

MRS. DEWEY: (*backing away in horror*) Oh. God. Dear. God. This is not how, Lee.

LEE: Here, Mrs. Dewey.

MRS. DEWEY: You poor man. Now you are bride to his darkness. God have mercy.

> (*She goes.*)

LEE: As in the beginning, so in the end. Standing on the cusp, past and past, the same bag, the ending of the story in the bag.

> (*SONIA, wearing her white dress, enters with her bundle. She sits and arrays the pretty cotton dresses on the ground like fanning beds of flowers. Stricken, hollowed, but*

strangely heartened, LEE watches her.)

SONIA: Right about now all the *turistas* come out of the *mesones* into the square. Ready to buy their colorful curios to take back across.

LEE: Mercy, sweet mercy in Pima. Sonia.

SONIA: You see any *turistas*?

LEE: Forgive me, Sonia, I never meant--

SONIA: Do you?

LEE: No. *No turistas.*

SONIA: *Ama y yo,* we sew them in our house. The fabric comes from Jalisco but the embroidery is all ours. The lace here. I did that.

LEE: Beautiful.

SONIA: All by hand. Those little purple roses are not easy. *¿Como te llamas?*

LEE: *Leandro.*

> *(SONIA gazes innocently at him and smiles. DRU in the motel room, rousing herself from the bed, watches piteously the scene between them.)*

SONIA: *Leandro.*

LEE: And in her smile, the pity, the shame, the obligations of blood and time vanish, oh, for that look you give me, oh, for that tenderness, Sonia, *mi amorosa, mi hermana*, for that touch I would die, I would give this heart to you, I would turn it into sweet bread for you, I would carry you away that sacred home, that hive of all desire, that creche of baby satan, Belen. Belen. Belen.

> *(LEE stands over SONIA, each in their bliss, as DRU weeps for them.)*
>
> *Lights fade to blackout.*
>
> **end of play**

Notes on Contributors

DOUGLAS LANGWORTHY is the Literary Manager and Dramaturg at the Denver Center Theatre Company, where he manages the theatre's new play development program. Prior to Denver, Douglas served as Dramaturg and Director of Play Development at McCarter Theatre in Princeton, NJ for two years and Director of Literary Development and Dramaturgy at the Oregon Shakespeare Festival (OSF) for seven. While at OSF he developed a new adaptation of Dumas' *The Three Musketeers* with Linda Alper and Penny Metropulos and a new translation of Brecht's *The Good Person of Szechuan*, both for the 1999 season. In the 2004 season, he collaborated with director Ken Albers on a new adaptation of Friedrich Dürrenmatt's *The Visit*. In 2007 he collaborated with Penny Metropulos and Linda Alper to write lyrics and book for the new musical *Tracy's Tiger*, based on the novella by William Saroyan, with music by Sterling Tinsley. Douglas has translated 15 plays from the German, which include *Spring Awakening* by Frank Wedekind, *Medea* by Hans Henny Jahnn, and *The Prince of Homburg, Penthesilea* and *Amphitryon* (National Theatre Translation Fund Award). He was also the dramaturg for Target Margin Theater in New York, which produced his translation of Goethe's *Faust*. For

Target Margin, he also co-wrote the libretto for *The Sandman,* a new opera with music by Thomas Cabaniss.

OCTAVIO SOLIS is a playwright and director living in San Francisco. His works *Ghosts of the River, Quixote, Lydia, June in a Box, Lethe, Marfa Lights, Gibraltar, The Ballad of Pancho and Lucy, The 7 Visions of Encarnación, Bethlehem, Dreamlandia, El Otro, Man of the Flesh, Prospect, El Paso Blue, Santos & Santos,* and *La Posada Mágica* have been mounted at the Mark Taper Forum, Yale Repertory Theatre, the Oregon Shakespeare Festival, the Denver Center for the Performing Arts, the Dallas Theater Center, the Magic Theatre, Intersection for the Arts, South Coast Repertory Theatre, the San Diego Repertory Theatre, the San Jose Repertory Theatre, Shadowlight Productions, the Venture Theatre in Philadelphia, Latino Chicago Theatre Company, the New York Summer Play Festival, Teatro Vista in Chicago, El Teatro Campesino, the Undermain Theatre in Dallas, Thick Description, Campo Santo, the Imua Theatre Company in New York, and Cornerstone Theatre. His collaborative works include **Burning Dreams**, cowritten with Julie Hebert and Gina Leishman and **Shiner**, written with Erik Ehn. Solis has received an NEA 1995-97 Playwriting Fellowship, the Roger L.

Stevens award from the Kennedy Center, the Will Glickman Playwright Award, a production grant from the Kennedy Center Fund for New American Plays, the 1998 TCG/NEA Theatre Artists in Residence Grant, the 1998 McKnight Fellowship grant from the Playwrights Center in Minneapolis, and the National Latino Playwriting Award for 2003. He is the recipient of the 2000-2001 National Theatre Artists Residency Grant from TCG and the Pew Charitable Trust for **Gibraltar** at the Oregon Shakespeare Festival. Solis is a Thornton Wilder Fellow for the MacDowell Colony, a New Dramatists alum and a member of the Dramatists Guild.

More titles from NoPassport Press

Antigone Project: A Play in Five Parts

by Tanya Barfield, Karen Hartman, Chiori Miyagawa, Lynn Nottage
and Caridad Svich, with **preface by Lisa Schlesinger, introduction by
Marianne McDonald; ISBN 978-0-578-03150-7**

Amparo Garcia-Crow: The South Texas Plays *(Cocks Have Claws and
Wings to Fly, Under a Western Sky, The Faraway Nearby, Esmeralda Blue)*
Preface by Octavio Solis; ISBN: 978-0-578-01913-0

Anne Garcia-Romero: Collected Plays *(Earthquake Chica, Santa
Concepcion, Mary Peabody in Cuba)* **Preface by Juliette Carrillo; ISBN:
978-0-6151-8888-1**

**John Jesurun: Deep Sleep, White Water, Black Maria – A Media
Trilogy** Preface by Fiona Templeton; ISBN: 978-0-578-02602-2

Lorca: Six Major Plays *(Blood Wedding, Dona Rosita, The House of
Bernarda Alba, The Public, The Shoemaker's Prodigious Wife, Yerma)* **In
new translations by Caridad Svich, Preface by James Leverett,
introduction by Amy Rogoway; ISBN: 978-0-578-00221-7**

Matthew Maguire: Three Plays *(The Tower, Luscious Music, The Desert)*
Preface by Naomi Wallace; ISBN: 978-0-578-00856-1

Oliver Mayer: Collected Plays *(Conjunto, Joe Louis Blues, Ragged Time)*
**Preface by Luis Alfaro, Introduction by Jon D. Rossini; ISBN: 978-0-
6151-8370-1**

Alejandro Morales: Collected Plays *(expat/inferno, marea, Sebastian)*;
ISBN: 978-0-6151-8621-4

12 Ophelias (a play with broken songs) by Caridad Svich; ISBN: 978-
0-6152-4918-6

NoPassport is a sponsored project of Fractured Atlas, a non-profit arts service organization. Contributions in behalf of [Caridad Svich & NoPassport] may be made payable to Fractured Atlas and are tax-deductible to the extent permitted by law.

For online donations go directly to
https://www.fracturedatlas.org/donate/2623

CPSIA information can be obtained
at www.ICGtesting.com
Printed in the USA
LVHW100446260123
737853LV00001BA/10